FRANKLIN PARK PUBLIC LIBRARY
FRANKLIN PARK, ILL.

Each borrower is held responsible for all library
material drawn on his card and for fines accruing on
the same. No material will be issued until such fine
has been paid.

All injuries to library material beyond reasonable
wear and all losses shall be made good to the
satisfaction of the Librarian.

Also from Janet Mullany and Harlequin HQN

Bespelling Jane Austen

And from Spice Books

Tell Me More

JANET MULLANY

Hidden Paradise

HARLEQUIN®
entertain, enrich, inspire™

Recycling programs
for this product may
not exist in your area.

ISBN-13: 978-0-373-77719-8

HIDDEN PARADISE

Acknowledgments

Thanks to my editor, Emily Ohanjanians,
and my agent, Lucienne Diver, and all those who listened patiently
to my whining (thanks again, Lucienne),
especially Pam Rosenthal and the Tarts.

This is dedicated to Alison, Steve and other family members who won't and probably shouldn't read this one, and to my late dad, who shared my love of Jane Austen.

One

Lou, Montana

She would not answer the phone.

Not now, when she was coming awake to the slide of skin against skin, coming awake to the possibility of coming, sleepy and lazy, his cock prodding against her.

"Yes, like that," she said. Or maybe he said it. Maybe they both did, finely tuned to each other, reading minds and touches.

"Tell me to open my legs." That was her, quite definitely. He liked it when she gave orders, or when she talked dirty and got crude, because she didn't do it all the time. There was an element of surprise, of the unexpected, and he reciprocated with his own sort of crude roughness. Sometimes, afterward, she'd find red welts on her breasts from his stubble—she'd remember much later in the day, when her bra rubbed against the abraded skin.

She'd feel what he did next later, too—the push of his fingers inside her before she was quite ready. At least, she thought she wasn't, but he knew her better than she knew herself and laughed softly when she gasped in surprise and shock. Gasping and greedy, both of them now, and then the shock of cold air seeped in from outside as he lifted the quilt and climbed on top of her. Again, she thought she wasn't ready, but she was. Quite definitely ready.

Don't answer the phone. Ignore it. If they really want to talk, they'll call back later.

"Shove it inside me. Hard." She told him what to do, but she was helpless and at his mercy as he hoisted her legs onto his shoulders.

He caught and held the moment, extending it with exquisite care. His cock reared high, thick and ready, but he slowed to look at her pussy.

"Pretty," he murmured. "Pretty."

She loved him for thinking her pussy was pretty when it was flushed and wet and the seam swelled apart into a crevice. Sometimes she heard the tiny crack it made as it swelled and opened, a sound like a small kiss, as he kissed her or even just looked at her, sometimes hours before they'd even touched or undressed. She could melt with that special look across a room full of people, or just the two of them alone, a look that said *tonight, or in the next ten minutes, I am going to fuck you good.*

His eyes gleamed with anticipation.

She raised her hips and told him again to shove it in her hard, like this was the last time, so this time it had to count, it had to be worthwhile. He slid his hand up his shaft, almost as though he was unaware of his action.

But he knew exactly what he was doing, conscious of every moment, every scent and touch and sound. And he knew precisely the effects each small movement had on her.

Words and her imagination were her allies now, shifting

the power back to her. She whispered to him to do it now, *now*. She would allow him to pretend she was one of his hot little undergraduates, like the one who'd let her legs fall apart, oh so casually, revealing a narrow band of thong, while he was teaching. Because in real life, when that had actually happened, he'd looked once and then away, and wondered if he'd imagined it. At home, he was slightly embarrassed, more embarrassed by his excitement, as he related the tale.

In the safety of their bed, where anything could happen, she whispered to him that this time he would look again. And again. He would watch a strap of her sundress fall, a pink tongue emerge to lick glossy lips. With absolute precision, in a suddenly empty auditorium, her hand, tipped with shiny bloodred nails, would undo his zipper and release his cock.

Now—

The fucking phone again, shrilling in her ear, ripping the moment away from her. She rolled across the wide expanse of empty bed to grab the receiver. "What?"

"You need to have some fun, Loulou."

But she had been having fun, even if it was only a dream. "Don't call me Loulou." Grumpy, half-asleep, she shifted the phone to her other ear and turned to look at the clock. "You do realize it's half past six?"

"Half past one here, Lou. Nuncheon time. Rise and shine."

"Oh, shut up, Chris." She contemplated briefly the in-dignity of her name—a name that suggested either a toilet, a cancan dancer, or one of Jane Austen's mildly unlikeable characters, the fickle poetry groupie Louisa Musgrove. The room was dim and cold with the quiet silvery quality that suggested freshly fallen snow.

"So come on over and play with us."

"Who's 'us'?"

"Peter, of course. The daft old queen has started interviewing footmen. We want to get a historically correct matched set—hire them like buying a team of horses, same height and coloring. Some quite delicious possibilities, darling. Other friends from London and the States are joining us, as well. A journalist, Viv, our terrifying costume person, a lovely lady who'll teach us manners and act as chaperone—not that you need one, you're so well behaved—and some very handsome men."

"It sounds like a gay wet dream. All those tight pants and high collars."

"Some of the men, and with you specifically in mind, are straight. It's up to you to find out who."

She sat up in bed, pulling the comforter around her neck, and hoped the stove wasn't out downstairs. "So long as they know first. I'm not some sort of guide into sexual preference."

"And the house, honey. Oh, the house is magnificent. Georgian splendor, original plasterwork, minimal plumbing and electricity. Except for the kitchen, which is all set up for fabulous, historically authentic food—"

"Lard and butter—"

"And dozens of eggs. Huge amounts of red meat. The first salads of the season, exotic fruit from the greenhouses—that is, in a few years. We're buying in at the moment. Do come. We need our Austen expert on hand. We'll put the sparkle back in your eyes and gunk in your arteries."

"I don't know. I don't know what I want to do." She got out of bed and padded across the room. She had no curtains or blinds. You didn't need them when you looked straight out across the Rockies, at a pristine white wilderness and a blue sky. "I can't get away until the snow's gone."

"Oh, to be in England now that April's here. Come over in June. We'll have staff then."

"Stop it, you vile seducer."

"That's my girl. Peter sends kisses. Must run. But you'll think about it, promise?"

"Okay."

Chris's voice turned serious. "Lou, he's gone. We loved him, too. Come back into the land of the living. Come and have fun and adventures in Paradise. Kiss kiss. Bye-eee." He ended the call with the curious upward breathy farewell she'd noticed on the phone with other English people.

Lou pulled on a pair of thick socks and a sweater and jeans lined with flannel over her pajamas and headed downstairs. The stove was lit, barely. She coaxed it into life with some choice morsels of wood, placed a kettle on to boil for coffee and let the dogs out. They frisked in the fresh snow with great enthusiasm as though they hadn't done the same thing every morning for the past five months.

She picked up the picture of Julian with the dogs that she'd taken last summer and smiled back at him while running through the list of chores for the day. Muck out and feed Maisie the Morgan horse, oatmeal for breakfast, drive the tractor out with hay for the cattle, ski up to see Julian, ski back home, have a sandwich, shower, do some work, dinner. Read. Bed. Obligatory session with vibrator to stop things atrophying, and another day would be over.

"So, you big jerk." She stood in the meadow where she'd scattered Julian's ashes last fall when the aspens were a glory of gold and the sheltered hollow still had a few wildflowers in bloom. "I still miss you, but you know what? I'm beginning to forget bits of you. I forgot what your penis looks like, so I had to go online and find some. Don't think I enjoyed it. Some of them were quite grotesque. You'd think if they were that butt ugly the owner would edit them into something better, but I guess it's like no one thinks their baby is ugly. Or perhaps dicks are like snowflakes—all basically the same but each one is different. Speaking of snow, we got some last night. Again.

"I went into your studio yesterday and looked at your stuff. I still haven't cleared anything out. I wish you'd come haunt me. You won't haunt me in the studio, you won't haunt me in bed—what use are you anyway? Here I am increasing my carbon footprint with a plug-in vibrator because you won't manifest. The dogs would like to see you again, too.

"Chris called this morning, trying to get me over for Paradise Hall's trial run in the summer. Remember when I wrote the copy for the website and brochure? I'll be doing another version soon. He's planning to open officially with a big Christmas bash, taking things slow. Right now things are pretty primitive in the house. He's already lusting after footmen."

A chill breath of wind whipped the snow at her feet into a miniature funnel.

"Is that you, finally coming around to haunt me?" She sighed. "I've got to go. Things to do. You had some fucking nerve, dying and leaving me with all this. I worry about stuff, whether the roof will be okay, whether I have enough oil to last the cold weather, where the phone number for the feed guy is, veterinarian bills. All the piddling little things. And you know you never threw a damn thing away and it's all junk. I keep finding old envelopes with your to-do lists on them, printouts of emails— *Why?*

"Oh, good. I'm in the anger stage of grieving. I'm progressing. But you know what? I don't want closure. I don't want to forget. *I want you back.*"

She brushed away a tear, startlingly hot in the cold air, from her eye. She didn't want tears freezing on her face. She waited for something, a sign, but nothing happened.

She whistled to the dogs and slowly, clumsily—Julian would have managed his skis with so much more grace— turned around and launched herself upon the two lines that cut through the snow, back to the empty house.

Maybe, just maybe, Julian might come to her again at Paradise Hall.

Rob, Seville, Spain, two months later

OH FUCK, OH FUCK. HIS HANDS were slippery with sweat and nervousness and he bit into the foil package of the condom, hoping he wouldn't bite through the damn thing. That would be really embarrassing and probably taste awful, too.

"*Oh, fuck,*" said Gisella or whatever her name was, writhing around like a belly dancer on the narrow bed, gorgeous, and if only he could get the bloody condom taken care of and hold her breasts again, and all that hair, ripples of it like a da Vinci sketch over the pillow. He thought it was Gisella, he knew it was Italian, but it seemed sort of stupid at this point to stop and ask her to spell her name. Just like it would seem sort of stupid to get off her and take his jeans all the way off, even if it meant he'd be able to move around a bit more freely. Perhaps next time he'd be better at it. He was allowed to be fairly stupid the first time, after all, but not too stupid. Like coming too early, or before he got inside or...

She murmured something. It sounded incredibly sexy, but then at this point anything would, particularly in Italian. For all he knew, she could be asking him to open the window or something, although probably she wasn't. She raised herself up on one elbow and helped him roll the condom on—*oh fuck, oh fuck,* for a moment he thought he'd come right then, seeing her fingers with those long red nails on his cock—and then his mobile rang.

She plucked the phone from the bed and he grabbed it from her, and did what he immediately regretted—he looked to see who was calling.

Don't answer it.

It was his sister, and he had no idea why he answered it, but he did, and regretted that, too.

Oh fuck, oh fuck. His condom clad penis drooped as he listened to his sister rant and rant and cry.

Oh, fuck.

So much for getting laid.

Peter, a week later, Paradise Hall, Somerset

"Robert Temple. And we call you—Bob, Bobby, Robert?"

"Rob."

Bonny sweet Robin. The phrase crept into his mind unawares—shades of Good Queen Bess, or in his case, Good Queen Peter. The kid was sweet, though. Young, too—nineteen, nice clear English skin, brown hair with a hint of copper flopping over his forehead, gray eyes—an innocent Hugh Grant type, although even Peter could tell that he wasn't *posh,* to use the English term. He had the local accent, that soft burr, and the address he gave on the application was in the new part of the village—tacky little houses crammed together—not the historic, older part.

Peter glanced at the kid's curriculum vitae—God bless the English, they couldn't just say résumé, even if it was mostly

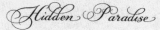

minimum-wage student jobs. "And you're off to Cambridge in the fall. The autumn."

"Yes, sir."

"Oh, Peter, please. At least until you're on duty." He winked, a mistake—he sounded like some effulgent old queen, which is what he suspected he probably was. "Congratulations," he added. Cambridge was still a big deal here. "What's your major?"

Another blunder. They didn't use that terminology over here. "I'll be reading history."

"Excellent!" Now he sounded patronizing. "I mean, a sense of history will be an, an asset. And you've been a waiter. That will be useful, too. I see you've been abroad. May I ask why you didn't stay in Seville for the summer?"

The kid's face closed down. "Family trouble."

Oh, dear. "I see. Well, let me tell you about the house and what we're doing here." He gave the standard spiel about how guests would be able to go back in time and live the life of Regency ladies and gentlemen, enjoying the pleasures of the age and, it was implied, each other, should they wish. What happened at Paradise Hall, in other words, stayed at Paradise Hall and very firmly in the early nineteenth century. "You may find that the isolation from the modern world, the role-playing, and the dressing-up aspect may go to the guests' heads. As you know, it was a bawdy age, as well as an age of elegance—people were very forthright about physical matters. So discretion is absolute. And if you're asked to participate in an activity that is unacceptable, remember you can always say no, and please come directly to me if you have any sort of uncomfortable experience."

Rob looked at the brochure Peter had handed him. "'Paradise Hall, where anything can happen,'" he read aloud.

"Two centuries ago things were different, passionately so."
He looked up. "I'm cool with that."

Peter tried not to let his imagination run riot. What did
these kids get up to? It made him feel old.

"Good," he said, and moved on to safer territory. "You're a
local, so I expect you know about the history of the house—
originally Jacobean, remodeled by Adams, and there's an un-
documented tradition that Jane Austen stayed here."

Rob nodded. "When I was a kid, we thought it was
haunted," he said. "'Course, we'd say that about any old house
in the village that stood empty. Changed a bit, though."

"Oh, it's fabulous," Peter said, aware that he was falling
into the role of the queer old uncle who liked interior design. "You'll love it. You'll work hard, but we pay well, and
you'll get excellent tips."

"I think they called them vails then," said the future Cambridge history undergraduate.

"Absolutely. Vails. Let me give you the grand tour…" God
help him, he sounded as though he were about to coyly slip
away and come back in drag as Danvers. He deepened his
voice and tried to sound more masculine. "And I'll introduce you to my partner, Chris Henckley."

"What an adorable boy," Chris said, gazing at Rob, who
swung one leg over his bicycle and pedaled away. He and
Peter stood in the stable yard, while doves cooed and fluttered overhead. "On a bicycle, too. How sweet. But troubled,
I think, don't you, Peter?"

"There's some family crisis, from what I read between the
lines. He's straight."

"Oh, yes, it sticks out half a mile."

Peter refused to crack a smile at Chris's double entendre.

"He's barely legal, for God's sake. I hope I'm making a wise decision hiring him as head footman."

"He's nineteen. They start young here. Oh, come on, honeybuns." He slid a hand into the back pocket of Peter's Levi's. "I will not fuck the help, I promise, even if they're as fuckable as young Master Rob. But think how he'll look in livery. I can't wait. I just hope Viv doesn't eat him alive when she measures his inseam."

"Mmm." Peter slid away and headed back into the office, once the estate manager's, that opened onto the cobbled yard. He tapped the keyboard of the computer and the screen sprang to life. He had mail, a perky message informed him.

Chris peered over his shoulder. "Oh, excellent. The widow Loulou is emerging from her deep winter to join us."

Two

Rob

"You're Rob Temple, right?"

He turned to the girl who was crammed against him at the bar. "Yeah. You're…" She looked familiar, someone from school, or from the posh part of the village.

"Di Brooks."

"Oh, right."

"We were at St. Matthews."

Primary school. He'd probably thought the height of eroticism then was being given a glimpse of her knickers.

"So you're working down the old house. Me, too."

He nodded and tried to catch the eye of Baz behind the bar.

She leaned forward and yelled, "Oy, Baz, get us two pints, will you?" She shoved her glass and Rob's forward.

Baz swiveled, took the glasses in one hand and Rob's last ten-pound note with the other.

"I was going to buy you that," Di said.

"It's okay."

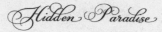

"Sorry about your house and all."

So the whole village knew. He'd ridden home from Paradise Hall and, without thinking, had found himself about to push open the gate of the family's house, their former house, blinking at the for-sale sign. His mum would have been furious at the weeds in the front. A kid's football, probably Graham's, had lain abandoned in one of the flower beds, and Rob had picked it up and stuffed it into his backpack. He'd ridden away, wanting to bawl like a little kid.

"'S'okay. What are you doing up at Paradise Hall, then?"

"Lady's maid." The glasses arrived back in front of them, froth running down the sides, along with a very small handful of change. "I've just done my first year at the London School of Fashion. So it's good experience. I'll be mending stuff and helping the women guests dress and all."

"Cool," he said, and took a good look at her. Pretty, brown eyes, brown hair with lighter, toffee-colored streaks in it, skimpy short sundress, those clacky sort of heels and long bare legs. "I'm a footman."

"I bet those two gay blokes just loved you. They seem okay, though."

He shrugged. "I'll see you tomorrow, then."

"Whatever. I'd better get back to my friends." She nodded her head toward a group of girls, all like her, pretty, sexy, laughing in a corner. A few guys hung around, looking, but not approaching, under the pretext of a game of darts. "Thanks for the pint."

"So you're going posh on us, then," Baz bawled at him, the sudden rush at the bar dispersed.

"What?"

"Cambridge."

"Not really."

"They pay well up the old house?"

"Not bad." They paid exceptionally well, but he wasn't telling Baz that.

"Them couple of pansies have been in a few times."

"They're okay."

"Keep your back to the wall, son." Baz winked, wiped the counter and, having dispensed his advice, went back to the other end of the bar to join an impassioned discussion about football.

Rob drained his glass and glanced over at Di in the corner. She raised a hand to push back her hair, bangles sliding down her arm, and laughed with her friends. She leaned back, her skirt riding up. Great legs. He wasn't the only one watching. Blokes hovered around like wolves around a herd of lambs on one of those TV nature programs.

He went outside and unlocked his bike, reluctant to leave the warmth and friendliness of the pub—or rather, the relative anonymity of the pub. He hoped his dad would be asleep by the time he got back to his sister's place, or passed out, like he had been the past few nights. He pedaled down past the village green, and turned onto the lane that led to the estate—formerly a council estate, housing for poor people, badly built and cramped.

He could understand his mum being mad at Dad, lying about the business and the mortgages on the house. Although, what sort of woman would be so clueless about the family finances? Someone like Di wouldn't let a bloke get away with that sort of shit. On an impulse, he steered onto the grass verge and punched in his mum's number on his cell.

No reply.

You stupid bitch, he thought, *you bloody, stupid, selfish bitch,* and disconnected, leaving no message. He pulled the football out of his backpack and threw it hard over the hedge into the darkness of a field. A football wouldn't stop Graham sniveling all day and wetting the bed at night.

Only his mum coming back would cheer Graham up, but apparently she'd abandoned them all.

Lou

LOU'S JET LAG GAVE HER A FUZZY sense of unreality and heightened senses. The sunshine was intense, the crunch of tires on gravel deafening as the limo dropped her off at a stone house next to a pair of imposing wrought-iron gates.

"You have a nice holiday, miss," the driver said.

She fumbled in her billfold for a tip, squinting at the unfamiliar bills, but he'd driven away, the smoked glass of the window rolling up.

The door of the house swung open, revealing a woman with lipstick so vivid it appeared cut into her pale skin, and dead-black hair cut in a severe, angled wedge. She wore a pair of cowboy boots, a leather miniskirt and a vintage Sgt. Pepper T-shirt. A cigarette dangled from bright red lips.

"Welcome to Paradise Hall. I'm Vivian. You must be Lou. Don't tell the boys I was smoking. Come in. Good timing, I've just brewed up. Cup of tea? I know you stopped for lunch on the way down, but how about something to eat?"

She led Lou into a room with a flagstone floor and a minimal sort of kitchen at one end. Tailors' dummies stood around, draped in fabric, gossamer-thin silks and cottons, sumptuous satins and velvets. More fabrics lay on a large table scattered with scissors, pins, scraps of paper, manila folders and a complex hi-tech sewing machine.

Viv tossed the cigarette into the sink. She poured tea from a fat brown teapot into a mug and arranged scones and butter on a tray. "I've put milk in it for you—sugar? Your folder's on the table. Your day dress I'll finish off after a final fitting here, and you can take the sleeves off and accessorize it for tonight. How was your flight?"

"Fine, thanks." Lou found the tea hot and strong, invigorating and soothing at the same time. She flipped open the folder with her name scrawled on the tab, and sketches with swatches of fabric pinned onto them, pretty florals and delicate stripes, tumbled out. "I didn't bring much of my own. I..." She stopped, dumbfounded, as Vivian, having run her cigarette under the faucet, unzipped Lou's bag and rummaged inside.

Lou almost choked on her scone as she watched this woman, a stranger, pick through her belongings in the battered leather bag that had once been Julian's.

"Knickers optional," Vivian said. "No bra, no watch, no cosmetics. You'll have stays, which I made to your original measurements. This silk scarf is okay, most of your earrings are okay. The rest I'll keep here for you. We have a safe."

"But..."

Vivian plucked what looked like a folded length of white cotton and a pair of shapeless socks from the table and folded them over one arm. "There's a bathroom and dressing room upstairs, and you can take a nap up there afterward, while we prepare your day dress. It's silly, but we like to give guests the experience of walking up the drive to the main house in their Regency clothes, giving them a chance to ease into the Paradise experience."

Just what she needed, a bossy punk elf dominatrix. Clutching the steaming mug of tea, she followed Vivian upstairs and into another room stocked with racks of clothes and more dressmaking paraphernalia. A large, comfortable-looking sofa strewn with pillows and throws stood in one corner. Vivian opened a door that revealed a huge bathroom with a large cast-iron bathtub with claws and a rack of thick white towels. Blue-and-white-striped curtains fluttered at the window, allowing plenty of light to spill onto the flagstone floor.

"Take your time." Vivian turned on the faucets, and steam billowed into the room. "You look like a rose girl to me, but there's lavender and lemon. Enjoy. Give me a shout when you're ready and we'll have more tea and a fitting. These are your stockings and shift." She laid them on the towel rack, winked and left.

Lou stripped off her clothes, poured rose bath oil into the tub and sank into its comforting, foamy depths. The bath was equipped with an attachment to the faucets for hair-washing, which she managed with only a minimal amount of water sprayed around the room.

Heaven, just heaven, after the travel. She and Julian had never got around to really fixing up their bathroom—she would have loved a tub like this—but now it all seemed so far away. Even Julian.

She dozed off, woke to add more hot water, scrubbed herself luxuriously and experimented a little with the shower attachment. Not quite enough pressure, she decided, but she certainly was clean from head to toe and in every nook and crevice, and with a mildly excited tingle. After witnessing Vivian's bag search, she was glad that she hadn't packed a vibrator.

She dried off and dropped the cotton shift over her head. It was a silly, unsexy, shapeless sort of garment, but if you were going around with no panties, and everyone knew it, you didn't really need sexy underwear. Her first step into the Regency accomplished—she wondered vaguely if in future here she'd be bathing from jugs and bowls; Peter and Chris had been rather vague on plumbing matters—she padded across the flagstone floor into the next room. The sofa and pillows lured her in. How wonderful, to nap in the middle of the day on soft down pillows, wrapped in cashmere.

When she woke, the light had changed and she guessed a couple of hours must have passed. It was very quiet, apart from the birdsong, but she could dimly hear a man's voice from downstairs and a woman's reply, muffled by the thick stone walls of the house. For a moment, she didn't recognize Viv's voice, uncharacteristically soft and plaintive.

Lou hesitated. She was barely dressed and had no wish to expose herself to a stranger, or some sort of intimate scene. She looked around the room for a shawl. Maybe she should return to the bathroom and retrieve the long-sleeved T-shirt she'd worn on the plane. Or she should just go back to sleep. Curiosity won. Even as she hesitated, she opened the door that led to the staircase.

"You *are* a naughty girl," the man was saying. An American accent, an amused, sexy purr.

"Yes, Darcy. I'm sorry, Darcy."

Darcy? This was ridiculous and intriguing. The door into the main room stood slightly ajar. She had to get a glimpse of a real-life Darcy. She tiptoed down the stairs to the doorway and peered through.

"How do you suggest I punish you?" The speaker stood leaning against the table, absolutely at ease in his Regency clothes. And he looked terrific in them, tall and lean and muscular, his black hair mussed forward. He wore a blue coat and buckskins and boots. Everything fit like a glove, revealing a noticeable bulge at his groin.

Vivian stood in front of him, head hanging, tracing a

pattern on the floor with the toe of one boot. "Maybe you should fuck me, Darcy. In a very degrading sort of way."

"Hmm." His mouth quirked upward in an involuntary grin for one moment. "Are you wearing panties today?"

"Oh, yes, Darcy."

She lifted her skirt to reveal a skimpy leopard-print thong.

"I guess it's quite wet."

"I'm afraid so, Darcy."

He straightened up and took a step away. "Too bad, honey. Take it off. You'll go bare-assed the rest of the day."

"Yes, Darcy." She pushed the thong down and stepped out of it.

"And keep your skirt up." He dropped one hand to the front of his pants, cradling the erection that bulged against the leather.

"Yes, Darcy." Vivian stood, obediently waiting for his next command, her skirt rolled around her hips.

"On the table." He removed his coat and dropped it onto the flagstone floor.

"Don't do that," Vivian said in her usual voice. "Put it on a chair. And fold it, otherwise I'll have to iron it. I am busy, you know."

"Sorry." He straightened the coat out, folding it neatly onto a chair, and removed his waistcoat. "Okay. On the table. Ass up, I think."

"Yes, Darcy." Vivian pushed papers and fabrics out of the way and arranged herself on the table, her bottom raised. She was facing to Lou's right, fortunately—how embarrassing if she'd positioned herself facing Lou.

Darcy stood behind Vivian for a moment, as though admiring the view, and unwound his neckcloth. He laid it on the chair with his other clothes, and then bent to rummage in the coat pockets, pulling out a pair of leather gloves. He slapped them experimentally on his palm.

Lou's breath caught. Was he going to…?

"Like I said," Darcy said, "you've been a bad girl. I'm going to have to spank you."

"Yes, Darcy."

"And then I'll fuck you."

"Yes, Darcy." Her voice quivered with expectation. "May I pull my top up, Darcy?"

"I think not. I don't want you enjoying this by rubbing your tits on the table."

"No, Darcy. I'm sorry."

He grinned, and brought the gloves down on Vivian's bottom with a sharp crack. She gave a short squeal of surprise.

He paused to unbutton his cuffs, and slapped her again.

Fascinated, Lou watched as he removed his shirt—getting in another slap, while the shirt hung from his other arm—and tossed the garment onto the chair. His chest was spare and muscular, dusted with black hair. He coordinated slaps with unbuttoning his buckskins and Lou waited, breathless, to see his cock emerge.

Oh. She hadn't seen an erect cock, apart from her half-hearted internet explorations, in…months. She stifled a small moan—nothing compared to the sort of noises Vivian was making, shrieks and groans and continued requests for Darcy to "Stop, stop, please. I promise I'll be good." It all sounded rather theatrical to Lou's ears. She wanted to laugh, but at the same time she was embarrassed at how excited she felt at the electric response that thrummed between her thighs.

Darcy's cock arched out, blue veined and strong, from a nest of dark hair.

Lou curled her hand, imagining the spring and tender silk-iness of it in her palm, his groan as she caressed him.

Darcy shoved his partially unbuttoned buckskins down, revealing the curve of his buttocks and part of a black-furred thigh, and produced a condom from a pocket. Not very his-torically authentic. Shouldn't he be messing around with a nice bit of sheep gut tied with a red ribbon?

He tossed the gloves onto the table, needing both hands now to roll the condom on, while Vivian moaned and writhed on the table. One hand on his cock, he reached forward to pull Vivian's T-shirt up and pinch her nipples.

Lou's own nipples tingled, reminding her rather forcefully of their existence.

Darcy positioned himself and pushed forward.

Lou's breath caught. She imagined that slow slide, the sen-sation of being filled, stretched, penetrated, invaded, fucked. *Oh.*

And then the withdrawal, right to the brink, almost out—and back with a sudden push, a vigorous back and forth, a hearty, galloping sort of rhythm while Vivian moaned and he groaned—pausing to slap her ass—and then off again. The muscles stood out on his arms as he braced himself, palms flat on the table. His buttocks clenched and flexed.

This man knew what he was doing. Lou could see him assess Vivian's pleasure, wait for her, adjust to a rhythm that pleased her and bend to whisper in her ear, and bite it, maybe—she couldn't quite see—and sustained her rather noisy orgasm for what seemed like a long time.

Once upon a time, Lou had done that, too. Or rather, had it done to her. Her clit and nipples had particularly vivid memories of that sort of thing, and were whining at her that they wanted some now, right now.

Now he increased the speed of his thrusts—his turn.

Darcy turned his head to the doorway where Lou stood, looked her straight in the eye, grinned and winked seconds before he came.

Three

Mac

When Mac looked at the doorway next, the skinny blonde woman had disappeared. He'd liked seeing her interest, her shock and, above all, enjoyed the fact that she'd blatantly watched, her nipples poking through her shift like bullets. She hadn't done anything overly porno like feeling herself up while she watched, and somehow her restraint had made it more exciting. He'd got that tingle-at-the-back-of-his-neck feeling that someone was watching quite early on in the game. Vivian, he suspected, had known all along, even though she had been as noisy as usual.

He disposed of the condom and pulled on his shirt again.

"Bloody hell," said Vivian. "I'll be black and blue, you bastard."

"And pantyless." He snagged her thong from the floor and stuffed it into his pocket. "Spoils of war."

"I do have other pairs, you know."

"There you go, ruining my fantasy." He helped her off

the table and aimed a kiss at her mouth. As he expected, she dodged away.

"Don't get all sloppy over me," Vivian said. "Cup of tea?"

"No, thanks, but I'll use the bathroom." He said it purely to see her reaction, knowing the blonde was in there. He guessed Viv had got an extra thrill from knowing someone might walk in any moment.

"Go outside. There's a guest using it."

"You mean, I could have had a threesome?"

"Dream on." She picked his vest and coat from the chair and handed them to him. "I have things to do." She took his neckcloth and tied it expertly around his neck, far better than he could do, straightening out his collar and lapels.

"When can I interview you?" he asked.

"You keep coming to interview me and fucking me instead. Maybe you should just send your editor a video of us."

"Can I check my email?"

"No. You've had enough fun for the day. Sod off back to the nineteenth century."

"Okay, okay."

She evaded another friendly kiss and shoved him out the door.

Typical Viv. She didn't like kissing, didn't like affection; she liked fucking—no, she liked orgasms. She made sure she got one, too, one way or the other. This time, he felt she'd fucked the table—grinding her pussy against the wood—as much as she'd fucked him. She didn't even like to talk much after she'd come, when she'd revert back to being efficient, tough Viv. He could understand in a way why she wanted to play the victim in fantasy, all quivering lips and downcast eyes, when she was such a ballbuster in real life.

Trouble was, he wanted to laugh half the time. And some

of the time, he wanted to shout *"What about* me, *Viv? There's a guy at the other end of this dick. Talk to me, for Christ's sake."* Perhaps it was some sort of karmic payback for acting like a jerk in the past with women who'd wanted affection and conversation and cuddling in bed. He'd always done his best, but quite often he drifted off to sleep while wondering what the hell they really wanted.

Had he been the male equivalent of Viv? He hoped not. Women liked him, and not just to gratify themselves on his dick, or so he'd always thought. But Viv didn't seem to like him particularly, and that bothered him. Maybe his last divorce, ostensibly so amicable and rational and grown-up, had changed him in some way.

Uncomfortable, he ran a finger around his neckcloth and contemplated removing it as he strolled along the drive, beneath the branches of the huge horse chestnuts that grew on either side. He hated ties and this was far worse. But a gentleman should be properly attired at all times. Yeah, he was a gentleman, or at least he'd been one for five days (the amount of time he and Viv had been fucking) and would be one for another couple of weeks. Maybe becoming a Regency gentleman, all testosterone and manly pursuits, had brought out his inner bastard. You wore clothes like this, you strode around as though you owned the universe and you became what you imitated.

Hell with that. He was a journalist, one of a dying breed of those who wrote for print, a modern-day Grub Street man—not that the prestigious magazine he was writing for would appreciate the term—not some rich jerk from two centuries ago. He should really get down to work, making notes and writing up stuff. Although, it was refreshing to be mostly out of touch with his editor.

The house came into view, creamy stone and a red sand-stone portico and steps at the front. Two figures dawdled across the gravel in front—Rob the footman and Di the ladies' maid. Local kids, nice, mistrustful of him, of course. He remembered his mom, at his last birthday, raising her glass and crowing, "Never trust anyone over thirty!" He'd given her a smacking kiss and called her an unrepentant old hippie.

He extricated his watch—he couldn't bend, shoulders rounded, to get it from his pocket, not with this tightly fitting coat—and saw he had enough time to duck into the kitchen and beg some bread and cheese before the afternoon's activities. He couldn't believe he'd once wondered what people did all day long back then, being gentlemen—he still wasn't sure what the ladies did. Riding lesson, dancing lesson, boxing lesson, change for dinner and then maybe he'd meet the new arrival formally with his pants on. He remembered her name now, Louisa Connolly, Paradise's historical adviser. Peter and Chris referred to her as Lou. Loulou. He had her résumé somewhere in his notes. He remembered them saying they'd met her at some Jane Austen conference in the States.

As if on cue, Chris appeared on the portico and descended the steps, resplendent in his Regency outfit that included the tightest of tight pants and a gaudy striped vest. He stopped to chat to the two servants and straightened Rob's collar. That was Chris, all touchy-feely and flirty, while poor old Peter glowered in the background.

And there were lots of people in this house to get touchy-feely and flirty with, whatever your sexual orientation.

Lou

STAYS MADE YOU STAND UP straight, and that wasn't all. Lou found she couldn't bend particularly easily and her breasts were presented ridiculously high, like apples on a tray. She had to negotiate a reticule, a parasol and a bonnet that wanted to slide off her head, and walk along the gravel drive that led from Vivian's gatehouse to the main house, wearing thin slippers that reminded her of childhood ballet lessons. The posture, too—shoulders back, head up, don't look at your feet if you could even see them past your ridiculously upthrust breasts. *Bosom,* that was the word. Now she had a bosom. Never one for lounging on beaches, she now had to worry about tender skin presented to the ravages of the sun, and was glad of both the parasol and the lawn scarf tucked into her neckline to protect her pair of apples. She was thankful she didn't have a Montana rancher's tan, thanks to daily, religious applications of sunscreen on exposed flesh.

The gown, though, was gorgeous—fine cotton, a pale blue stripe on a cream background, simple yet elegant. It floated as she walked and it rustled in a seductive whisper.

The house was stunning in the glow of late-afternoon sun, friendly and impressive all at once. Had Austen really stayed here? She knew Chris and Peter longed to substantiate the myth, but now, after the house had passed through several sets of hands and suffered the ripping away of walls and floors during renovations, she doubted any new evidence could be found. No, let the myth remain. At the very least, it was a good conversation point.

She lifted the skirt of her gown to negotiate the steps, wondering if she were revealing her garters, ridiculous ribbons that had already untied once on the walk. The door of the house swung open, and Chris, resplendent in a gold-and-maroon vest, a blue coat and buff leather pants, bounded out to meet her.

"Loulou, my love, how wonderful you look!"

"You, too, Chris. I love that watch fob pointing straight at your package."

"Isn't it fabulous! Come on in, darling, we're gathering for dinner and you can meet the others. Rob, dear, take Miss Loulou's—or rather, Mrs. Connolly's—parasol and gloves and bonnet for her. This is Rob, our head footman, ready to meet your every need. He'll take you upstairs so Di can get you ready for dinner."

The young man bowed and took the items from Lou. "If you'd like to follow me, ma'am."

She followed him up the stairs, noting his broad shoulders and muscled calves. If he felt uncomfortable in his livery, showy gold braid and dark blue velvet, he didn't show it. He seemed remarkably self-possessed. And cute. Heck, he was cute in the same way that some of Julian's students had been—young and serious and clean.

"How long have you been at the house, Rob?"

He stepped onto the first landing. "A couple of weeks, ma'am."

"Are you enjoying it?"

"Yes, ma'am." He gave her a sweet smile.

"Do you come from around here?"

"Yes." He stopped and opened a door. "Yes, ma'am, I mean. This is your room. Miss Di is your maid."

He handed the parasol and other items to a young woman who stepped forward and curtsied. "I'll help you get ready for dinner, ma'am," she said.

The room held a beautiful four-poster bed hung in a toile fabric, red print on cream, which was also used for drapes and to upholster a couple of chairs in the room. In authentic style, the room was sparsely furnished, with a washstand in one corner and a chest of drawers with a mirror against the wall. A table and a chair stood at the window, a location for ladylike pursuits such as writing letters or reading the latest fashionable novel. Lou moved to the bed and patted its surface—a modern mattress, to her relief. She opened the drawer in one of the small cabinets on either side of the bed, and found an assortment of condoms.

So much for ladylike pursuits. She slammed it shut, annoyed and touched that Peter and Chris were anticipating sexual escapades for her. Or perhaps everyone received a condom care package. She wouldn't put it past them.

"Great room," she said to Di, who had looked up, startled at the sound of the slamming drawer.

Di unpicked the tacked-on sleeves on the dress Lou wore, and deftly brushed and pinned up Lou's hair and twisted a scarf and a couple of artificial flowers into a headband. She removed the lid from a small pot, revealing a red, waxy substance. "This is for lips or cheeks. It's made from beeswax, very authentic. I'd recommend you rouge, ma'am."

Lou agreed; all her efforts with sunscreen and more recently, weariness from travel, had left her looking pale. She turned down an offer of lamp blacking for her eyelashes. Di told her, grinning, that none of the ladies had wanted to use it, but at least one of them had smuggled in some mascara.

Peter, clad in clothes similar to Chris's, but slightly less showy, moved forward from the shadows of the hall and tucked her hand into his arm as she descended the staircase. Lou kissed him with great affection. "You look great, but you look tired, honey. Is that distinguished gray I see at your temples?"

He smiled. "Oh, it's been a strain, dealing with everything. You know, construction and permits, or rather the mysterious English equivalents thereof. Thank God, Chris understands this stuff. But we're nearly there. I feel like a proud papa. Julian would have loved the place."

"I know." She paused as they entered a drawing room. "Oh, it's gorgeous. Look at that plasterwork. Is it original? And the furniture—not all antique, surely."

"Most of it. Not the beds, though," Peter said, "as you probably noticed. Modern, to withstand 'heavy bonking' as they say here. Now let me introduce you to the others."

It was truly like going back in time. The group of people at the other end of the room looked as though they had stepped out of an old painting or a Jane Austen movie. Some of the men still wore their daytime buckskins and blue coats; others wore satin britches with matching coats, white stockings and buckled shoes. The women shimmered in low-cut gowns.

She met a good-looking couple from London, Ben and Sarah, both actors, who were there primarily for their decorative appeal, Lou suspected. Another couple, Cathy and Alan, who seemed shy and uncomfortable in their Regency clothes, were also recent arrivals. The design team, Jon and Simon, Lou figured were probably gay and a couple in more than their professional lives. She wondered exactly who Chris and Peter, with the most loving of intentions, had in mind for her.

Vivian, wearing a shot silk gown that gleamed dark blue and green as she moved, and with her hair tucked into a matching turban topped with a scarlet ostrich feather, gave Lou a brief inspection. "Very nice. I'll send the rest of the clothes up tomorrow."

Another man stepped forward from the shadows of the room. He'd changed from his buckskins into equally form-fitting trousers, made out of some sort of silk knit, breathtakingly clingy, with an elaborately ruffled shirt and a swallowtail coat above. Only a man with such a gorgeous body—and she'd seen most of it earlier that day—could get away with that style. The silk knit revealed the subtle outline of his genitals, which stirred against the fabric as he walked toward her. *Christ, sex on a stick.*

"Mr. Darcy, I presume," Lou said, hand outstretched.

He stopped and blushed. "Uh…"

"He does look the part," Peter said in appreciation. "Lou, this is Mac Salazar. He's doing an article on us for *Georgian Living,* so be nice to him. Mac, this is Lou. She's our Austen expert, so you must spend some time with her."

Peter stepped away and sent Rob over with a tray of champagne.

Mac handed her a glass. "Should we be discreet and pretend our first meeting didn't happen?"

"It's certainly not the sort of meet cute Austen wrote about." He might talk of discretion but his eyes shone with mischief and energy. An attractive man, she thought, and not only because she'd seen him half-naked and lustily enjoying sex.

He grinned. "Chris and Peter told me a lot about you."

"Yes, we're good friends. Where are you from?"

"Chicago by way of London. I got this commission to do an advance piece on the house, so here I am. What are you doing in…Montana, I think Peter said?"

"Oh, long story." She sipped her champagne. "My husband and I lived on a ranch and we taught at a school a couple of hours away. He died suddenly last year." She could say it now, the short version, stark and matter-of-fact.

"I'm sorry. Do you think you'll stay there?"

"I don't know." Her glass was empty. "Don't you want to ask me about historical authenticity at Paradise?"

"I guess so. After you've settled in, we should set up a time for an interview. It's an interesting concept, time travel with no chance of getting stuck in the past, or treading on a bug and changing the course of history."

"It's a very sexy period." She was halfway down another glass now and the room was beginning to take on a subtle, mellow glow that was half sunset, half alcohol. "Mainly because of popular culture, of course. People say there's no sex in Austen. They're wrong. Her books are full of sex, but it's all subsex. Subtext."

"That's the champagne talking." He took her glass from her hand.

"Champagne and jet lag. I can't drink. Never could. You should have seen me at Julian's faculty parties." She focused on his face. "Why does she call you Darcy?"

"It's my middle name."

"Mac Darcy Salazar?"

He nodded. "My mom likes Austen." He bent his head and whispered in her ear, as though admitting to a perversion, "So do I."

"Real men read Austen." Another glass was in her hand, cloudy liquid with a slice of lemon and a sprig of mint—lemonade, and just in time. She was suddenly very thirsty. She took a long swallow. "Am I slurring my words?"

"Not at the moment. Let's go eat." He offered his arm.

She smiled at him and took her place at the table. Candlelight danced off silver and crystal, flattered pretty faces into beauty, emphasizing hollows and sculptures, the fall of a lock of hair. She rubbed the smooth linen of the tablecloth between her fingers. *This isn't real. This is a fantasy. In real life, I'd have been dead of an infected paper cut or toothless by thirty-five. But what a fantasy.*

The door flew open and footmen, led by Rob, streamed

into the room. And yes, Peter had managed to hire a matched set, equal in height, all good-looking and young. They placed large platters of food on the table—pies, roast meat, bowls of vegetables and some sort of jellylike dessert—the first remove of dinner.

"Aren't they adorable?" the woman opposite Lou said. Sarah, the actor, she remembered. Sarah plucked at Rob's sleeve. "I'm a vegetarian. What can I eat?"

From the expression on Sarah's face, Lou thought she'd like to eat Rob, vegetarian or not.

"That's a leek-and-cheese tart, ma'am, in front of you, and salad."

"Mmm." Lips pouted, Sarah cut into the pastry. "Would you like some, Lou?"

"Sure. Thanks. Have some asparagus."

Mac stood to carve a joint of lamb. "Baa, baa," he intoned. "Sure you don't want some fresh meat, Sarah?"

"Oh, shut up, Mac." Sarah tossed her head. "Carving, it's such a guy thing. Lou, tell us about yourself. Who do you fancy?"

Who, not *what.* Sarah wasn't offering her food, apparently. If Lou hadn't seen Mac and Viv earlier in the day, she would have been quite shocked at Sarah's lack of inhibitions.

"Ben's quite good," Sarah said. "I think he fancies Mac, though, don't you, darling?"

Ben, who Lou could swear was examining his reflection in the shiny surface of his knife, gave a secretive smile.

"Sarah," Chris bellowed from the other end of the table, "stop behaving like a procuress. You'll give Lou entirely the wrong impression."

"Or the right impression." Mac flipped a slice of meat onto

Lou's plate. "Do you really think Austen's characters fucked like bunnies, Lou? Give us the official academic reading."

"Stop showing off, Mac," said Vivian.

Lou noticed that Cathy, who sat next to her, was staring, entranced, at the bulge in Mac's pants. "Hi, I'm Lou," she said by way of distraction. "We didn't get a chance to talk before dinner. I love your gown."

"Thanks. Yours is nice, too." Cathy paused. "We—me and Alan, my husband—we won this contest in the newspaper to come here. It's a bit grand, isn't it? And all these people waiting on us. It wasn't what we expected. We thought it would be more like a hotel."

"It's not quite finished, yet," Lou said. "It will be much more luxurious then, when all the en suite bathrooms are finished."

"Oh, it's horrible now," Cathy said. "That shower is like the one we had in college, and there are all these bits of wiring sticking out of the walls. Did you know there's only one proper bath in the house?"

"Use the bathhouse," Mac said. "Get in there with your husband and scrub his back, honey. No hardship there. Or double up with me. I won't complain." His carving duties over, he sat and helped himself to asparagus.

"I don't think it's hygienic," Cathy said primly. "You're swimming around in that nasty water that smells like rotten eggs that everyone else has been in."

"Are you going to come back at Christmas for the grand opening?" Lou asked. "Everything will be gorgeous then. You'll love it."

"Oh, no." She looked down the table to where her husband was deep in conversation with Peter. "Alan thinks we should, but it's so expensive. He gets on ever so well with Peter and Chris."

Lou heard the uncertainty in her voice and noticed that Peter had his hand over Alan's on the table. Getting on a bit too well, she thought. She was surprised at Peter's behavior. Of the two, it was solid, dependable Peter who she would have thought least likely to stray. Chris, on the other hand, flirted with anyone—men, women—it was part of his personality, to be charming and entertaining.

"You could always come and use the bath in the gatehouse," Vivian said to Cathy in a seductive purr. "I'd love to have you."

"Hands off, Viv," Mac said. "She's a married woman, you home wrecker."

Cathy gave him a quick, grateful glance. She stared at a dish on the table, a pale, molded creation, garnished with watercress. "What's this—ice cream?"

Lou tasted it, sweet and gritty on her tongue, and nodded. "Nice. Pistachio, I think, with a bit of lemon. They liked to mix sweet and savory then in each remove—that's what they called the courses. Sorry, I'm reverting to being a teacher. Try it."

Cathy dipped her spoon into it and took a tentative taste. And another. "Oh. Oh, my God, that's so good."

Cathy's face, which Lou had thought too sharp and pointed to be really pretty, softened to a voluptuous dreaminess as her pointed tongue flicked across the surface of the spoon. Across the table, Mac fell silent and watched her.

Lou wondered exactly what was going on in those knit pants.

Even Rob, standing at the sideboard, had forgotten his servant persona enough to stare at Cathy with open interest.

The moment was broken. Chris, a conspiratorial smile on his face, grasped a small silver bell that stood by his plate. "Rob, dear," he sang out. "Second remove, I think."

Four

Peter

He balanced his laptop on his knees and ran over the schedule for the next day. The urge to lay the laptop aside and fall into sleep was overwhelming, but he knew that if he neglected this ritual, his night would be haunted by dreams of things left undone, domestic catastrophes and scheduling nightmares.

The shower turned off and Chris entered, shaking his wet hair. He wore his blue pajama bottoms, the ones Peter liked, low on his hips. He patted his face dry and yawned. "You old fussbudget."

"All done." Peter clicked out and laid the laptop on the bedside table. He drew back the bedclothes.

"Like an old married couple," Chris commented. He leaned to kiss Peter. "Uh-oh, what's up, lover boy?"

He hadn't even realized he'd turned his face aside to receive the kiss chastely on the cheek. "Nothing. I'm tired. Sorry. Rain check?"

"Okay." Chris settled into bed beside him, sweetly scented with shampoo and soap, his skin slightly damp. "Not that tired, I see." He grasped Peter's semi-erect cock and gave it a quick squeeze. "Inspired by the lovely Alan?"

"Not my type."

"Sure. Playing genial host, were we?" Chris's voice was light, but Peter caught an undercurrent of something—alarm? Jealousy?

"Honey," he said carefully, "we're both tired. Let's not say anything we'll regret, okay? Let not the sun go down on our anger and all that good stuff. I was flirting, yeah. He's a tad bi-curious, that's all."

Chris slid down in the bed, hands behind his head. "It's not like you."

"But it's like you." Immediately after the words were out of Peter's mouth, he regretted them.

"Tit for tat?"

"Something like that." He slid down in the bed. "Honey, you flirt. You flirt with *everyone*. I don't. Not usually. So when I do, you notice."

"Okay, okay." Chris turned and fumbled with the button at Peter's pajamas.

He really wasn't in the mood but he recognized it as a gesture of reconciliation, if not desire. "You don't have to," he said, hand on Chris's wrist.

"Sure. Fine." Chris released him and turned over, the moment lost, and stretched to switch off the bedside lamp.

"I love you," Peter said, a little hesitantly, a little too late, into the darkness.

There was no reply.

Lou

"I CAN'T REMEMBER MY ROOM," she said to the footman, the good-looking one. They were all good-looking. And she could remember her room, its quiet elegance, the handsome bed, the soft cooing of doves and the scattered shadow from the trees outside. What she couldn't remember was how to get back to it. "Where it is," she amended.

"There's tea, ma'am, in the drawing room."

"No, too jet-lagged. Too...drunk," she finished successfully. "I need to go to bed. But I don't know..."

"It's okay, I can help you," said the Georgian footman, a phrase that made her giggle. So wrong, so right.

"How sweet." She linked her hand through his bent arm and kept going and going, and he straightened her up, supporting her. Rob, she thought his name was. "I don't normally do this."

"Of course not, ma'am. Up the stairs, now."

She stopped, suddenly. "Wait. My gown." She grabbed a handful of fabric to free her feet.

"You okay, Lou?"

With some difficulty, she turned, grabbing the banister for support with one hand and Rob the footman with the other.

"Mr. Darcy!"

"You're shit-faced," Mac said.

"In my cups. It's mostly jet lag."

"Oh, sure." He took a step up the stairs. "I'll follow behind, make sure she doesn't fall backward."

"I really hate it when people refer to me in the third person. You're not going to grab my ass, are you, Darcy?"

"Frankly, I'm shocked." He put a hand on her ass and shoved. "Hurry up. You're more likely to fall if you go slow."

"It's a novel experience, being escorted upstairs by two gentlemen," she commented.

"I'm glad to hear it," Mac said. "Okay, top of the stairs. Try to walk straight."

Down a corridor, a turn, dim lights, another turn. "I remember now," she said, lurching to a stop.

"No, ma'am, not this one," Rob said. "A few more steps, and here we are."

He opened a door.

"I can take it from here," Mac said, taking Lou's arm.

Rob turned away, with a muttered, "Good night."

"Take what from here?" She propped herself up against the door frame. Perfectly vertical. Well, maybe not so vertical as she began a slow, relaxed slide against the polished wood.

"Getting you to bed."

"Don't for one moment think you'll get lucky. I can manage. Front-lacing stays. Very sensible."

"Oh, yeah?" He pushed her forward into the room.

Giggling, she landed on the bed, perched, not sprawling. He went to the corner of the room.

"What are you doing?"

"Getting you some water. You'll have a hell of a hangover tomorrow if you don't hydrate."

"Crapulous. Bottle bitten." She took the glass from him. "All of it?"

"Yeah. Try not to puke."

Three glasses of water later, she found herself lying on her back on the bed, contemplating the tester. "Thanks, Mac. I'll be fine now."

He lifted her foot and unlaced her leather slipper, then the other, standing between her spread knees.

She sighed.

"What's wrong?" He bent and swiped at the side of her face, at the hot, wet tears that spilled from her eyes without warning.

"This could be so damn sexy." She sniffed. "I thought I'd find him here, but now I'm too drunk."

"Not tonight, gorgeous. I don't know why that makes you cry, but heck, you're drunk as a skunk. Okay." His hands hovered at her neckline. "Is there some sort of pin arrangement here?"

"No." She wiped her face messily and stood, hardly swaying at all. "Ties at the back. You called me 'gorgeous.'"

"Okay, slight exaggeration. Turn around." She did so, and felt the give and slide as he pulled the two ties undone, and her gown dropped to the floor. She giggled and reached for the drawstring of the petticoat, which followed the gown onto the floor in a soft rush, and then she fumbled at the front lacing of her stays.

He backed away, hands held out. "I'm done."

"You are?" She wasn't sure if she should be relieved or insulted. "You're a kind man, Mr. Darcy."

"Kind? I just undressed you. Your ankles are driving me wild with lust. If you weren't so damned drunk, my dishonorable intentions would be a lot clearer. Get some sleep. 'Night, honey." He bent and gave her a quick, swift kiss on the forehead as her stays loosened and fell from her hands. "Sleep tight."

Oh, great. He was speaking to her as though she was a toddler. But didn't being drunk reduce you to some sort of idiot infantile state anyway? She watched the door close behind him and tottered in her shift to the bathroom. Her eyes looked huge and shadowed in the dim light—the only lighting was from those cunning fake candles that flickered like the real thing. Much better for the infrastructure, no staining of paint, no guests falling drunkenly asleep and setting themselves on fire.

She dropped her shift on the floor and stumbled naked into bed.

Then it hit her. "Heck, Julian, I could have ended my celibacy with a threesome if I'd played my cards right. What a missed opportunity." The cool sheets stroked her body, caressed her. "And where are you? Still refusing to haunt me?"

"THEY'VE GONE RIDING, MA'AM." The maid, whose name she couldn't remember, fussed around with last night's gown, which Mac, presumably, had folded neatly over a chair. Lou couldn't remember much, only that she'd probably done or said something embarrassing, and that doubtless shameful memories would eventually crowd back. She groaned and covered her face with her hands.

"I'd like to have gone riding. If I wasn't hungover."

Di, that was her name, giggled. "We had bets on downstairs."

"On what?"

"Who'd be most pissed." Ah, yes, *pissed* for *drunk*; the beauties of the English language. "I bet on you but Cathy—Mrs. Saunders—she was pretty far gone, too. I think she was upset with Mr. Saunders ignoring her." She passed Lou a dressing gown.

"I don't think this is historically correct," Lou said, pushing her arms through the sleeves.

"You don't want to get cold," Di said diplomatically. "What would you like to wear?"

"I don't know. You choose." Lou, decently clad and propped up on the pillows, watched as Di smoothed fabric and imagined herself two centuries back. She absolutely wouldn't have let two gentlemen—or strictly speaking, one gentleman and one servant—see her in such a shocking state of drunkenness, and the shame of awakening knowing that at least one of them had helped her off with her clothes would have been overwhelming. As it was, she had a slight headache, but otherwise an overall sensation of relaxation. Soon she would get up and test the primitive shower, a cheap plastic contraption in one corner of the bathroom, and in proper Georgian fashion, take the air in the garden. She assured Di she didn't need help dressing, and the young woman bobbed a curtsy and left with her basket of laundry.

ONLY THE OCCASIONAL DRONE OF an airplane overhead indicated that two centuries had passed. The garden, Lou knew, had been carefully researched and planned and already the flower beds, with the straggly equivalents of familiar modern plants, were beginning to fill out. There was even a wilderness area of the sort in which Lady Catherine de Bourgh cross-questioned Lizzy Bennet, a shrubbery carefully planted to give an illusion of wildness, and the gleam of a building, a summerhouse, farther inside.

Footsteps, strong and fast, crunched on the gravel behind her.

"Good morning, Mr. Darcy," she said before she could stop herself.

His pace quickened and he came to her side. "You're clairvoyant, as well as being a brilliant scholar, Mrs. Connolly?"

"Neither. You can call me Lou if you like."

"Not here," he said. He smelled of sweat and horse and leather, and carried a riding whip. She wondered idly if he planned to smack anyone with it. "Here and now, you're Mrs. Connolly."

"I guess so. How was your ride?"

"I seem to be getting better. I don't feel I have to soak my ass for hours after. Our riding master said I was a natural. I have the thighs for it." He winked. "You ride pretty well, don't you?"

"Not real well and hardly at all sidesaddle."

He seemed quite content strolling at her side, tapping the riding whip against his leather boots. "You're feeling okay?"

"Not nearly as bad as I should, thanks. And I guess I have to thank you for getting me to bed. I'm sorry I was such a mess."

He nodded. "My pleasure."

"Really?"

"Well, shit, that came out wrong. I mean, I was glad to be of service."

"You're a knight in shining armor," she said, touching his arm before she realized what she was doing, amazed that as fully clothed as they both were, the brush of her gloves against his sleeve held such significance.

He gave a bark of laughter. "Tarnished armor. Where are we going?"

"I want to see the summerhouse. The boys sent me pictures of it." As they approached the small building, she heard the murmur of voices. "Oh, Cathy and her husband—I can't remember his name—are there. They may not want company. I think they're newlyweds."

"His name's Alan," Mac said. "Well, well. Looks like a lovers' tiff."

Sure enough, Cathy and Alan stood in the center beneath the domed roof, clearly visible through the arches that formed its construction.

"I want to go home," Cathy was saying as Mac and Lou approached.

Mac took her elbow and drew Lou to a halt behind a bush.

Alan gazed at the mosaic floor and kicked one of the marble pillars. "Come on, love—"

"I don't like it here. I don't like having to dress up and do what I'm told and not being able to wear knickers, and last night at dinner you paid me hardly any attention at all."

"But everyone else did," Alan said. "You practically had an orgasm over that ice cream."

"What?" Cathy shook her head. "I can't help it if you—"

"If I what?" Alan advanced on his wife, unbuttoning his coat.

"Uh-oh," Mac whispered to Lou. "Make-up sex is imminent."

"I think we should go," Lou said, unable to tear her eyes from Alan and Cathy, now kissing, Alan pushing his coat off and letting it fall to the floor. "Maybe they know we're here."

"So what?" Mac said calmly. "Oh, yeah, here come the titties."

Sure enough, Alan fumbled at the drawstring of Cathy's gown, revealing small pointed breasts.

"You know," Lou said, "I'm tired of being a voyeur. Or should that be voyeuse? Twice in two days, and you're involved both times."

Mac's breath was warm on the back of her neck. Her hair

stirred as he laughed softly. "Don't you like watching people fuck?"

"Not particularly," Lou said, but was aware that she wanted to stay and watch this, watch Alan caress and tongue his wife's breasts, hear Cathy's soft sighs, and see her head tip back, eyes closed, just as she'd reacted to the ice cream at dinner. Cathy's nipples had hardened to dark points.

Alan stepped away and tore off waistcoat and neckcloth—at least, his intentions showed some haste, but unwinding the foot or so of muslin took some time. Cathy meanwhile unbuttoned the front flap of his breeches, pushing them down over his hips.

"Damn, I don't think he's going to undress her," Mac said.

"Why don't you go in there and show him how to do it?" Lou said. "No! I didn't mean that."

"I'm shocked," Mac said. "I think they would be, too. Hey, it's oral sex time."

"Shut up," Lou said. "You're like an annoying sports commentator."

Alan pushed Cathy onto one of the stone seats in an alcove of the summerhouse, lifting her legs over his shoulders and burying his face between her thighs. Cathy's hands gripped the stone and she moaned, her muslin gown folded up around her waist.

Lou involuntarily squeezed her thighs together. Oh, yes, she remembered what that felt like, the luscious wetness, the sight of Julian's head bobbing between her spread legs and her pubic hair darkening with his saliva and her own juices.

"She's coming," Mac whispered. "Look at her face."

"I can't. It's too private." But she did, and watched Cathy's head tip back and her fingers clench and whiten on the edge of the stone bench, heard her cry out, her face ecstatic and blank.

The couple was still for a moment. That moment when Julian's lips would close on her clitoris in a slow caress of completion, calming the shocks. Sometimes he'd dart his tongue out to slide it inside her, lapping, promising more.

Alan, breeches now around his boots, stood and lowered himself to penetrate Cathy, his mouth on hers. *Taste yourself, Lou.*

Did her breathing hitch as Mac's did? And then guilt and shame took over: What was she thinking, watching this, and watching this in the company of a man who she barely knew? She'd leave. She'd leave now. No, immediately after they'd finished.

Alan's cock slid in and out of Cathy's pussy, hard red flesh engulfed by glistening pink.

Lou was still here. But she wouldn't subject herself to any post-game discussion with Mac. Absolutely not.

"Look at her cunt," Mac said softly. He brushed against her. Was it deliberate? Yes, he had a hard-on. The bulge in his breeches stirred her muslin skirts.

It's your hormones, she told herself. He wasn't even someone she liked particularly, or at least knew too little about him to know whether she'd like to know him more. Only hormones. Nothing to do with him, nothing to do with the couple fucking a few feet away, both of them groaning and Alan's back shining with sweat. Cathy's hands left the stone, gripped his hips and pulled him, positioned him, her feet digging into his thighs.

"I love you," Cathy gasped, and Lou turned her head away, eyes closed. This was too intimate, too painful. Cathy gave that same high cry, followed by a groan from Alan.

Lou kept her eyes closed. No more. Sunlight filtered by branches formed spangled, shifting patterns behind her eyelids, and scents of cool greenery and distant, subtle flowers overlaid with bergamot and male sweat filled her nostrils. Birds whistled and trilled.

"So, Lou." Mac's voice was a gentle whisper. He brushed against her again and one finger stroked her neck, the leather warm and soft against her skin. "I wonder what you look like when you come."

Five

"You wish," Lou said. Even to herself, it came out as unconvincing, her voice throaty with desire—no, not desire, pollen. Yes, that must be it, those damn oversexed trees jerking off shamelessly all around them.

"Look, I'm not suggesting we fuck," Mac said. "Peter and Chris told me about your husband, and I'm sorry. They said you're pretty fragile. Anyway, we're not each other's types and besides..."

"Besides what?" she asked, eyes still closed. "I know. You'll be saying next that you like me against your will, against your reason and even against your character."

"You've got to admit that I'm probably the only guy you'll ever meet outside your work who can identify an Austen quote when it's slapped around my head."

"Well, that's something." She opened her eyes. "So what are you suggesting? Do I possibly have something Viv doesn't?"

"Well." He stepped away from her, hands linked behind his back, and smiled. A friendly, sexy sort of smile that she told herself sternly to ignore. "It's up to you. We could make out or do…other things. You look really horny and I know I am. No obligations, nothing more."

"Or I could walk into Meryton to buy some ribbons."

He laughed. "Come on, Lou. Make up your mind. It's pretty damn uncomfortable in these leather pants."

"You really are a romantic, aren't you?"

"No," he said. "I'm honest. It's about all I can offer you, a bit of no-strings fun. Think of it as a physical necessity."

"Even worse. And where do you propose this lovely consummation of honesty and physical necessity take place?"

He grinned that wolfish grin. "I should tell you that your strict-schoolmarm act turns me on. I love a woman who can use the subjunctive correctly."

"Asshole," she said with more friendliness than she intended.

"You realize you keep looking at my cock?" He took her gloved hand and placed it on the fall of his breeches.

Her fingers closed around the hard length pushing against the leather before she could stop herself. "I've seen it in action. Remember? And it was certainly on display at dinner last night."

"Good thing there was a tablecloth to give me cover," he replied. He took her hand off his cock and tugged her forward. "How about the summerhouse? Alan and Cathy gave it a test run and it seemed to work for them. Nicely set up, with those stone benches and the view over the lake."

"A nice view for whom?" she asked. But she walked forward with him, hand in hand, their feet sinking into leaf mold. "I guess there might be some sort of cosmic balance if someone else watched us."

He handed her up the stone steps into the summerhouse.

Mac

WHAT WAS HE DOING? DESPITE HIS good intentions, it was still his cock driving him forward, to do something he might regret with a woman he didn't even know and who might not even like him. Same old, same old. He'd look damned stupid if he backed out now, although the temptation to run from her was almost overpowering. He could always take care of things later, alone.

Her hand was still in his. Naturally, idiotically, they still had their gloves on. Amazing how readily they could fall into their roles, half-crazy with lust but with not a stitch of clothing removed. He cleared his throat.

"Yes?" Cool as a cucumber, eyebrows raised. Wait, remember her last night, sprawled on her bed and crying, vulnerable, talking nonsense. Did she remember that?

She removed her hand from his and slowly began to work at her glove, twisting the fingers and easing the fabric from her hand. He watched with all the attention of a teenager in a strip club as she peeled the glove off and fluttered her fingers a little, airing them out. Then the other. It wasn't meant to be seductive, he was fairly sure of it, but he couldn't tear his eyes away.

"Well?" She stowed the gloves in a pocket at the side of her dress. "Don't tell me you're turning chicken on me." She raised her hands and unbuttoned what he thought was part of her gown but was, in fact, a sort of short jacket over it. What was the name of that piece of clothing? He couldn't remember for the life of him. Pelisse? No, he didn't think so. Spencer, that was it.

She folded the garment and laid it on one of the stone benches. Nice to see someone else was scared of Viv.

He stripped off his own gloves with more haste than elegance, quite unlike her slow unpeel and reveal. There wasn't room for them in his pants pockets, so he shoved them into his coat pockets and then started the laborious process of shrugging and wriggling the coat off.

She sat on a stone bench and watched him. "Let's establish ground rules."

"Okay." Coat off, he removed his waistcoat and sat opposite her.

"Contact?"

"What?"

She rose to her feet and he tried not to shrink back as she covered the space between them in a few swift strides. She pulled at the knot in his neckcloth and loosened it, slipping her hand beneath the folds and loops of muslin to unbutton his shirt. Her fingers fluttered on his chest, cool and gentle. "Who does what to whom?"

"Kiss me." His voice was throaty and uncontrolled. Immediately, he was mortified. He'd asked her to kiss him?

She tipped her head back to look at him, her lips parting. Her bosom, ridiculously high from her stays, lifted a little more as she sucked in a breath. The muslin scarf at her neckline, fine white cotton with subtle shiny white dots on it, parted to reveal a shadow of cleavage. Something was definitely wrong with him, that he was taking note of her clothes and the fabric first, and what lay beneath after. Maybe he'd learned more from Viv than he knew, or else he was about to channel Henry Tilney and advise her on laundry.

"You don't have to do anything," he said. "I mean, if you want to, I could, well, I—"

"Oh, shut up, Mr. Darcy." She raised herself on her toes. "Your reputation is entirely safe with me."

"My reputation?"

"I won't let anyone know you succumbed to sentimentality."

Her lips brushed against his as she spoke, a gesture that would have seemed almost innocent if her hips had not ground against his erection. Her tongue darted against the corner of his mouth, soft and wet.

He thought for one shameful moment he was going to explode in his pants.

He stepped away, loosening his hands from where they'd clamped on to her butt, and cleared his throat. "Yeah, look, we don't have to—"

"Yes, we do. I do." She glared at him. "What's wrong?"

"I'm, uh, surprised." Yes, he was surprised and lustful and a little afraid of this volatile creature. "What exactly do you have in mind?"

"You want me to spell it out?" She sat on the stone bench again, and propped one ankle on the opposite knee, pulling at the laces of her slipper. It dangled briefly from her foot and fell to the ground.

Another quick gesture released the ribbon holding her stocking up—not very sexy, these Georgian stockings, with all the allure of a tube sock and much the same shape. She unrolled the stocking and wiggled her toes. And that, somehow, was amazingly sexy. Her toenails were unpainted, her feet and calves muscular and pale.

A quick flash of white thigh and white petticoat—he remembered her petticoat floating from her last night and the sudden shock of her corseted breasts, round and constrained, almost under his nose—and she started on the other foot. "Come on," she said, "you wanted to see what I look like when I come. So do something about it."

She raised one foot onto the stone seat, turning so she sat sideways, and lifted her skirts. Fabric rustled as she raised skirts, revealing long pale thighs. She ran her fingertip up the inside of her thigh, back and forth.

Her fingertip slowed.

He groaned. He couldn't help it.

"Do it to me," she said breathlessly.

Today she wore a gown that pinned at the front. She undid the pins and laid them carefully aside, one-handed, her other hand on her thigh. The fabric fell, revealing the top of her petticoat and her stays, and she released one breast, pausing to stroke the nipple.

"Okay," he said. "Okay." And he was beside her, having made those few steps across the summerhouse, pulling her skirts all the way up around her waist, loving the way her thighs parted for him, the way she turned to reveal herself to him.

She made a small, excited sound as he gazed between her thighs, at the tuft of dark blond hair and wet, plumped lips. She could wait a little, he decided. He leaned to take a nipple into his mouth, feeling it swell and harden against his tongue.

She made a sound of appreciation, of pleasure, and her hips moved slightly in invitation. He hooked her raised leg over his arm and touched her where she was wet and warm and her clit was a raised, hard ridge beneath opulent silkiness.

"Yes," she said, and reached to adjust his finger a fraction of an inch. "You... Yes."

He moved his mouth to her neck and collarbone, then back to her nipple.

She raised one hand to her bodice and fingered her other breast, and he wondered if she could come like that, if she would come like that, and would he feel cheated? He bit gently on the nipple in his mouth and knew from its sudden swell and her quickened breath that she was almost there.

Her legs flexed, hard, and she moaned loudly. She was there, she'd gone, her eyes half-closed and he slowed his pace.

"Wow," he said.

"That was so...so sexy." She smiled at him, all her former tension gone. "And so fast."

He loved seeing her so relaxed, her breasts and her splayed legs, unaware of how sexy she looked. Probably. Meanwhile, his cock shoved painfully against his pants. He stood and moved away from her and tried not to look at her.

She shifted, and her eyes took on her familiar wariness. "What?"

As much as he wanted release, he wanted to touch her again, take his time, make it even better for her. Suck her nipples and kiss his way down her to bury his face in that gorgeous pussy. He wanted to wring more soft cries of pleasure from her and feel her warm skin heat beneath his hands, but he fell silent. He shook his head and stood, looking at the view over the lake.

She tucked her breasts away and pinned her gown back into place, but she delayed putting on her stockings and slippers again.

"We won't make a habit of this," she said. "It was one time only, right? It was very nice, but—"

"Sure." He tried to keep his voice casual.

"You're offended. I'm sorry."

"No, no," he lied. "I know, it's nothing personal."

"How could it be? I've known you all of twenty-four hours."

"During which time, I've undressed you, seen you cry and seen you come." He knotted his cravat, fished his gloves out of his pocket and walked away from her before he made an even greater fool of himself.

Very nice. What the hell had he done to deserve that?

Lou

LOU SMILED AS HE WALKED AWAY. What strange, delicate creatures men were, at the mercy of their cocks and yet so vulnerable. She remembered his touch, the way the tendons flexed on his forearm and the glint of sunlight that lit the lock of hair on his forehead, his face intent as he pleasured her.

And now he'd gone stomping off in a huff of male outrage. She closed her eyes. What did she look like when she came? He'd wondered, and now he knew. She ran her hands lightly over her bodice, meaning to tie her muslin scarf and tuck it away, but she encountered her nipples, still hard even through corset and petticoat.

Well, well.

She could do it again. She could open herself to the dappled sunlight and the breeze—her clitoris zinged as she increased the pressure on her breasts. She squeezed her thighs together.

She knew he'd been about to ask her if she would touch him, or if he could do more to her, and now she wished her hackles had not risen. The thought of that mouth—how soft his lips had been, how lovely the scrape of his chin would be against her thighs. His cock would press against her thigh, through her skirts, then beneath her skirts, and press and slide inside her, if she said yes, and she knew she would.

And she wouldn't once think of Julian. Next time, absolutely not.

Oh, who was she kidding? She might have come here chasing a ghost, but Julian was no closer to her here than in

Montana. The only difference was that here every corner and room, every view outside, was not dull with memories, weighing her down with regret.

Paradise Hall had already worked its magic, its promise of escape and sensual adventure. Lou shook her head and laughed, sliding a bare toe over the stone floor. She should really go back to the house and see what was on the schedule for the morning or the afternoon or whatever time of day it was. With this unchanging, translucent leafy light, she had no idea of the time.

She bent to retrieve her shoes and pulled them toward her with her toes while retrieving her stockings and garters. Decently shod once more, she eased her gloves over her fingers—how he'd stared and she hadn't thought she was doing anything particularly seductive when she'd taken them off— and placed her bonnet atop her head, letting the strings dangle. She should probably investigate what food was on offer, too; maybe she wouldn't be so foolhardy on a full stomach.

But it hadn't felt risky or dangerous. The only really uncomfortable moment was when she'd told him that it was a one-time-only thing. Mac obviously was used to being the one who called the shots in a relationship, if five minutes of friction could be called a relationship. Or two minutes, to be accurate.

But he kissed well.

As she took the path away from the lake and toward the house, a familiar ticking and metallic hiss arose behind her. A bicycle, and, as she turned, the head footman, in jeans and T-shirt, riding it. She stepped aside to let him pass as he slowed and came to a halt next to her.

"You're quite an anachronism," she said.

He smiled. "I shouldn't be here, ma'am. But the path round the back is too muddy for the bike."

"Where have you been?" she asked. "Not that it's any of my business, but how do you entertain yourself off duty?"

"No problem," he said. He dismounted and wheeled the bike beside her. "I've been down the village. Played some football with my little brother."

"That's nice of you."

"He's a sweet kid." He stared at the handlebars of his bike.

"How many brothers and sisters do you have?"

"One of each. He's seven. My sister's older than me, and she's going crazy with Graham—that's my brother—underfoot. Her place is too small for all of us. And he needs... Well, I'm here."

"Are your parents away?"

"My mum is. And my father, well. He's got some troubles with his business. He's depressed."

"I'm sorry." She touched his wrist. He gave her a startled glance from clear gray eyes. "Thanks for your help last night. I really appreciate it."

"It's okay." He shrugged. "I'd better go round the back, ma'am." He pulled the bicycle away and slung his leg over the saddle, turning swiftly down a side path.

Lou sighed. Another male fleeing her presence after revealing a little too much of himself. *I'm here,* he'd said. Taking on unexpected responsibilities at a time when he should be out exploring the world, not trying to repair the damage of a dysfunctional family. As a teacher, she'd become something of an expert reading between the lines of inarticulate students who sat in her office and threw out disjointed comments about why a paper was late or a grade not met. She had learned early on to distinguish between those with

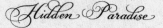

genuine problems and those too lazy or arrogant to put in the requisite work.

The house came into view. There was dancing this afternoon, she remembered, and smiled at the thought of the guests all stepping on each other's toes in every way possible.

Six

Rob

He flung open the door to the footmen's dormitory and bellowed, "Hands off cocks and on with socks!"

To emphasize his point, he banged on the gong that stood
just inside the door, a Victorian artifact that Chris and Peter
had declared absolutely unsuitable for use in the house, but
which Rob found invaluable in getting his charges awake.
He'd discovered early on that the only way to get his crew
moving was to behave like a jerk. As the din faded away, he
shouted, "Eleven-thirty, gents. You're on in half an hour.
Clean shirts and neckcloths. Inspection in the butler's pantry in twenty minutes."

Tousled heads rose from pillows accompanied by scowls,
belches, farts, the sounds of the awaking young male. Another local kid, Ivan, was the first to drop from his bunk,
swaggering naked across the room, erection swaying, rubbing
his eyes. Rob ignored him. His team of footmen, grumbling
and wearing anything from pajamas to boxers, spilled from

tangled bedclothes, clutching towels and toilet bags, on their way to the adjoining shower room.

Ivan paused near Rob. "Get any, then?"

"Piss off," Rob said, avoiding the urge to step back to avoid the waving penis.

"That Di. She's hot, man. If you won't do her, I will."

"Right. She thinks you're a hairy git. Get going." Sometimes he wondered if he wore an invisible sign everyone else could see that announced his embarrassing inexperience. Even Di seemed to know and, either because of that or because of her boyfriend back in London, had appointed him her BFF for the summer, which was nice, but not quite what he—or Ivan, it seemed—had in mind. It was endearing, in a way, that Ivan, and probably the others, thought that because Rob had a tiny room to himself that he spent his spare time in wild and indiscriminate sexual pursuits. He didn't have the heart to tell them the lame truth, that he woke early to read and then most days rode his bike out to see Graham.

"Or that new guest," Ivan the permanently erect continued. "That Lou or whatever her name is. Looks like a goer to me."

"Mrs. Connolly to you. Eighteen minutes," Rob said. He glanced at his wrist where a watch no longer resided, and straightened the cuff of his livery.

"Well, then." Ivan, having decided the conversation had reached its natural conclusion, ambled toward the shower, scratching his backside.

Rob made his way to the butler's pantry, an archaic term for a featureless, modernized space that was the meeting room of the footmen, and consulted the list on the bulletin board. The guests, he saw, were having a dance lesson this afternoon after lunch, served buffet-style upstairs. The regular kitchen staff had set out the chafing dishes and Rob and his crew now had to make sure all was well, explain what the food was if necessary and replace any popular dishes. After that, the footmen would get to eat the leftovers, take a few hours' break and then make themselves available to any of the male guests who needed help with dressing for dinner. He knew it wasn't anything like the hours footmen had to work two centuries ago but it made for a long day, ending well after midnight. One good thing, though—lifting all those trays and carrying them up and down the stairs from the kitchen was as good as going to the gym.

He ran water into the electric kettle and plugged it in on the kitchen counter at one end of the room. The least he could do was give his lads a cup of tea when they appeared. *His lads.* He very vaguely remembered meeting his great-grandfather, a veteran of the first world war. He must have been very small, but he remembered sitting on the old man's lap, fascinated by the frail, knobbly hands that turned the pages of a scrapbook showcasing the faded sepia photographs of young men long dead, hearing the pride and sadness in his quavering voice. *My lads, they were.* Until now, he'd never appreciated the bonds that arose in a group of men living in close quarters, working for a common goal. He grinned at his own pretension. Sure, exactly the same, but without gas warfare and mud and rats and exploding mortars day and night. Rob wondered what had happened to the scrapbook, hoped it hadn't been thrown out when his family had left the house.

The door opened and the first of his footmen straggled in, hair wet, jacket over his arm, reaching for a mug and a tea bag. The rest followed. Rob ran over the schedule, warned them against overindulging in the guests' wine—"finish up the opened bottles only, please, gents"—then had them line up for livery inspection. Another day was to begin.

"YOU'RE SURE THIS DOESN'T have any animal products of any kind, Rob?"

"Absolutely, ma'am. Saw the chef make it with my own eyes. Olive oil and lemon, a bit of tarragon."

Sarah poked at the pile of salad on her plate with a fork. "There's egg in there."

Then leave it on the side, you silly cow. "I'll get you a fresh plate."

"Thank you, Rob. You're the best."

He resisted rolling his eyes and handed the plate to one of his lads, who, he was pretty sure, would take the salad to the kitchen, dump it onto a clean plate, remove the egg and stir it around a bit, and take his time returning.

There were two newcomers for lunch, a woman and a skinny guy carrying a violin case, who'd come to teach them to dance. She was short, plump, with flyaway graying hair beneath an elaborate lace cap, and introduced herself as Becky the dance mistress and her assistant as Charlie. Nearly everyone else was here, Mac glowering more than usual and occasionally darting a glance over at Lou, who was in an animated conversation with the others and rather obviously ignoring him. So what had happened last night after Mac had dismissed Rob? He cringed again as he remembered Mac's dismissive tone last night. No wonder people hated being in service. It was too easy to think about this job as being a glorified waiter or hotel worker. In reality, it was a lot more than that.

After the footmen had cleared away, Rob returned to the room with pitchers of water and lemonade and more glasses.

He directed the lads to move the tables from the center of the room and took his station by the drinks. The guests were straggling onto the floor in pairs. Mac seemed to have disappeared.

"You," Becky said to Rob, "there's a lady waiting."

The lady was Lou. They expected him to dance with her? He began to stammer something about being on duty, but Becky, the lace flaps of her cap lifting in the air like an elephant's ears, bore down on him and grabbed his arm with a grasp of steel. "Yes, you, young man. You don't leave a lady without a partner."

He bowed. It came naturally now, and the woman made a clucking sound of approval. "Very nice. Gentlemen, bow to your partners. No, that's rubbish. Young man—your name?" He answered her and she continued, "Okay, everyone, watch Rob bow."

He felt like an idiot, but bowed again. He'd come to appreciate bows, how you could express a range of expression with the simple gesture, from genuine appreciation to a hint of incivility, all the way to understated insolence. He supposed it was the same for the women, curtsying. Lou dropped into a graceful sort of bob, a movement that didn't express much at all. The women apparently did better than the men, as Becky gave a nod of approval.

"And," Becky continued, "you must all have your gloves on. Absolutely no bare skin contact."

It reminded Rob of dealing with his lads, the same groaning and complaints as gloves were extricated from reticules and pockets. Made decent to Becky's specifications, they all lined up again and went through a series of baffling exercises: ballet positions, which the women could all do and the men were hopeless at, and a step that looked graceful when Becky did it—despite her decidedly ungraceful form—and which, as performed by everyone else, made most of them look like a bunch of lurching zombies. "One, two, three. One, two, three—bend your leg on three—one, two, three…"

Chassé. That was easy. Setting, a one-two-three hop, felt ridiculous. They walked through a mystifying combination of taking hands, changing directions, turning, circling.

"So now you have the basics," Becky said. "Back to your starting position, please. Face your partner and join your right hands. First position."

It was ridiculous, him standing like a duck and holding the gloved hand of a woman he didn't know.

Becky came down the line, inspecting them, just as earlier Rob had checked his lads for grease stains, dirty gloves, poorly tied neckcloths. She stopped at Rob and Lou. "And the most important thing of all. Eye contact. Lingering hand contact. This is as close to sex, standing up in public, as you're going to get in this period. It's partner swapping and flirtation and naughty goings-on. Remember that."

Dutifully, Rob met Lou's gaze and held it.

"Right," Becky said. "Let's do it. Bow or curtsy to your partner.…"

Charlie played an introductory ripple of notes on his fiddle, and they were off, Becky yelling instructions and pushing them into position.

It wasn't that bad, although most of the dancing he'd done was at clubs, usually with a beer bottle in one hand. This was different to say the least. More like a football game, lots of footwork that wasn't that difficult but it was how you performed it, weaving a pattern with your teammates. But even better, you got to touch women in a way that made the brush of gloved hands or the touch of elbows or shoulders much sexier than it should have been; a smile from another woman seemed full of seduction. Occasionally you had to hold a man's hand, or look into his eyes and hop about, and that wasn't nearly as gay as Rob would have thought. He supposed it was the equivalent of hugging a teammate after a goal.

Lou smiled at him. He smiled back and their gaze lingered and smoldered as they both turned away, circled, returned, clasped hands once more. "You're good at this," she said. Her skirts brushed against his calves.

They came to a stop as Cathy—who, with her husband, Alan, was next to them in the set—made a wrong turn. "I don't get it," Cathy said as Lou pushed her back into position.

"Listen to the music," Rob said, surprising himself. "It tells you what to do."

"Where should we be?" Alan said. "Cathy, come back."

"No, this way."

"You're going back up the line now," Lou said. "So you do what the others did before. You're couple one now." She and Rob did some more shoving and rearranging before Becky, realizing her charges were falling into disarray, called them to a halt.

"Well played, pardner," Lou said to Rob, and he found himself glowing with pride. She was slightly flushed and he caught a whiff of her scent, ripe and sexy, feminine sweat and lavender as he led her to the drinks table. The group, relaxed and laughing, exchanged friendly insults at each other's incompetence.

"It's like football," Rob said to Lou.

"Soccer?"

"Yes."

"Interesting analogy."

"Yeah, it's personal, you and me, but it's also about what everyone else is doing. If we go wrong, we mess up everyone, but we can get back into position. I bet she gave us an easy one to start off with," he said. "Would you like some lemonade, ma'am?"

"Absolutely right, young man, I did. I'll have you all bending it like Beckham before long," Becky said, patting him on the shoulder. "And I'll have a glass of lemonade, too."

Seven

Mac

He strode through the woods, toward the lodge and Viv, furious at himself, with Lou, with all of them. He took his hat off and swatted at a few flies that buzzed around. Not nearly as bad as a Michigan summer, but there were a surprising amount of small annoying bugs that had a particular interest in getting up his nose and no one had window screens here. He was damned if he was going to spend time hopping around like some sort of fairy and subjecting himself to more insults from women who couldn't make up their minds.

He loosened his neckcloth. To hell with formalities. He was going back—or going forward, rather—to the twenty-first century. He unbuttoned his waistcoat. Things would change. He'd play the Austen game as required, but only for the reason he was here.

The lodge came into view and with it a strange, tinny, discordant sound. Viv's radio. How easy it was to become accustomed to silence, birdsong and the rustle of wind in leafy branches, the pad of leather-soled shoes on wood floors, the feminine whisper of cotton garments.

He slid his coat off and banged on the lodge door before pushing it open.

Viv, a cigarette in one side of her mouth and pins in the other, and wearing a tight-fitting pair of jeans and a navel-baring T-shirt, looked up. "Hello, big boy. Let me finish this." She gestured to a dressmaker's form and removed a pin from her mouth to attach a fold of fabric. "Pretty, isn't it? Put your coat down. Carefully." Task completed, she turned to him. "And what can I do for you?" She rested her elbows on the worktable, breasts thrust forward, legs apart, a blatant invitation.

"What I should have done days ago." He placed an item on the table, a small recorder, and pulled a reporter's pad and pen from his breeches pocket.

"Honeymoon's over?" She reached to turn off the radio. "Thanks for asking. Of course this is a convenient time for me. Cup of tea? Fire away, Clark Kent."

He turned on the recorder. "Interview with costume mistress Viv Fairfield— Heck, what's the date, Viv?"

"Eighteenth." She spooned tea into the teapot and grinned at him, then perched on one of the high stools at the table, ankles demurely crossed.

He left the lodge an hour later, enthused by Viv's love for her profession, impressed by her expertise and faintly annoyed that he'd let the interview slide for so long. After all, he was here to work, just as Viv was. And yet she'd managed to balance sexual gratification with a single-minded dedication to her craft that he couldn't hope to match.

He was excited to write this up. But first, he'd visit the

bathhouse, once the pride and joy of the owners of the house. How many Georgian landowners had the fortune to possess a hot spring on their property? But instead of commercial development, the owners of Paradise Hall had chosen to dam the spring, creating a bathing pool for their own use. Peter and Chris, after consultation with historians and archaeologists, had built a simple round wooden structure with a vented roof to protect bathers' privacy and make the hot spring usable for most of the year. The new adjoining building, built of local stone, contained a modern spa because, as they both said, Georgian women didn't have a lot of fun stuff to do.

Mac could see their point. Historical accuracy could only take you so far in a commercial venture. This wasn't a crowd that would go for embroidery and crafts and piano practice. He nodded to a couple of spa employees who sat outside in the sun, their cigarettes incongruous with their mobcaps and gowns, and lifted the latch to the bathhouse door. Inside, it was dim and moist, steam rising from the water. A pile of towels lay on a bench. He sat in one of the wooden cubicles and toed off his boots. The water held a faint scent of musk and sulphur and a square of blue sky showed through the vent in the roof. Two hundred years ago, they would probably have drunk it, as well as bathed in it. Clothes off, towel nearby just in case anyone wandered in, he descended the stone steps into water that was the temperature of a hot bath, soothing and peaceful. In the middle, where it was deepest, you could float, buoyed by the high mineral content, or lounge on the stone steps, cork pillows covered in toweling provided for your comfort. He wedged a pillow behind the back of his neck and stretched out. Nice.

He smiled at the large sign on the wall that announced, in

a florid italic, that ladies and gentlemen who chose to bathe should remain within the bounds of decency—drawers or shifts, depending on gender. What a joke. Those thin cotton garments would be transparent within seconds. He liked the idea of a woman rising from the depths, a wet shift clinging to her breasts, hair like dark seaweed, a seductive mermaid sheathed in folds of transparent linen. He closed his eyes and let himself enjoy the image.

Lou

TWO HOURS TO DRESS FOR DINNER was a little excessive if you weren't messing around with cosmetics, merely planning to change a gown. Lou wondered if it had been built into the day as an official sex break. What an odd combination of activities Peter and Chris had put together—high culture with a bedside drawer of condoms. Last night's piano performance had starred an up-and-coming young European pianist, borrowed from a music festival nearby, and Lou had been sorry to have missed it. Or this, a historically correct bathhouse, based on Thomas Jefferson's in Virginia, next door to a state-of-the-art spa.

As she approached, a woman in a print gown and mobcap looked up guiltily as she stubbed out her cigarette in a clay container holding a rosebush. "We're closing in fifteen minutes, ma'am. Do you have an appointment?"

"No. Another time, maybe."

"Bathhouse is still open if you're interested. Have a good evening, ma'am." She darted back inside the modern building.

Lou lifted the latch to the bathhouse door and slipped inside into a moist, warm atmosphere. As her eyes became accustomed to the light, she realized with a shock that she wasn't alone. A man lay half in and half out of the water, one knee bent, dark hair tumbling over his forehead, which gleamed with a slight sheen of sweat. Adonis, she thought. Her breath caught at his beauty, the ivory and shadow of his body, that familiar flex of the forearm. But this time, he was caught up in his own pleasure, fist wrapped around his cock. His rib cage lifted as he sucked in a breath, then fell as he released it in a sigh. This was no urgent rush to release but a deliberate, leisurely quest for pleasure, a slow sensual slide of his fingers, thumb flicking up to massage the sensitive area beneath the tip.

She must have made some sort of sound. He froze, eyes flying open, head turning.

"Oh, shit," he said, and dropped his other forearm over his eyes.

"I'm sorry. I—" She backed away, but couldn't stop herself staring at him. "You're so beautiful." There. It was said.

"What?" He lowered his forearm and blinked at her. His other hand, meanwhile, continued its slow slide. "Give me a moment, will you?"

She stood, staring at his hand, the slick of dark hair on his chest, the elegant lines and planes of his body. She'd seen him partially undressed, but naked and pale in the dim light, caught at this most intimate of activities, his nude body had a vulnerability that touched her. "Would you like…" she said as a slow heat rose in her.

"What I'd like, Lou, is either privacy to finish this off or for you to join me. Could you make a quick decision?"

"I suppose I owe you from this morning."

He frowned. "It's not a barter system. It's sex. What would you like?"

"I'd like to touch you."

"Okay." He stroked himself, but his demeanor had changed. Now the act was provocative, seductive, playing to her. "Better get your dress off. It might get wet. Not just from the water." He grinned, now playful.

She unpinned her gown and tossed it onto a bench in one of the cubicles where she sat to unlace her shoes, and rolled her stockings down. Petticoat and stays off, she hesitated.

"Up to you," he said. "Depends whether you want to follow the rules." He nodded toward the sign on the wall.

She hesitated. It had been so long since she'd been naked for a man. Her body was okay, she knew, lean and strong, and he'd seen most of it. He might as well see the rest, and didn't the situation demand a sort of fair play—his nakedness in exchange for hers? She pulled the shift off over her head and saw his eyes darken and his hand tighten around his cock.

"Oh, yeah," he said dreamily, a sigh of admiration and pleasure. "Come here."

She walked toward him, nipples tightening beneath his gaze, hips automatically adopting a sway, enjoying the heat in his eyes, the catch of his teeth on his lip. She knelt next to him and cupped her breasts. "Tell me what you want."

He took his hand from his cock and reached for hers. "Make me come, Lou. Like this. Please."

She froze for one moment. This was a stranger, a stranger's body. Not Julian's, an unknown man's.

"Please," he said again. He shifted his hand over hers, so that his cock slid in her palm, against her fingers.

He was familiar yet new, as contradictory and as amazing as the hard ridges and tender outer skin she held. From strength to sweetness, a trust offered, masculine strength and vulnerability.

She stroked and clasped and heard his groan of appreciation. Their hands slid together. "Touch your nipple," he said, his voice thick.

"Is that good?" she whispered, although she knew the answer. She could see it in the clench of his jaw, the tension in his body, the flexed muscles. His back arched, his hand tightened around hers, and he cried out as semen splashed onto his chest and belly. His hand fell away from hers and he groaned again as she gave his softening cock a gentle squeeze. Then he pushed her hand away, opened his eyes and laughed, stretching, more relaxed than she'd seen him yet. He reached for a towel and handed it to her.

"Wow," he said. "Wow, that was pretty amazing, Lou." He pushed up onto one elbow and regarded her nakedness. "You look good naked."

"So do you," she said.

"Thanks." He scratched his chest and took the towel from her to wipe himself off. "Want a swim?"

"Wait." She got up to bolt the door. "I don't know why you didn't think of doing this."

He shrugged. "I didn't come in here specifically to jerk off. It just happened. Why did you come here?"

"I wanted to see it. The boys had sent me photos of the construction. You were a bit of a surprise." She walked toward him, once again enjoying the heat of his stare, and noticing the stir of his cock.

"Well." He settled the pillow beneath his head. "Now we're officially jerk-off buddies."

She laughed. "I guess we are." She sat beside him on the stone steps and dabbled her feet in the water.

"How was the dancing?" he asked. "Did I miss much?"

"Fairly disastrous. I don't see how we'll be ready for the grand ball in five days. Becky, the dancing instructor, is bringing in the people she dances with from a reenactment society, so we'll have some people who know what they're doing. I danced with Rob."

"Oh, yeah?" He cocked an eyebrow at her. "The kid has the hots for you."

"I don't think so."

"He does. And according to Viv, virtually everyone lusts after young Rob, or so she said today."

"You saw Viv today?" She shifted away from him.

"I interviewed her. It's what I'm here for, you know."

"And you were so horny you had to jerk off after?" Irrationally, she felt betrayed, embarrassed.

"No, I was so horny after this morning I had to jerk off."

"Hours later? Sorry, Mac, my experience of guys is that they don't wait hours."

"Look," he said, "I'm not competing in some sort of blueballs contest. I wasn't going to lurk in the woods with my pecker in my hand like some sort of pervert, and then by the time I got back to the house I was hungry, and after that the maid was making up my room, so… But why the hell does it matter to you, Lou?"

"I don't know," she said. And it was true. "I'm confused by you. I'm confused by my reactions to you."

"That makes two of us," he said.

"Oh." She didn't want to think of the implications of straying further into this strange territory of intimacy. "How was the interview?"

"Great." He sat up. "She's really interesting and brilliant at what she does. She's done a lot of stage work, building costumes for operas, which she says is pretty much what she's doing here, making clothes that look good but can be adapted for different body types. And she knows a heck of a lot about historical tailoring and so on. Apparently she had a big fight with Chris and Peter because they wanted a sort of generic look and she wanted historical accuracy. But they eventually compromised."

"You sound as though you never talked to her before," Lou said.

He gave an embarrassed laugh. "I didn't. It was always instant lust. But with you—I think I can have both. If you'll let me. And, yeah, I know I've known you all of two days, but think about it, Lou, okay?"

She slipped into the water and pushed off, floating. "Don't you think it's the artificiality of all this? Wearing gloves but also wearing clothes that suggest nudity? I mean, your outfit pretty much screams 'Look at my crotch.' And we know it's not real. Soon enough we'll go back to normal life."

A surge in the water and the brush of his leg against hers indicated that he'd joined her. "Possibly. I won't push you, Lou. But keep me in mind." His hand closed on hers and they floated side by side.

She let her head sink into the water so her ears filled with a gurgling dim roar. "I don't want a relationship."

"Tough. We have one already." His voice was distant.

She released his hand and pushed away from him, reaching the center of the pool in a few easy strokes. He was right, she thought, they did have a relationship although she wasn't quite sure what it was. She reached with her foot for the bottom of the pool and found herself out of her depth, in more ways than one, she reflected.

Water sloshed as he joined her, his body bumping against hers. She trod water, while he stood, his superior height giving him the advantage of standing. Oh, what the hell. She hooked one leg around his hip and stretched out before him, enjoying the admiration on his face.

"Is there anything I can do for you? Always happy to oblige. But I don't have any condoms here," he said.

"That's rather presumptuous of you."

"Come on, Lou." His hand smoothed over her belly, dark against her skin. "Sooner or later, we'll get around to it. You've only to say the word."

She raised her other leg around his waist and her hands to his shoulders so they were face-to-face, mouth to mouth. How easy it would be to take that final step, with his erection bumping against her belly and her own silky wetness. "What if I only fuck good kissers?"

He lowered his mouth to her neck, nuzzling, lips soft, the stubble on his chin grazing her exactly as she wanted it to. When he reached the corner of her mouth, he stopped. "How am I doing?"

"Okay."

"Just okay?"

"Do it some more and I'll let you know."

His mouth nipped and nibbled, teasing, nudging and retreating, soft and insistent. Was it her lips that moved against his, inspired to respond, or the actions of his clever, carefully attentive mouth?

"And?" He didn't move his mouth, but spoke against her lips, with a brief flick of his tongue as punctuation.

She moved her mouth from beneath his. "I'm not sure. I haven't had long enough."

He continued with a sweet deftness, exploring the sensitive contours of her lips and their tender inner surfaces, his tongue reaching out to touch hers. And then he withdrew, with a kiss to the side of her mouth, a brush of his wet hand against her nipples.

"Sure there's nothing else I can do for you?"

She untangled herself from him and swam away. "Later. We'd better get ready for dinner."

"I'd never have thought you were such a tease." He launched himself to the side of the pool. "Hey, how about getting to know each other?"

"We don't know each other?" she said, just to be aggravating. She grabbed a towel as soon as she reached the side and turned her back to him.

"No. We don't."

She snuck a quick glance at him to see him toweling his hair, his penis semi-erect. Mmm, nice. But neither it nor its owner was something she felt inclined to get to know more at the moment.

"I'll see you at dinner." Amazingly, she was dressed sooner than he was, stays hurriedly laced, stockings and garters in her pocket.

He looked up from pulling on his boots. "Go easy on the alcohol, Lou. I might break my rule about not fucking drunk women."

Peter

IT WAS THE STUFF OF FANTASY. He'd tried not to feel guilty about enjoying interviewing and hiring footmen so much and continued to try—again, unsuccessfully—to not feel bad about how sexy he found them in uniform. Or, as they were now, half in and half out of uniform, sprawled around the Servants' Hall. He felt a wave of tenderness at their youth, their unconscious beauty as they sat in their shirtsleeves around the table, polishing off the remains of dinner. Unbuttoned shirts revealed a sliver of chest, strong necks; rolled-up sleeves displayed handsome young well-muscled arms.

Rob rose to his feet. "Everything okay upstairs, sir?"

"Oh, yes. Fine, fine. Please, don't let me disturb you," he added, as others laid napkins aside and reached for discarded coats and wigs. "We'll be ready for tea and coffee in the drawing room in about ten minutes, and Chris will ring when it's time. But I wanted to thank you all for a splendid job thus far tonight. Well done, everyone."

"Thank you," Rob said. A few others murmured thanks but Peter winced as he caught a few sideways glances and sniggers. *Silly old queen.* Well, that's what he was, but it hurt, that these young men couldn't be more grateful for what he and Chris provided. He'd even hired Alex and Dejan, from Russia and Serbia respectively, despite their poor English, because he'd had a fit of guilt about their countries' sufferings—and they were both really hot, as Chris so often reminded him. Wasn't this better than working on a construction site or whatever else their options might be?

"I thought we might talk about the schedule for the ball, Rob," Peter said. "If this is a convenient time, that is."

"No problem." Rob stood and shrugged his coat on, adjusting the heavy, gilded cuffs. Peter winced as he saw Rob give his team a warning look, anticipating the chorus of suggestive comments that would arise, and that now might be delayed until they had left the room.

"So how do you think things are going?" Peter asked as the Servants' Hall door closed behind them.

"Okay," Rob said.

"That's good," Peter said with a touch too much enthusiasm.

Rob retied his neckcloth as they walked through the

kitchen, an incongruous figure among humming, top-of-the-line dishwashers and all the other paraphernalia of a commercial kitchen. He nodded at the chef, who sat tapping at a laptop as they passed. "They're still giving me grief about having to leave their mobiles in their lockers."

"Too bad," Peter said, remembering the first night with guests when the raucous shrill of a cell phone rang out in the dining room. "The guests don't even have access to their mobiles unless it's special circumstances, and then they have to get them from Viv. Is everything okay with Viv?"

"She bitches about spot cleaning our coats all the time," Rob said. "But it can't be helped. Spills happen when you're a waiter, which is what we are. And we sweat a lot, running up and down the stairs."

Peter cleared his throat. "I guess." He produced his ring of keys and unlocked the office door. Business, he reminded himself, not fantasies of clean young male sweat. He ushered Rob into the office and clicked to the footmen's schedule on the laptop.

"Oh, please, sit down." Peter pulled forward a second chair. The poor kid had been on his feet for hours, after all. "I'm thrilled that you're our head footman. I couldn't have chosen better. Now, on Saturday I see that two of the footmen have the night off. Is there any way we could do some rescheduling? I need as many staff as possible."

"Sorry, Paul's sister is getting married and I promised Ivan he could have the day off to play cricket. He's on the village team and they have a big match. He said he'd try to make it back by ten, and maybe sober."

"Oh, dear. Well, we'll make do, I suppose." Rob's elbow was inches away from his, his hand on the desk.

"It'll be fine. Keep dinner simple and fairly light, according to Chef, right? No problem with the buffet supper if we can serve it on the terrace...."

Peter's mind wandered as Rob talked. He found himself staring at Rob's hand, the red scar of a healing burn across the knuckle, fine golden brown hair on the fingers. Before he could stop himself, he touched the burn.

"That looks rather serious."

Rob moved his hand away, frowning. "Nah, it's nothing. We burn ourselves all the time, but not as bad as the cooks. But that reminds me, we need to put in an order for the first-aid supplies. We're running low on gauze and antibiotic cream. Okay, how many for breakfast after the ball?"

"You remind me so much of myself when I was young," Peter blurted out to his embarrassment.

Rob regarded him calmly. "Thanks, I think." He removed his hand from the desk. "Do you...fancy me?"

Peter wanted to weep with mortification. He took a deep breath. "I guess I do. I'm sorry. I find you very attractive." Oh, shit. He was about to lose his head footman. Chris would never forgive him, on so many levels. "I'm sorry," he said. "That was entirely unprofessional."

"I'm not dumb," Rob said, and the kindness in his tone almost undid Peter. "None of us are. It's a bit of a joke downstairs that you hired us for our looks, but you know that. And I'm flattered and all that but I play for the other team. Sorry, mate. I mean, sir." To Peter's relief, he switched back to business again. "Okay, I'd calculate twenty guests for breakfast, right? I'll let half the lads off at ten so they can get a bit of sleep and then they'll be on duty at five for breakfast."

"Yes," Peter said. "Yes, that sounds fine. Thanks. Thanks for everything, Rob."

"I'll get back to the Servants' Hall," Rob said. He stood and straightened his coat. "Everything all right, sir?"

"Yes, fine." Peter forced a smile.

As the door closed behind Rob, Peter sank his face into his hands, elbows on the desk. Dear God. Was he out of his mind? What if Rob's brisk, matter-of-fact tolerance was skin-deep and he went back to the Servants' Hall and told everyone how the old fag had made a pass at him?

He rushed out after Rob and took one painful moment to bask in the young man's beauty as he walked away—the straight back and broad shoulders, the curve of his muscled calves.

Rob turned. "Something wrong, sir?"

"Rob." He grasped his sleeve. "This is just between us, right? No hard feelings, I hope. Look, I know you've got some problems at home. If there's anything I can do, just say the word. I can…." His voice died away at the look of contempt on Rob's face.

"You don't need to bother." Rob shook his hand off and walked away.

Oh, God, he was such a clumsy fool. He blundered back into the office, tears rising to his eyes. The other door, the one that opened to the yard stood open, and a couple of moths circled the overhead light, making rash bursts of flight and falling away from the heat.

Chris sat at the desk and, from the expression on his face, Peter knew he'd overheard at least the end of his encounter with Rob.

"Just what the hell is going on?" Chris said.

Eight

Rob

He came back into the Servants' Hall as the drawing-room bell jangled.

"All right, mate?" Ivan asked.

"Yeah, great." He looked around. "Dejan, where's the tray of cups and saucers?"

"Cups and…?"

"Yeah. For upstairs."

Dejan frowned and gestured to the table where the remnants of dinner lay. "Tea?"

"I'll do it, you berk," Ivan said, and ran to the adjoining room where the china was stored.

Rob rushed to the kitchen—it was always the same, however well prepared they thought they were, everything always happened at the last moment—and hefted the tray laden with a huge teapot and coffee jug, sugar and cream. He snatched a handful of teaspoons, loaded the cake stand with tiny cakes and dried apricots and chocolates decorated with gold leaf, and carried it all out, narrowly missing Ivan and his tray. They eyed each other.

"Wig's crooked," Rob said, and thrust the tray at Declan.

"Bugger." Ivan laid his tray on the table and adjusted his wig.

Rob armed himself with a couple of smaller trays and a cloth for spills, and opened the door for them. They began the trip up the narrow winding servants' stairs.

"Why the fuck didn't they put in an elevator," Ivan wheezed.

"Architectural integrity."

"Archi—what? Did the old guy make a pass at you, then?"

"You know what he's like." They paused on the landing at the first floor.

"I had ten quid on it," Ivan said in disgust. "Couldn't you give the old sod a pity blow job?"

"Sorry, mate. Wrong team." They emerged from the servants' staircase and paused to catch their breath. From the drawing room, they heard the sound of a piano and a woman singing.

"Wait," Rob said.

"Why?"

"Because you and Dejan are all red and she's still singing. We go in when they clap."

The pianist played a final chord and during the applause Rob opened the door and ushered in Dejan and Ivan and their trays. Neither Peter nor Chris was present, which was unusual, and the guests looked a little drunk, which was not unusual at all. At least Lou was pretty much sober tonight. She was sitting next to one of the guys who messed around with the plaster and paint, talking to him with great animation. Mac, meanwhile, across the room, gazed at her, and

Rob wondered why he didn't just go and talk to her. Like poor old Peter had done, clumsily touching him and gazing at him like some sort of pathetic spaniel. It wasn't the first time a gay guy had propositioned him—it happened, no big deal—but it was a big deal when it was your boss and he looked so sad and scared. Hell, he was even older than Rob's dad, and he felt more pity for Peter than he could for his own father.

"Tea, ma'am?" he said to Lou.

She took a cup from the tray without even noticing him. "Sixteen layers!" she said to the decorating guy. Jon Nesbitt, that was his name.

"You'll have to come and look at my samples," Jon said in his plummy posh voice. Would Rob talk like that, too, after Cambridge?

"Oh, I'd love to."

Christ, she was practically having an orgasm about looking at paint layers or whatever she was planning to do. He moved the tray away before Jon could take a cup and went to the next guest, the one Downstairs voted most likely to put out. Unfortunately, she also tied for the honor of most annoying and demanding.

"Hi, Rob." Sarah took a cup of coffee. "Is this organic?"

"Absolutely. And fair trade. Tastes nice, too," he said vaguely, staring straight into her cleavage. He couldn't help it. It was just there, all ripe and pillowy and gorgeous with its mysterious deep shadow, and she was sitting and he was standing, and if he wasn't careful he'd tip half a dozen cups of tea and coffee into its depths.

Dejan nudged him and Rob tore his gaze away and stepped aside. Sarah smiled at Rob, took one of the small cakes from Dejan's tray and flicked her tongue out to capture the sugared rose petals adorning the top. Rob stood transfixed, his limbs immobile—except for his cock, which was moving around rather too much—and wondered if he had some sort of hormonal infestation that made everyone come on to him. Even he, inexperienced as he was, knew Sarah, gorgeous, very silly Sarah, was all but inviting him to bed. It was so fucking ironic that a woman he fancied only in a general tits-on-parade way should proposition him. What was wrong with liking a woman you fucked? Something must be, because the women he did like—Di, for instance—didn't invite him to bed and they put up some sort of invisible wall that stopped him inviting them. How did you resolve this? Maybe you never did, maybe all guys were like this. All their lives.

Back to business. He nodded to Dejan to move on to the next guest.

"I might need some help later, Rob," Sarah said in a soft whisper. She licked her lips.

"Okay," he said, trying not to let his face stretch into a huge, stupid grin. Sometimes tits on parade was enough. "I'll be around, ma'am."

"Sarah," she said. "Call me Sarah."

"Not my place, ma'am. Not in company."

She smiled and he, sensing that the other guests were interested in the contents of his tray, left the view of Sarah's splendid cleavage to serve them.

"Nice teats," Dejan said, nudging him.

"Which ones?" Rob said. It was true, the room was full of nice tits, because that's how all the women were dressed and he was doing his best now to ignore them, since he was standing, the guests were sitting, and he was self-conscious about his excitement. He was glad Peter and Chris weren't around, because they'd certainly be aware of his condition.

The woman went back to the piano and rustled some music around and everyone stopped talking, giving Rob the chance to move back into the shadows, holding the small tray in front of himself. Things were getting pretty uncomfortable down there and he really wanted to adjust himself, but not in public. He could do that only by unbuttoning the flap and once he'd done that he knew the adjustment would need to turn into something providing a different level of comfort, and he'd have to wait until he was alone for that.

To take his mind off it, he tried to listen to the music, which was the sort of stuff his mum liked. She'd love this sort of thing, the culture and everything. To get his good mood back, he thought about Sarah and exactly how he was going to hook up with her when he was off duty. And what about her husband? Rob didn't fancy getting beaten up by him, but he didn't look like the sort of guy who'd get into a fight over his wife. He wouldn't want to mess with Alan, though, and he and Cathy were all over each other, occupying a small sofa in a corner, and not paying any attention to the music at all, only to each other. Lou sat fanning herself, obviously all steamed up about plasterwork and layers of paint, and Mac continued to watch her from the other side of the room.

At the end of the next song, Chris and Peter came into the room, and Rob wondered if he was the only one who could sense the tension twanging between them. But they went into their usual genial hosts act and, as Rob expected, Peter kept his distance, approaching Dejan for a cup of tea. More standing around, more tedious music—Cathy and Alan had the right idea; they'd slipped quietly from the room when Peter and Chris had come in.

Sarah didn't give Rob another glance. The whole situation reminded him of being caught in the middle of some complicated game where everyone except himself knew the rules. Where was he supposed to find her after? Had she been serious? He sent Dejan and Ivan to the kitchen for more tea and coffee and refreshments and leaned against the wall, tired of standing, and immensely relieved when the singer announced that the next song would be her last. After that, the guests, yawning and gathering up fans and gloves, left the drawing room in couples or groups. Rob watched Sarah for some sort of sign but she left in a group of people that included her husband without another glance at him. Or maybe she did, but there wasn't enough light in the room, other than where the candlesticks were massed, to see. So it seemed as though the next move would be up to him. *Great.*

Lou

"CAN I HELP?" SHE SAID TO Peter as they left the drawing room.

He paid her no attention but stared at Chris, who had an avuncular—possibly—hand on Ben's shoulder and seemed to be sharing a joke with him and Sarah.

"Honey?" she said.

He turned to her, and she saw how drawn and tired he looked, the lines in his face etched deep. "Lou, there's no fool like an old fool."

"How would you know?" She tucked her hand into his arm. "Want to talk about it?"

He nodded. "Let's go...not into the office. The dining room." He plucked a candlestick from a table in the hallway and they made their way through the dark house. "I'm beginning to wonder about you and Mac," he said.

"There's not much to wonder about," Lou said. "I think

I'd be better off sticking to the footmen." His silence told her she'd blundered. "Oh, shit, Peter, I'm sorry."

He pushed open the dining-room door and set the candlestick on the sideboard. "I've rather screwed things up, I think."

"How?" She sat opposite him, the polished surface of the mahogany table cool to her fingertips and elbows.

"There's a lot of stress in this endeavor," he said. "Lots of worry and details and…well, things haven't been too hot in the bedroom recently. We're both tired, we talk shop all the time and it's not exactly romantic, you know? And…"

"And you don't fuck the help," Lou said.

"If fucking the help was a problem, I think we could deal with it. I'm in love, Lou. I've fallen in love and I still love Chris and he can't understand it and I can't, either. It doesn't make any sense at all." In the near darkness, he swiped at his face and she saw him attempt the semblance of a smile. "They all know downstairs, of course. He—that is, the one I— Well, he's been pretty decent about it. He turned me down very tactfully. Shit, Lou, I don't even know him, and I'm sighing and fantasizing over him and I can't get him out of my mind. It's Rob."

"Well, he seems a sweet kid," Lou said.

"He is. And Chris found out, about an hour ago. Maybe I wanted to get found out. Adulterers often do. He overheard part of a conversation, heard me coming on to Rob, and… well, it's a mess, Lou. Chris and I have pretty much been faithful to each other—he's flirted a lot, I've flirted a little, but this time I've done damage."

Lou reached for his hand. "I'm so sorry. You'll have to talk to Chris, but you know that."

"Yes. He's mad as hell. It doesn't jeopardize just our relationship—it's this, all this." He made a gesture around the room. "We've sunk our savings and our hearts and souls into this place, Lou."

"I know." She raised his hand to her lips and kissed it. "You're one of the best people I know, Peter. Chris, too. Yeah, you've done damage, but you can make it good again. I know you can."

"It's just so damn depressing, Lou. Here I am, I'm fifty-two, and I'm still making the same damn stupid mistakes. I should know better. I should have kept my mouth shut. I should have suffered in silence." He gripped her hand. "You and Julian, you did okay. I always thought of you as the ideal couple."

"That's funny. We always thought of you as the ideal couple. I still do. Keep the faith, honey."

He released her hand. "Thanks."

Lou, staring at the reflection of the candle in the windows, caught a sudden movement from outside. "Who's out on the terrace?"

Peter turned. "Ah. It appears to be a madman, dancing by moonlight. Your madman, I believe. Go for it."

She borrowed the candle and, following Peter's directions, found a side door. Outside, the night was clear, the moonlight brighter than the flickering light of a single candle in a corridor paneled with dark wood, and she saw her madman dancing, apparently with his own shadow, on the terrace. He muttered to himself as he stepped and paced.

"One, two, three, four…" He referred to a slip of paper in one hand. "Set? Oh, yeah, set. One-two-three. Cast off… sounds like fucking knitting. One, two, three, four."

Lou leaned against the balustrade and let herself enjoy the sight of Mac, painted by moonlight to silver and sable and

ivory. The tails of his coat swished around his thighs. Tonight, he wore dark knee breeches and cream stockings that
hugged his handsome legs. A lock of hair fell forward over
his brow and he frowned and brushed it aside. He raised one
arm—presumably to join hands with three other nonexistent
dancers—and caught sight of Lou.

He stopped. "Congratulations. You've caught me indulg-
ing in solitary pleasures again."

"Are you enjoying yourself?"

He stopped and peered at his slip of paper. "Damn. Lost
my place." He held out his hand to Lou. "Care to join me?"

"It's easier with other dancers." She took his hand. They'd
both removed their gloves, and the touch of bare hands was
an unexpected delight.

"Viv gave me the steps," he said. "She said I should catch
up, since I missed the lesson."

"And it's much easier with the music," Lou said. "But I
guess you should be commended for effort."

"Thanks. Let's take it from the top."

They parted, danced toward each other, then away, weaved
among imaginary dancers, and met again.

"Oh, hell," Mac said, and slipped his arms around her
waist, bringing her close to him. They slow danced together,
thighs and hips bumping, counting forgotten. "Let's go to
bed."

"With each other?" She tipped her head back to look at his
face. That lock of hair had fallen forward again. She raised
her hand to smooth it back into place.

"No, with half a dozen footmen. Of course with each
other. Come on, Lou, don't tease me anymore."

"I haven't been teasing you. Not much."

"Sure. Ignoring me all night to talk to that paint geek."

"That paint geek is one of the U.K.'s leading experts on Georgian-era paint color and restoration. I've wanted to talk to him for years, and I would have thought you would, too, for your article. Come on, Mac, it isn't all about you all of the time. I can't believe you're serious." She tipped her head back to see his expression.

"For what it's worth, neither can I." His eyes were dark, troubled.

Something screamed, far off in the direction of the trees. "What the hell was that?"

"Fox," he said. "Just think, Lou, all around us, critters are screwing."

"Or killing each other."

His hand smoothed up and down her back. He tilted his hips at hers. "Nature's a wonderful thing. Let's get natural together, Lou. Like I said, it's bound to happen sooner or later. I'd like it to be sooner."

"And what if I want those half dozen footmen?"

"I guess it could be arranged. So long as I could watch."

"So much for moonlight and romance."

"You're the one who brought up bringing in the help, Ms. Romance. Real thoughtful of you, but this time I won't be needing any help."

Sure enough, the erection pressing against her belly held the promise of being absolutely adequate. She made the decision, then. Was Paradise Hall responsible for her awakening, or was her desire for him an escape from her emotional winter—like the season itself, so long and cold and dark?

"You're thinking," he said.

"And that's a bad thing?" She slid a hand from his lapel to the shirt ruffle above his waistcoat, absorbing the warmth of his skin. "I may be using you. Or, how about if I want more than just a quick vacation fuck? Or if you do?"

"Then we deal with it. We're both adults. Let's go inside."

The candlestick she'd left on a shelf by the door flared, subsided and died as they entered the house, plunging them into velvety darkness. His warmth and scent, dampened linen, male sweat, engulfed her as their mouths met. This was wrong, the rational part of her mind told her, all wrong. He was far too possessive for a guy who wanted to get laid— and he could achieve that elsewhere, as she knew only too well. *Why me?* And the perfect dance of tongues and lips gave her the answer. His hand fumbled at the back of her gown and then moved to the front, freeing a breast and rasping his thumb over the nipple.

"Stop." She pushed him away, afraid he'd strip her naked there and then, and that she'd do the same to him. "Wait until we get upstairs."

"Which way?"

She took his hand and led him forward, the darkness fading a little as her eyes adjusted. Cool air washed over her exposed breast, tightening the nipple. She raised a hand to tuck herself back into the bodice of the gown.

"Leave it out," he said in a low, lustful rumble. "I want it ready."

A door stood ajar, letting in a little light, but only a very small amount, enough for her to see a steep set of stairs. Servants' stairs, she was pretty sure, but going in the right direction, with another flight leading down into pitch-darkness.

"This way." She lifted her skirts to ascend the stairs, and predictably his hands, hearing the slither of fabric, slid up her legs, stroking her thigh, cupping her butt.

He gave a low hum of appreciation.

"Not on these stairs. Too steep." She spoke in a whisper, although she wasn't sure why.

"Hold that thought, then."

The stairs curved into pitch-darkness and ended. She spread out her hands to assess where they were and what sort of space they were in and almost screamed as her fingers and then her exposed breast brushed against warm skin. Mac? No, he was behind her and this felt different, smoother, scented with a clean soap smell, and was almost certainly a bared male chest.

"What—"

"Shit. Sorry," the owner of the chest said in a whisper. Whoever it was released her and a faint greenish light illuminated Rob, wearing only a pair of boxers and holding a cell phone. They were standing on a landing, with the staircase going up the next flight. "Sorry," he said again.

"What the fuck!" Mac moved forward, threatening, the alpha male.

"Shh!" Rob jerked his head toward a closed door.

A slow grin spread over Mac's face. From the other side of the door came the unmistakable sound of a couple making love, a bed creaking, groans, panting. "We could be singing 'God Save the Queen' and I don't think they'd notice." He addressed Rob. "What the hell are you doing here?"

"She invited me to… Well, I thought she did." Rob jerked his head toward the door. "There's a hidden door to this room. But it's locked. What are you doing here? This is the servants' staircase."

Lou leaned against the wall, overcome with giggles. Both Rob and Mac gave her curious glances, although Rob's gaze fixed on her exposed breast. She pulled her bodice back up to cover it.

"Are you up for a threesome?" Mac asked. "Looks like they started without you."

Even in the dim light from his cell, Lou could see Rob blushing. "I thought… Well, I'm not even sure what she meant, now. She said she'd need me later, whatever that meant. May I help you get back to your rooms?"

"Does every room have a hidden doorway?" Mac asked.

"Most of them. I'll show you if you like. Not now," he added, glancing away in embarrassment. "If you go up the next flight, there's a door opening into the main corridor. You'll know where you are then."

He directed his cell phone to the staircase and gave a longing glance at the doorway.

"Is it Sarah?" Lou asked.

He nodded. "Good night."

He brushed past them and Lou noticed his hair was wet. Silly Sarah, leading the nice kid on like that. The sound of his bare feet pattering down the stairs died away.

"Well, come on." Mac, who had been paying rather careful attention to the sound effects from the bedroom, grasped her arm and pulled her in the direction of the stairs. "Or do you want to go read Rob a bedtime story?"

"He's sweet," she said.

"Yeah, I noticed you checking him out."

She ignored him. Chances were that after they'd had sex he wouldn't be nearly as possessive. At least, she hoped not. He was in pursuit mode right now.

"So, Mac," she said casually as they began the ascent up the stairs in pitch-darkness, "how are your relationships with exes?"

"Great. Her family invites me and my mom over for Christmas."

Well, that didn't sound like a stalker.

"And the other one travels a lot but lets me stay in her guest room when I'm in London—"

"We're talking ex-girlfriends, right?"

"No, ex-wives. Now, the girlfriends—"

"You've been married twice?" she said as they arrived at the next landing. "What happened?"

"I was very young the first time." He pushed open a doorway and they arrived in the upstairs hallway, which was illuminated by candelabra, and they were able to see each other again. "Think of it as me being road-tested."

"Or housetrained. Whose room?"

"Mine."

"Do you have protection?"

"Yes." He stalked ahead and she followed after, trying to read his mood.

 Nine

Mac opened one of the doors and bowed. He straightened and laughed. "It's becoming second nature."

"Inviting women to your bedchamber?"

"That's first nature. I meant bowing." He patted her shoulder. "Relax, Lou. Want a drink?"

She considered. She envied him his ease, his grace, as he slipped off his coat. A drink might help, but one thing was for sure—if she was going to go through with this, she wanted to be fully aware. Desire prickled in her breasts and belly but manifested outwardly as a keen nervousness. Thankfully he seemed only mildly amused and not offended by her sharpness.

Without waiting for a reply, he twisted a cork from an already opened bottle and poured two glasses of wine. He handed one to her and reached for a small framed picture of a child with unruly dark hair and a mischievous, gap-toothed smile, showing it to her without a word.

"Your daughter?" she asked.

"Yes. That's Rosie. She's five." He beamed with pride.

"She's cute."

He replaced the picture on the dresser. Lou watched as he shifted gears again, switching from proud father to seducer, clinking his glass against hers. "Sit down," he said. "You're doing your nervous hover."

"I do not do a 'nervous hover.' What do you mean by that anyway?"

He sprawled on the bed on one elbow, glass in that hand, and unbuttoned his waistcoat. "You know what I mean. Make yourself comfortable."

She sat down on the bed. Nervous hover, indeed. She took a sip of wine. "Why did your marriages break up?"

He paused in unbuttoning. "This doesn't really put me in the mood, Lou, but since you asked… Number one, we were both very young, still students. We grew up and found we'd grown away from each other. Number two, Jennifer, Rosie's mom, got pregnant and I insisted we get married for practical reasons—she's based in London, I'm mostly in the States. Jennifer and I get on real well, but then she fell in love with someone else. So we divorced. All very friendly. Her new husband's a nice enough guy but I'm still Rosie's dad."

Waistcoat unbuttoned, he shrugged it from his shoulders and removed the neckcloth that he'd loosened earlier that evening. Lou found herself transfixed by the curl of dark hair that appeared in the placket of his shirt. He kicked off his leather pumps.

"You want to take your gown off?"

She shook her head.

"What's on your mind, Lou?"

"I can't believe I've spent almost all the time I've been here deciding whether or not to have sex with you." She curled her fingers into his. "It'll be my first time since…"

"It's okay. I'll be gentle." He grinned. "I'll be whatever you want."

She leaned forward and kissed him. "You're sweet, Mac Salazar."

He stared at her in mock horror. "You sure know how to wreck a guy's ego, Lou. This morning you tell me my sexual services were 'very nice.' You extract a confession about my ex-wives. Now you tell me I'm 'sweet.' You want a fuck or not? Because I can feel my balls shrinking by the minute."

She glanced at the fall of his breeches where, contrary to his claim, no shrinkage at all seemed to be taking place. "I think you'll manage."

"We could always do each other's toenails or something," he grumbled, but with a hint of a smile. "So...you want to tell me about him?"

"Okay." This was familiar ground for her. She felt she'd done nothing but tell the story, in tears, in disbelief, in anger, for almost a year now, in pieces as it unfolded. "His name was Julian. We were together for five years. Together in the sense that we both had jobs in different states and we spent a lot of the time on the phone, online, grabbing weekends together, spending vacations together, trying to get jobs nearer to each other. Then he got a tenure position and bought the ranch. So I moved in to write my dissertation. We got married.

"We put in a garden, started the summer jobs, cutting firewood for the next winter. We rode, hiked. It was fun. We talked about having kids, planning a real future."

She paused, remembering those days, the two of them making up for lost time, making the necessary forays out to look after the animals, then back to bed for hours and hours. Sheets wrinkled and sticky, dirty plates and mugs sliding onto the floor, the phone ignored, computers shut down.

She gave Mac the short version, the simple statement that he had died in a car crash in the fall. Nothing about the phone call, the terrifying request that she come to the hospital immediately. The long night of waiting, holding Julian's inert hand in a room of blinking lights and the rhythmic hiss of the respirator. The meetings with the hospital staff, calling his parents, his sister, making the hardest decision of her life—when to turn off the respirator—and Julian making a journey so different from the two-hour drive home. He'd traveled beyond them all.

She'd come home alone to the ranch. Outside, the garden they'd planted together withered and died.

Now the hand of the living man curled into hers. "We'd been married just a few months.

"The boys—Peter and Chris—came over for the funeral even though they were going crazy with the renovations here. We scattered his ashes on the land, the same place we got married. I love him. I miss him. I want to tell him things all the time and then I remember he's not here anymore."

Mac raised a thumb to swipe a tear away from her cheek.

"I'm sorry," she said.

"No need to apologize."

"I'm tired of crying. Tired of grieving. Tired of feeling like I'm only half-alive and drifting. He's gone, and I came to Paradise, hoping I might find him here again. He loved the idea of what Chris and Peter were doing with the house. And although I feel better here than I did at home, Julian isn't here. He's gone. I'm having difficulty letting go."

"And that's where I come in?" He poured himself another glass of wine. She raised her own to her lips and sipped.

"You said you don't fuck drunk women. But do you fuck women yearning after dead men?"

"You have good reasons for being sad," he said to her surprise. "You're probably feeling all the right sort of things, but I don't want to push if you're not ready. Change your mind if you want, Lou. I'm still fine with it."

"I haven't put you off?" She stole another glance at the bulge in his breeches, still in evidence.

"I'm a guy," he said. "It's biology."

"Oh, if it's biology," she said, "who am I to argue with mother nature?"

"Yeah." He took her glass and placed it on the bedside table with his. "Time for you to stop being straitlaced." He tugged at the strings at the back of her gown.

So her tears hadn't put him off. Well, of course he'd seen her cry before—and she wasn't about to recite the list of other things he'd seen her do—and she helped him unlace her corset. "What about you?" she said.

"I'm doing just fine," he said, dispensing with his clothes with a rapidity that would have made Viv curse, and pulled the bedcovers back.

"Not undressing." She paused as he pulled her shift over her head. "I mean, what about you? You told me about your marriages, but where are you now?"

"Look, honey, I've only got one thing on my mind at the moment. I can't multitask under these conditions, but I'll tell you one thing—I want an emotional connection with a woman. I don't want to be some sort of screwing monster even if I come across as some sort of Lothario. And you…"

She waited.

"I'd love to see you in real stockings."

"Spoken like a true guy," she said.

He laid her on the bed, arranging her, looking her over with heated intent. He bent to take her garters in his teeth and pulled them untied, one leg and then the other. With brisk efficiency, he unrolled her stockings and tossed them aside, kneeling between her spread legs, his cock dark and hard. He placed his forefinger between her breasts and ran it down her torso, her belly. "I'm normally pretty good at foreplay," he said, "but I think I'm going to last about two minutes, tops. Okay with you if we worry about finesse and all that good stuff after?"

"Sure."

He reached into the bedside drawer for a condom, rolled it on with swift assurance, and his tongue entered her mouth a split second before he penetrated her, spreading her thighs wide.

"Mac—" She tore her mouth from his, panicked by his weight and immediacy, the sense of being filled, stretched, invaded.

He crooned something sweet and sexy and soothing that turned her panic into excitement. When he lowered his mouth to her breast, she cried out in surprise and pleasure— not an orgasm, not even close, but a sort of relief that all was well between them. His body was rough and smooth mixed, his jaw a fierce scrape, his chest springy with curly hair, his hip silky and hard beneath her hand.

"That's right," he said. "Let it go."

She squirmed beneath him, surprised at how this unfamiliar man created familiarity with his smooth, careful thrusts. When he bent his head to lick her breast, she pushed him away, afraid of being overwhelmed. *I'm being fucked. I'm fucking. It's different but it's the same.*

"Okay?"

"Yes." She wanted to tell him to get on with it, to forget about being considerate and tender, because that would be too much, an invitation into a territory of intimacy for which she was ill-prepared. But when his breathing halted and became harsh, his body tense, a brief sense of disappointment that it was about to end, so soon, flashed through her mind.

He dropped his head to her shoulder, sucking in a breath. "Okay?" he said.

"I'm good."

He grunted and rolled off her, collapsing on the bed beside her, his chest rising and falling. "Oh, my God," he said. "Two minutes? More like twenty seconds. Sorry, Lou. Couldn't last any longer." His body shone with a faint sheen of sweat. "It's not usually a problem for me."

She poked him with her elbow. "Stop being such a guy. It's not a competitive sport."

He pushed himself up to a sitting position and poured a glass of water from the carafe on the bedside cabinet, offering it to her and then draining it when she shook her head. Muttering something about the condom, he left for the bathroom. She lay on the bed, eyes closed, and listened to the toilet flush, the sound of running water and the pad of his bare feet on the floor as he approached the bed again.

"That couldn't have done much for you," he said.

"I didn't come, if that's what you mean." Now her whole body tingled and pricked with expectation, as though dormant nerves had awoken. She knew he stood at the foot of the bed, observing her. Was he looking at her spread thighs, at the dampened hair and the plumped, slick lips of her sex? At her breasts, the nipples erect, and the dampness on her skin?

The bed shifted as he moved onto it, but still at the foot. Her skin hummed with anticipation.

"Open your eyes."

She did. He stood with one knee on the bed, positioned between her feet. His cock stirred and lengthened at her gaze.

She raised one knee, oh so casually. His gaze was riveted between her legs, his cock lifting and darkening. As though unaware of his action—although, she suspected he was not—he palmed himself. The bed dipped as he lowered himself to her, his breath hot on her inner thighs.

"Nice," he said, and dropped an oddly chaste kiss on her mound. But there was nothing chaste about what followed, as his tongue delved and licked and tantalized in a luscious, leisurely exploration.

"Please, please," she gasped.

He stopped, his face innocent. "Am I doing something wrong?"

She grabbed his head and returned him to his proper place. "Just keep going. Like that."

And then she didn't need to issue any more orders and he didn't need to tease because she was there, crying out and arching against him and then falling to earth once more, drowsy and replete.

"Oh," she said. "So nice. Thank you, Mac."

"You have such lovely manners. I like that about you." He rolled his head onto her thigh. "I guess that was okay."

"Mmm." She pushed his head off and raised herself on one elbow to appreciate him sprawled on the bed, his cock dark and erect against his belly. "Don't move." She reached for the bedside drawer and found a condom.

He propped his head on one hand. "What do you have in mind, Lou?"

"This." She unrolled the condom and eased it over his penis. He raised a hand to help her. "Sorry, I'm out of practice."

He pulled her head to his, his tongue searching hers. She could taste her own scent on him, his urgency, his desire. This time she was the one who kissed, who directed and explored, while slowly lowering herself onto him. He became impatient and jerked his hips up.

"Stop that!" she said with mock ferocity. She tasted his neck, his collarbone, the fragrant roughness of his chest hair, and swirled her tongue around one nipple and then the other.

He shifted beneath her. "You're killing me, Lou."

"I haven't even started." She returned to his nipple, this time using her teeth, but very gently, moved to the hollow above his collarbone and bit a little harder to show what she could indeed do if she felt like it, and settled fully upon his cock.

He sighed, and took her breasts in both hands, his skin dark against hers, and chafed her nipples with his thumbs. "I guess you're calling the shots this time."

"Mmm." She slid, loving the fullness within her, the sight of him stretched beneath her at her mercy. "I nearly always come like this. Lots of times. And I want lots of orgasms from you, so you'd better start reciting baseball scores or whatever it is you do to hold out."

"Poetry," he said, teeth gritted as she moved.

"How effete."

"Nothing effete about *this,* honey." *This* twitched inside her, a delightful reminder, although she was in no danger of ignoring his presence.

She moved slowly and carefully, seeking the path to her own pleasure, made all the sweeter by the sight and sounds of Mac, who strove to remain still or respond to her prompts—he did well and he'd do better. She pushed away the thought that maybe she wouldn't have the opportunity to teach him or learn from him after this night; she must concentrate on the moment, because life was uncertain.

Pleasure flooded her, took her over, ebbed and returned and returned.

"Is four enough?"

She blinked and looked down at Mac. "Oh, hi."

"Yeah, I'm here, too." But he smiled. "You look like you're dreaming when you come. Innocent."

"You watched me?"

"Sure. I loved it. How about I fuck you now?"

But he was turning her, rolling her over, still joined. He loomed over her, considering, and then withdrew. "Hands and knees, honey. I'm going to take you fast and hard and recite poetry all the way through."

She scrambled to get onto her hands and knees and he took his time, stroking her bottom, running an inquisitive finger down her crack. He leaned into her and fondled her breasts, his cock rubbing her vulva. "I want to make you get noisy. Maybe it's the dressing up. You come in a genteel way. I want to make you scream."

"Oh, yes," she said.

He laughed and plunged into her, big and hard, and she reached to clutch his butt, telling him to wait.

He slowed. "Okay for you?"

She caught her breath. "Can you go a bit slower? It's nice but I'd like to be able to walk tomorrow."

"Sure. Sorry, I forgot you're out of practice."

He was quite gentlemanly at first and then she became accustomed to his strength and the power of his thrusts and welcomed his roughness—he slapped her butt a few times, which sent delicious shivers through her. His breathing became labored.

"Want to make you come first," he muttered, and reached for her clitoris, rocking her hard and the ascent became urgent, painful for a moment, and then she cried out, and he shuddered with her, against her.

They dropped to the sheets still joined, both of them out of breath.

He laughed and withdrew. "Shit, Lou, you've wrecked me. Stay here. I'll escort you back to your room if you really want, though I might have to crawl."

She stretched beneath him, breathing in his smell, and flexed her legs and arms, slightly sore, very relaxed, very content. "I don't want to move."

"Me, neither."

"But I've got to go to the bathroom."

They peeled themselves from each other and Lou made her way to the bathroom, as small and primitive as the one in her room. Her legs, she noted, were slightly shaky, and the reflection in the mirror revealed her breasts reddened from Mac's attentions, her hair disordered, lips swollen. As she finished washing her hands Mac ambled into the bathroom, scratching his chest.

"Hey," he said, "want to take a shower?"

They both regarded the small plastic shower stall.

"It's rather small," Lou said.

"So much the better." He leered. "I could prop you up in the corner, and..."

She shook her head, rubbing toothpaste onto her teeth. "Tempting, but I'm tired."

He put his arms around her. "That's okay. And anyway, I want to keep your smell on me for as long as possible. I want to curl up with you and let our smell ferment."

Hand in hand, they returned to the bed and straightened

out the wrinkled and disordered sheets, working together as smoothly as a long-married couple. A thought she found disturbing. He offered her a shirt to sleep in, which she declined, not wanting the coarseness of the fabric against her sensitized skin—or so she told herself, luxuriating in the coarse and soft and smooth textures of Mac's body. He gathered her in his arms, curling his big body around hers and making her feel fragile and protected. His closeness made excitement stir, as did his genitals brushing against her buttocks, tightening. He made a small sound of approval and his hand brushed against her breast, a question, an invitation.

The sex she could have summoned up, imagined—maybe—but this intimacy made her uneasy. She resented his comfort, his relaxation into sleep. Why was it so damned easy for him?

"What's wrong?" he mumbled. "Thought I'd got you good and relaxed."

"Not sure."

His hand touched her breast, lingered, fingertips at her nipple. "I'll do this," he said. "And you…you do this." He directed her hand between her legs. Both hands at her breasts, he teased, slow and sexy. His leg dropped over hers, parting hers so she sprawled open, her hand at her clit. His fingertips pulled and caressed and he murmured sleepy encouragement to her to get herself off. Wasn't it the best way to invite sleep? She didn't think she would come again that night; she never thought she'd masturbate in the arms of this man she barely knew, but she did, reaching a fast and joyful climax, and falling into oblivion.

Ten

Mac

He had no idea what the time was; it was light and out-side birds whistled and twittered, which meant it might be anytime after four in the morning. Sooner or later in this house a clock would chime or a servant would knock at the door and another day of gentlemanly pursuits would begin. He wondered if he should wake Lou and see if she'd like to ride—he could lend her a pair of his breeches, or she might have a habit for riding sidesaddle. She'd probably be a better rider than him, with her life on the ranch.

She turned and burrowed her head beneath the pillow, re-vealing the delectable curve of her ass; quite an ass she had for a slender woman. The idea of getting dressed and dealing with a large, unpredictable animal with steel on its hooves was becoming less attractive by the moment, what with Lou in his bed. She might not come back after this night. Perhaps she had used him to exorcise her ghosts and she'd tell him his services were no longer required. Or perhaps not. Seize the moment: seize that luscious ass.

He seized it and slipped back into the bed with her. She gave a grunt of annoyance and pulled the bedclothes over herself.

"Lou," he whispered. "Lou, honey, I have something for you."

He pushed his cock against her leg just in case she'd missed it.

She made no response, and he got his arms around her and held her, her hair tickling his face. He remembered her last orgasm before they fell asleep, her excitement, the sound she'd made when she came. He'd like to watch her touch herself in daylight. Would it be different? Would she perform for him? His cock gave an appreciative twitch. He'd like to do a lot of things with her, in fact, particularly when she was awake. And come to think of it, she'd probably like to go horseback riding, and he'd like to see her enjoy herself.

Lou

SOMEONE WHISPERED HER NAME.

"Too early," she mumbled. "Oh, hi, Mac."

"I got you fixed up." Something landed on the bed beside her, a tangle of fabric and a pair of boots. "You're going riding in drag, so you don't have to go sidesaddle. Young Rob's an enterprising lad. I hope the boots fit."

"He knows I'm here?"

"He met us last night on the stairs, remember?"

She remembered now, the shock of Rob's bare skin against her hands, so warm and surprising in the dark, and then the presence of the man who sat beside her on the bed, wearing a thin pair of cotton drawers. She sat to examine the clothes, breeches and coat, turning the boots in her hand. "They look a bit big."

"You can borrow some of my socks. Stockings. Come on, Lou. You know how to ride, so they'll let me out alone with you."

"I'm not that good at English style." But the temptations of wearing pants and riding later, and Mac now half-naked beside her, and a tray with two cups and a pot of coffee, strawberries and brioche, brought her fully awake. "I'm impressed."

"I like to look after my women in the morning," he said, pouring coffee.

"Your women? You have a few spares around?"

"Figuratively speaking." He handed her a cup. "I'm not sure I need more than you this morning. I'm all yours. Have a strawberry. Have me."

He watched as she bit into a strawberry and she flicked her tongue around the fruit, teasing him. He sprawled on the bed beside her, watching her with a smile on his face, and reached to wipe juice from her chin with his thumb.

"This is lovely," she said. "Pure hedonism."

He pulled apart a brioche in a scatter of crumbs and golden crust and consulted a sheet of paper, printed in a font that imitated eighteenth-century handwriting, with the Paradise Hall logo at the top. "Here's my schedule for the day. Riding this morning, fencing this afternoon. Very macho, except then we have dance practice. After dinner apparently we will have music of Beethoven, Haydn and Mozart performed by a string quartet. Very cultured. There's one thing missing."

"What?"

"Hot sex first thing in the morning." He tugged at the sheet covering her breasts.

She tugged back, unaccountably shy.

"I want to see you naked in daylight." He tossed his schedule aside. "Let me look at you, Lou."

She had never been particularly shy about her body—and hadn't she walked around naked last night with no self-consciousness, dazed and relaxed from sex? Mac's sharp intake of breath told her what she needed to know.

"You're stunning." He reached out reverently to touch her belly.

She tugged at the drawstring on his drawers, baggy thin white cotton, and ran her fingers down the line of dark hair that ran from his navel. Her fingertips brushed against the head of his cock, which lolled, half-erect, against his belly.

He'd been so generous, so attentive to her needs. Now she would give him the same care, the same pleasure. He gave a pleased sigh when she bent to kiss where her fingers had touched and when she flicked her tongue against him. His cock stiffened, pushed against her lips. He breathed her name, his hand stroking her hair.

"Take these off."

He complied, lifting his hips and kicking the drawers aside.

Another happy sigh as she took him into her mouth. He tasted slightly of sweat and musk, dark, exciting. She swirled her tongue over the smooth head, the strong ridges and veins, tasting, learning him and what he liked. He liked to have his balls cupped, she found, and he gasped when she ran her fingernails over the base of his cock and scratched gently at his scrotum.

"You want me to come like this?" he murmured. "Because I will, Lou. Oh, God, Lou, that's nice."

She stopped, only to nibble down the length of his cock and dig her fingers into the dense hair at its base.

His eyes were dark and dreamy. "Kiss me."

She raised herself to bring her lips to his, tasting the dark and sweet, coffee and strawberries, and meeting the thrust and curl of his tongue. She gripped his cock, her hand sliding, as his body tensed against hers.

He pulled his mouth from hers to whisper that he was going to come, soon, and where did she want it?

She tongued his lip.

In her hand, his cock swelled and he made a helpless sound against her mouth, on the verge of a climax, entirely at her mercy. She bent her head to his cock again, took him deep, and his hand returned to her head, fingers knotted in her hair as his body tensed. His cock pulsed; he cried out, semen spurting against her tongue, salty and warm and vital.

She raised her head to look at him, lying spent beneath her, his cock subsiding while he sucked in air.

He opened his eyes and smiled at her. "Wow. That was nice. No, *nice* is an understatement. That was phenomenal. Anything I can do for you, Lou?"

"I need a shower," she said. "I think you do, too."

"Great idea." He grabbed a handful of condoms.

She raised her eyebrows. "Isn't that rather ambitious?"

"I thought we'd keep some in there. Just in case, you know, some other time…" He grinned and stood, stretching, in what she thought was a deliberate display but which she appreciated anyway. She took his hand and rose from the bed.

Some other time. She didn't want to ponder the implications of those words. Did he intend them to sleep together—to have sex together—on a regular basis for the duration of the stay? Right now, with his hand caressing her bottom, them both stumbling off balance as he bent to nuzzle her neck, that seemed like a good idea, but…

"Lou, will you stop thinking!" He lowered his head to tongue her breast.

"I'm not thinking," she said, and now she certainly wasn't. His cock, already half-erect again, bumped against her hip.

"You are. You're wondering what my intentions are."

"That's a new name for it." She grasped the part of him that best expressed his intentions and stroked.

"It's better with soap. Come on."

They crammed themselves into the small shower in the corner of what would eventually be a luxurious bathroom but which was now minimal. He eased her into the corner and turned the shower on, letting loose a feeble stream of cold water. She squealed.

He had his mind on other things than the water temperature, hands cupping her bottom and sliding between her thighs, his mouth at her breast again. She raised a lather from the bar of sandalwood-scented soap and stroked his shoulders, his belly, his cock, the dimensions of the shower cramming them together.

He reached for a washcloth and wiped some of the lather away before donning a condom. She marveled at his regenerative powers as he pushed her into the corner of the shower, issuing instructions. "Leg up, around my waist. Yeah. Oh, shit. Can't get in you."

"Have you ever done it in a shower before, Mac?"

"Not as such." He mumbled something about seeing it done in movies. "Seems a pity to waste this condom. Turn around."

Ah, that made much more sense, if *sense* were the word to apply to this clumsy, urgent act. His hand, slippery with soap, caressed her breasts, creating aching excitement in her nipples. His cock bounced from her thighs to her buttocks, trailed down her crease and then he was inside her and she cried out with surprise and delight at the angle and that lovely sense of fullness.

"A—nice—dirty—clean—fuck," he said, thrusting. "Got to get these breasts clean, Lou. You're not howling with pleasure enough."

"I'm doing my best."

"I'm going to play with your clit." A dirty, leering whisper as one hand left her breast to travel down her belly. "I liked it when you got yourself off last night. But right now I'm in control and I'm going to make you come."

His finger touched and rubbed in counterpoint with his thrusts. She wriggled against him, trying to move, trying to hit the spot, and his cock slipped out. He cursed, she laughed, and then the moment turned from comedy to need and she helped him back inside.

He gave that breathy sound she now recognized with a sense of ownership as the moment before he lost himself entirely to pleasure, but she was ahead of him—*there, not so hard, slow down*—she was the one issuing instructions now, riding his hand and clenching him hard as she abandoned herself. His cock jerked inside her and he groaned her name.

She turned her head to his for a long, grateful kiss, water streaming over their faces. "Clean enough?" he asked.

"We haven't even started washing yet."

"Here." He withdrew from her, and a moment later a dollop of herb-scented shampoo landed on her head. His fingers were long and strong and skillful—but she knew that already, those fingers had given her so much pleasure—as he slowly massaged her scalp.

"Now that's the sort of sound I want to hear when I'm fucking you," he said.

"I don't plan what sort of noises I'm going to produce," she said. "But you are so very, very good at this."

"I'm good at lots of things. I'm good at you, Lou. Good in you." He tilted her head back beneath the shower.

"But I don't know whether you're good *for* me."

"I am, baby. I am."

In a way, he was. Her body hummed and tingled at his touch, any sort of touch. The first man since Julian, the first man to bring her back to life and touch her secret places, to make her cry aloud with pleasure. He was good for her, she enjoyed his lovemaking, his body and his touch. She liked to look at him, lean and naked and powerful, and for the most part she enjoyed his company and conversation. But it was nothing more. It should not be anything more, not now. It was too soon.

Her turn to massage his scalp and receive a low sound of pleasure. "In the nineteenth century—Victorian, I think, not during Austen's time—there was a science based on the shape of the skull, to determine a person's character," she said. "And this...yes, you're very horny. Smart but mostly horny." She directed the showerhead to his head, the wet hair slick against his scalp. "Why did you become a journalist?"

"It was the guys in hats." He wiped water from his face and reached for the soap. "In the old black-and-white movies, there's always a bunch of guys in hats with notebooks shouting out questions. I wanted to be one of those, finding out the truth, working deep into the night with a cigarette in my mouth and a green eyeshade. A fearless investigator."

"You're a romantic."

His hands, creamy with soap lather, fondled her breasts.

"Are they dirty again?"

"Very. Yeah, I was a romantic, all right. Timed my graduation from journalism school with the death of print and I've been freelancing ever since, froufrou stuff for magazines like the piece I'm doing now. Which reminds me, I need to interview you as the history consultant."

"Probably not here." She took the soap and caressed his buttocks. Between them, his cock stirred and shifted against her belly. He wanted her again and she, despite the ache of little-used muscles in her thighs and belly, wanted him. She stepped away as much as she could in the tiny space and directed the showerhead to rinse off the remaining soap.

He turned off the shower and took her in his arms again. "I should shave."

"Shave later."

"You sure you want to ride this morning? Horses, that is?" His unshaven face scraped her neck and shoulders.

"Yes. It'll be fun." She pushed him away and reached for a towel.

"We can have more fun here. You can put on the pants and we'll pretend you're my page boy."

"How depraved," she said with a thrill of excitement, even though she knew he was joking. She toweled her hair, shivering in the cool air, and ran back to the bedroom, wrapped in the towel. A large chest of dark wood held a collection of linens. She pulled on a shirt and a pair of drawers, both soft linen, scented with lavender, and used her own garters to hold a pair of woolen stockings in place.

In the mirror, she saw herself change into a creature with a distinctly masculine appearance, particularly with the coat disguising her shape. Mac looked on with appreciation as he tied his neckcloth. "Amazing how sexy a woman in pants looks now," he commented. "Ankles get me really hot, too."

"I've always thought the erogenous zone of the Regency

was the nape of the neck," Lou said. She tied her own hair back as she spoke, noting the abrasions on her neck from Mac's stubble. "Haven't you noticed how the poses in portraiture and fashion prints emphasize softness and submission, bent heads and so on?"

"Hmm. Maybe you're right." He looked at her with a slow grin. "We may have to do something about that."

"But not now." She pulled on her boots and stood to test them. A little big, but she'd manage without extra stockings. He looked as handsome as ever—somewhat Byronic and depraved with stubble on his chin and a lustful gleam in his eye. But she could ignore that. *Should* ignore that.

They left the room and ran into Di the lady's maid with an armful of gowns and linens as they walked along the corridor to the main staircase. She gave a quick grin, hastily disguised, and dropped a curtsy. "Clean clothes and your day's activities are in your room, ma'am. Please ring if you need any help." She regarded Lou with a critical eye. "I can take the coat in for you if you want to wear it again. And tailor the breeches."

"Thanks, but they're borrowed," Lou said.

"Enjoy your ride," Di said, and continued past them.

They left the house, feet crunching on the gravel, into a beautiful early-summer morning. Lou paused to smell a creamy pink rose dotted with drops of dew.

"You remind me of that rose," Mac said. "You, naked."

He sounded so serious and embarrassed by his own sentiments that Lou was touched; she couldn't imagine such a comment from him without a degree of cynicism. "Thank you," she said, and took his hand.

"If anyone's watching, this won't do my sexual identity any

good at all," he said, but continued to hold her hand as they walked around the side of the house and into the stable yard.

A black horse, bridled and saddled, stood in the yard, tethered to a ring, chewing on a bag of hay.

"My old buddy Ajax," Mac said, patting the horse's neck.

"My old buddy Mac!" A tall blonde woman emerged from a doorway. "I thought we'd go out by the river again today and find a... Oh, good morning." She bowed; although she looked fairly modern for a stable setting in breeches, boots and a tweed jacket, the clothes were historical facsimiles. Lou remembered that Peter had had to hire mainly female stable staff, as they were the most qualified of the applicants, and dress them as their male counterparts of two centuries ago.

"Oh, hi, Annabelle," Mac said. "This is Dr. Lou Connolly."

"Oh. Yes." Annabelle shook Lou's hand with a distinct lack of warmth. "Peter said you were an experienced rider but maybe I should come out with you, since you don't know the countryside."

You jerk, you screwed her, Lou thought.

"No, that's fine," Mac said. "I know the trails and Lou's good with horses."

"I have Dr. Connolly down for sidesaddle riding tomorrow," Annabelle said. "But it's okay. I was just saddling up Jasper. You do know how to ride English style, do you, Dr. Connolly? We don't have any Western saddles here."

Lou assured her she was fine with English style and Annabelle went back inside the stables to emerge from one of the loose box doors with a tall, rangy chestnut.

"I hope you can handle him. He's quite fresh."

"We'll be fine." Lou took the reins from her. She knew Annabelle wouldn't jeopardize her job or any of the horses, but she could feel the woman's resentment and jealousy, and suspected she might be up to some sort of practical joke. Sure enough, when she slipped her fingers beneath the girth, it was loose enough that an attempt to mount would have deposited Lou on the cobblestones.

Lou ignored Annabelle, stroking Jasper's neck, and getting to know the horse, who snuffed at her sleeve and coat, inquisitive and friendly. She was reminded inappropriately of Mac burying his nose in her navel, her armpit, and bit back a laugh. She lifted the saddle flap to tighten the girth, aware that Annabelle was helping Mac to mount with rather a lot of close bodily contact, as though staking her claim.

"I think you need your stirrups adjusted, Mac." Well, that took more hand-thigh contact than Lou would have expected.

The girth tightened to her satisfaction, Lou swung herself into the saddle. With the stirrup raised higher than it would be for Western style, she hoped her extra effort in mounting wasn't obvious, but to her annoyance Mac and Annabelle were engaged in a low-voiced exchange. Annabelle finally giggled and released the lead that tethered the horse to the ring, slapping Ajax on the rump.

As Lou had guessed, Jasper was the horse that preferred to take the lead, which was why Annabelle had chosen him for her ride with Mac. She loosened the rein to let him trot ahead, with only a quick squeeze of her calves to encourage him. Beneath her, he was strong and lively; not so smooth a ride as her own Morgan horse, Maisie, but pleasant enough. She turned in the saddle to smile at Mac, who sat his horse well for a beginner.

"Having fun?" Mac asked as the clatter of hooves on the

cobbled stable yard gave way to a soft pounding on a bridle path and they entered a quiet, shaded area.

"Yeah. It's good to be on a horse again. Bring Ajax forward and we'll ride together."

As Mac and Ajax came level with them, Jasper snorted, ears back, and Lou urged him slightly ahead. "He likes to be boss. It has nothing to do with me, but do you have some unfinished business with Annabelle?"

He shrugged. "Sort of. We made out a bit."

"Oh, for God's sake. I felt sorry for her. She wasn't expecting you to turn up with someone else."

"Look, I couldn't very well send her a text, could I? Or call her. Should I have sent a footman? Come on, Lou."

"You're right. It's a lovely morning. Let's not spoil it by bickering." Sunlight glinted through the trees, which thinned out to parkland, grass dotted with stately oak trees.

He reached to pat her knee. "I'm sorry. I guess I was untactful."

She smiled. "You up for a canter? Come on, then."

Mac

MAC WATCHED AS SHE DRUMMED HER heels against the horse's side and rode forward. She could ride almost as well as Annabelle.

He really shouldn't have kissed Annabelle and stuck his hand in her shirt and... Well, all the rest of it. Although there was something about Annabelle that attracted him, a blonde, horsey quality like an English upper-class Valkyrie.

But Lou... He watched the gentle spread of her butt as her coattails lifted, the way her breeches-clad legs pressed against the saddle. *Down boy.* He really didn't want to experience a hard-on on horseback. Riding was an uncomfortable enough experience in itself.

He thumped his heels into Ajax's sides and the horse switched from a trot to a canter. Hands down, heels down, head up, lean forward a little. This was far more comfortable than posting to a trot with the awareness that he could do his balls some serious damage on the saddle horn if he misjudged the rhythm. Ajax shook his mane as though agreeing.

The path approached a thicket of trees again, and they slowed to a walk.

"So what is it about girls and horses?" Mac asked, coming to ride next to her.

"Obviously the sensation of a huge, powerful animal pulsing between our thighs and driving us to ecstasy," she said, entirely straight-faced. "Really, Mac, dumb question. Why don't you give it some thought?"

"Being in power? In control?"

"Partly. But it's more than that. Horses are very intuitive creatures. Beautiful and muscular and you have a pact that you do no harm to each other and you try to understand each other, even though you're so very different."

"Like men and women?"

She tilted her head. "Possibly. At least we're the same species, whatever pop culture may tell us. And I bypassed the whole adolescent horse thing so I may not be the best person to ask. I only started riding when I moved to the ranch, though I've done quite a lot." Her face saddened. She was thinking about him—Julian—again.

"Do you think you'll stay at the ranch?" he asked.

She shrugged. "I'm not sure. It's on the market, but my asking price is high and I doubt I'll get an offer. I'd miss having the horse and dogs and cattle. A neighbor's looking after

them for me. That's something I'd miss, too, if I moved—
neighbors who look out for you. In bad weather, your lives
can depend on each other. You don't get that sort of community in a city. And then there's my dissertation—as yet
unfinished."

"What's your dissertation on?"

"Jane Austen and the stuff of domesticity."

"The what?"

"It's about houses and things—the sort of things women
made and owned," she explained, and sighed. "I don't really
want to talk about it. I gave a paper on the topic at a conference in the States where I met Peter and Chris, and the idea
grew, but it doesn't seem like part of my life anymore, even
though I'm here."

The path divided ahead of them. "If we go to the left, we
can go around the lake. It's pretty."

He watched her face as the lake came into view, vivid
rhododendrons dipping to meet their reflection in the dark
water. On the wooded rise above was the summerhouse, a
perfect miniature Greek temple. A pair of swans floated, se-
rene and barely moving.

"They mate for life," she said with such longing that he
felt he was intruding upon her most intimate thoughts. He
reached a hand out to her but she didn't notice, and at that
moment Ajax stepped away sideways, snorting loudly, as if
reminding him just in time not to be an idiot.

A splash broke the silence and the swans turned to see who
might be invading their territory. Someone's head broke the
surface of the water, hands rising to push back wet hair. It
was that kid, the footman, Rob, who began a circuit of the
lake, moving easily through the water.

"Let's get moving," Mac said, aware now of how Lou

stared at the swimmer, whose buttocks occasionally flashed clear of the surface.

"Oh. Okay." She tugged at her horse's reins and began to talk of how American riding style differed from English, as though resuming an interrupted conversation.

So she did fancy the kid after all.

Eleven

Back at the house, Lou turned down Mac's suggestion of more sex. He suggested a shower and lunch together, but they both knew what he meant. Besides, she should dress as a woman again. Her masculine clothes weren't that comfortable and now she smelled of horse. She reminded Mac that she had a date with someone else—and was amused at his possessive glower—and no, she didn't want to come watch him fence, because that was about as interesting as watching paint dry.

"Isn't that what you'll be doing, Lou?" He leaned against the sandstone pillar on the porch, idly slapping his riding crop against his boots, stubbled cheeks made even darker by the brim of his hat.

He looked so stunningly sexy in a non-PC way she had to look away and collect her thoughts. "Nonsense, this paint dried years, decades ago. Go have fun with the other boys. I'll see you at dinner."

Back in the house, two maids in modified historical clothing pushed a very modern housekeeping cart down the corridor. Lou smiled at them and entered the quiet of her own room. She wished she hadn't started thinking about her dissertation. This room would be a good place to write, if she didn't feel so frozen and, well, bored by the whole idea.

Another pretty cotton gown, clean stockings and linen awaited her, along with a list of the day's activities. The fabric reminded her of old-fashioned wallpaper, but not in an unpleasant way, with its muted colors, stripes and stylized sprigs of roses. She remembered Mac saying she was like a rose, and how embarrassed he'd been by his spontaneity, and smiled as she tightened the drawstring of the gown.

She tied her hair back with a length of lace she found among the ribbons and odds and ends in a small wooden box on the dressing table and wondered if she'd caught a touch of sun from the morning ride. The scrapes from Mac's stubble had faded a little but her face looked pink and excited. Did thinking about Mac do this to her?

She left the room and one of Rob's footmen, the one who hardly spoke any English, directed her to the wing of the house still under restoration. Jon, wearing a pair of painter's overalls, sat at a cheap wooden desk in a room that was stripped to plaster and lathe, the floorboards dull and uneven. Tables held containers full of samples in small plastic bags. She noted with ridiculous excitement that the room had electricity and a computer.

"Lovely to see you, Lou," Jon said. He peered at her over half-glasses with a genial smile, his hair flopping onto his forehead. He had come into the business naturally, as the descendant of impoverished English aristocrats, brought up in a house like Paradise Hall. Last night, he'd told her he had probably wrecked his brain picking off layers of ancient, lead-filled paint in his bedroom as a small child. After that, it was the only profession open to him.

"I asked them to bring us some lunch and my partner, Simon, will join us," Jon said. "Meanwhile, look at this little beauty from the small dining room." He ushered her to the microscope. "This is our sixteen layers, with the original being the sort of mauve that was meant to aid digestion based on Goethe's color theory. That's the room we use for breakfast. Imagine seeing that paint color if you had a hangover. I much prefer the yellow."

She admired shreds of the past preserved in small plastic bags and awaiting analysis or stabilization and storage; a strip of gorgeous red silk brocade from inside a chair found in the attic, pushed into the stuffing of the seat and as brilliant as it was over two centuries ago; discolored, dull pieces of wallpaper and fabric ravaged by time and damp and rodents; hinges and door handles, nails and other pieces of archaic, rusted hardware.

"What to do with it," Jon said. "That's the question. The boys can't bring themselves to throw anything away, and it takes a weird sort of mind, like yours or mine, to appreciate this stuff. So it goes into storage. And sadly, much of the original decor of the house would be unpleasant to the modern eye. Oh, here's Simon. And lunch. Delicious!"

A footman placed a large tray on one of the tables and Simon helped him push boxes of samples out of the way and arrange chairs. They sat and helped themselves to cheese, a sharp crumbling white and a smooth soft one that oozed delectably onto the china plate, fruit and freshly baked bread, a cake decorated with fresh flowers and a jug of amber cider.

"Oh, dear, did you miss breakfast again?" Jon said as Simon worked his way through a huge plateful of food. "He works so hard. We'll take Lou to the blue room later, shall we? Although, it's not very blue at the moment. Simon's doing lovely work on the plaster and we'll show you the paint color we've chosen. Very classical and elegant."

Sometimes with upper-class Englishmen you really couldn't tell, but Lou decided they had to be gay. Or… both had that same floppy brown hair, sleepy hazel eyes behind half-glasses. "Are you related?" she asked. "You look so alike."

"We're always being asked that," Simon said. "Probably inbreeding. Don't we have the same great-great-great-great grandmama?"

"I think so. We're probably something like fifth cousins ten times removed. I should ask Nanny next time I visit."

"You have a nanny?" Lou said.

"Oh, dear, yes," Jon said. "She was invaluable when we restored the kitchen at my house to its Edwardian glory. She knows all the family stuff. Mummy's too busy with her charities."

Lou shook her head. "You are such a cliché."

"But we're not gay," Simon said.

"Only a little bit," Jon amended. "We do like girls."

"Now, don't put our guest off her lunch. I'm sure she doesn't want to hear about our perversions."

Lou spluttered over a mouthful of cider. They both looked at her with identical benign smiles.

"The thing is," Simon said, "we work together, we're in and out of each other's houses, we like each other's company. Naturally people think we're a couple. We even sound and look alike. And some women like that sort of thing."

"Double the pleasure," Jon said. "Are you interested, Lou? Because I'm sure we can fit you in."

"So to speak," Simon said. "Maybe after the blue room is painted—"

Lou could barely contain herself as she patted the neckerchief at the top of her gown dry. "Did Peter put you up to this?"

They exchanged glances. "Dear me, no. We thought of it ourselves," Jon said. "Peter hired us for restoration work because we're the best."

"At everything we undertake," Simon added meaningfully.

Lou looked at them both, owlish and earnest, and tried to fight back a giggle. Yes, of course some women would find them attractive. Some men, too.

"The emphasis is of course all on the lady's pleasure," Jon said primly. "No playing with each other's winkles."

"Oh, a little. Sometimes," Simon said. "Some girls like that. We can give a demonstration of our extraordinary prowess, Lou, anytime."

To her astonishment, he produced a BlackBerry and consulted it. "After I've finished the blue room, we're pretty much free. I think we're both recovered from Sarah—such a greedy girl, all those orifices begging for attention all the time. Quite exhausting. But if you need a reference, I'm sure she'll—"

"Thank you," Lou said, "but I don't think I'll take you up on it."

"Alternatively, you could observe," Jon said, and Simon nodded in agreement.

"You don't have to *do* anything," Simon said. "You don't even have to announce your presence to whichever lady requests our expert services. We have a very lovely screen—early-eighteenth century, and someone had the foresight to cut holes in it, probably for a very similar occasion—so you can stay hidden. Sometimes that's jolly good fun."

"Oh, yes," Jon said. "May I help you to a slice of cake, Lou? Simon, dear, do ring for the footman and he'll bring us some tea. Or coffee. Whatever you like, dear, we're happy to oblige."

"I'll have some tea, please," Lou said with as much seriousness as she could muster. She was trying to let go and embrace the Twilight Zone that was Paradise Hall, but this was a lot to wrap her head around. "Thank you for thinking of me."

"Ah." The two of them looked at each other, nodding, like mirror images.

"Mac," Jon said. "Now, I'd let him play with my winkle anytime he wanted."

"Except, I don't think he wants to," Simon said. "He is so deliciously macho. Well, I'll just give young Master Rob a ring—" he brandished his BlackBerry "—and after we've had a nice cup of tea we'll visit the restoration on the blue room."

SHE SPENT THE REST OF THE afternoon with Jon and Simon and then, during the period she'd come to think of as the sex break, sitting beneath the shade of a huge cedar tree, reading and napping. She let her mind wander into pleasant erotic fantasies of Mac, Mac and another man, which was rather appealing, and a threesome *was* something she'd always been interested in—but who could be their third? Her shifting dreams wouldn't settle on one distinctive set of features.

She didn't sit next to Mac at dinner. He wore those clingy knit evening trousers again and she refused to let herself stare at him. Sometimes pleasure delayed was better. He flirted with the other women and now and again looked down the table at her with appreciation and longing.

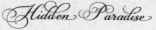

As the ladies left for the drawing room, the men stood. Mac brushed against her and pushed something into her gloved hand. It was a note. She concealed it in her fan and, while the other women chatted and drank tea, moved close to a candlestick to unfold and read it.

Wait for me in your bed.
Naked.

Mac

P.S. I like those earrings. Keep them on.

She smiled and tucked the tiny note away.

WELL, WHERE THE HELL ARE YOU, *Mac?*
She'd arranged herself like an odalisque on the bedcover and he had yet to show up. A modest pile of condoms lay ready next to the bed. Outside, thunder rumbled and a flash of lightning flared in the room and she saw something at the window. Rain slashed down, infusing a cool fragrance into the air.

She froze for a moment as the window rattled and then swung open. A figure stood there, dark and still, on the small stone balcony, before stepping into the room. He was naked, with a dark red dressing gown that billowed around him, and that he flung off as he strode across the room, bringing the scent of the rain and the storm with him.

"Mac." She rose, holding out her arms to him, and met him halfway. "Just like you told me, you're a romantic."

"Almost scraped my balls off on that damned ivy," he muttered. "I wouldn't do that for just anyone, Lou."

Drops of cold water flew from his hair and clung to his legs and arms. He folded her against his damp, cool body and pulled her into bed, where they were swaddled in cotton and down, scents of lavender and bergamot, the musky smells of arousal.

"You're cold." She ran her hands over his chest, enjoying the spring of hair and the hardness of his nipples beneath her palms, feeling his body chill against hers.

"Warm me up, Lou." He leaned in for a kiss.

She'd never met a man who wanted to be kissed so much, whose mouth and tongue became pursuer and pursued, whose kisses could range from playful to carnal and back. He tasted of coffee and toothpaste and sex as they twined together, limbs tangled, his cock rubbing against her thigh, her hip, her belly. She straddled his thigh briefly, riding him, and he reached down to dip his fingers into her.

"So wet. Like satin. Gorgeous." He lifted his fingertip to his mouth and licked, savored. "Want to taste yourself, Lou?"

She took his fingertip into her mouth as avidly as she'd taken his cock earlier that morning, and sucked the remnants of her musky juices, while he hummed with pleasure and lowered his other hand between her thighs. He zeroed in to the right spot with unerring precision and she opened wide for him. One finger, two, delved inside; his thumb flirted with her clitoris, nudged and circled and flicked.

She took her mouth from his finger and blew on it. "I'll come."

"Maybe." He played her, up on one elbow now to watch her face and follow her reactions. "If I let you."

"I'll come if I do this with my breasts." She raised both hands to her breasts and stroked and pinched her hard, sensitive nipples.

"Do it, Lou." His mouth nipped her neck. "So sexy. I love watching you touch yourself."

She anticipated the moment when he'd take control and delay her orgasm. How close would he let her get? She toyed with tricking him, stealing an orgasm from under his nose and as she thought of that potentially delicious moment she tightened around his fingers.

"Uh-oh. I think you've had enough." Sure enough, his finger and thumb withdrew. "Hands off your tits, Mrs. Connolly. You should be ashamed."

"You're so mean," she whimpered, delighting in their playful exchange.

And then his fingertips, shiny and wet and fragrant, were in her mouth, followed by his tongue, greedy and licking and sucking, his chin scraping against hers. His thigh dropped over hers, holding her legs open wide, her sex exposed and needy. Laughter vibrated in his chest as her hips moved, begging for attention.

Mac

SHE LIKED HIM TO TALK DIRTY and she shivered with pleasure when he pulled her mouth from his and asked her roughly if she wanted to be fucked. Her eyes were wide, face flushed, her chin abraded from his stubble.

"Oh, yes," she breathed, squirming beneath him. He had her wrists in his hands now, fragile and pale, the knobs of bone touching and vulnerable.

"Yes, what?"

She burst into laughter. "Now?"

"Very funny." He lowered himself over her. Shit, the condom. He'd almost forgotten. He reached for the foil package and tore it open. "For that, you get to put it on me."

"Yes, O master," she replied with a flutter of eyelashes, and tipped the condom onto the palm of her hand. He'd never found a condom sexy before, just a necessity, a gesture that combined courtesy with common sense. He didn't think he could get any harder, but when she touched him, stroking and smoothing the condom on his dick, he caught himself making a pathetic little girly whimper and she looked up at him, eyes shining with amusement. But he was beyond embarrassment now, torn between wanting to watch her slender fingers on his sheathed dick and wanting to plunge inside her.

Question was, who wanted whom the most? Who could hold out longest? He lowered himself onto her, nudging her thighs apart with his hips, stroking his cock down that sweet wet cleft. She gasped a little and squirmed, her hips tilted to receive him. He moved back.

"Meanie," she said, and nipped at his shoulder.

"Yeah, I can be real mean." He lowered his mouth to her nipple, sucked and swirled his tongue. Her wrists, held tight against the pillow, tensed. "Should I tie you up, Lou? Couple of neckcloths should do it." He blew on her nipple. "Make you put on those breeches and tie you up and flip you over and fuck you in the ass?"

"Oh, Mr. Darcy, and I thought you were so masculine."

"I am," he growled, and nudged his cock at her again. "Feel that?" This time, he pushed inside her a little and she was so warm and luscious he couldn't bear to withdraw, but he did.

She sucked in a breath. "You want me to beg?"

"Yeah." He stroked up and down her cleft, lingering at the hard ridge of her clit and lowered his head to her moist, parted lips. Her tongue flicked and tangled with his and she made a deep, surprised sound in her throat as her legs quivered against him. He moved his mouth to below her ear, to the moist fragrance of her neck and the tickle of her hair.

"Stop teasing me," she said. "Fuck me now."

He slid inside her and she cried out in surprise, tightening on him so that he had to stop and growl out how good she felt, fighting for control. He still held her slender wrists, his hands dark against her skin that almost matched the cream of the pillow.

"I'm not hurting you, am I?" he asked, conscious once more of her pale fragility.

Her breasts rose and fell, round and plump on her slender torso and he bent to kiss them, and then her armpits, burying his nose in the fragrant wisps of hair to snuff her scent.

She giggled. "Tickles." She wrapped one long leg around him, foot planted on his ass, and drew him forward. "Now."

Oh, now, absolutely now. Now as they joined and plunged and surrendered to each other but he wanted to please her, hear her cry out and shudder under him; now roll her over so she sat astride him and he clasped her to him and kissed her, drowning in her mouth, her scent, her taste.

Lou

IT MIGHT HAVE BEEN JET LAG OR something else, but she found herself suddenly wide-awake, confused by her surroundings, her heart thudding fast. She sat up, eyes adjusting to the dark, and reassured herself. Yes, she was at Paradise Hall—and a clock struck three, answering the next question; and this was Mac beside her; and the muscles of her legs were a little sore from riding, and from her enthusiastic lovemaking. The sweet scent of rain drifted in through the open window. Everything was okay, wasn't it?

Or was it? What was she doing, throwing herself into such

an intense emotional experience when she'd come here to find Julian? This increasing closeness with Mac, whatever else it might become, had the potential to cause trouble, she was sure of it. Before she became more entangled with him, she should end the relationship. As great as the sex was, she really couldn't continue anymore. The intensity scared her. This wasn't what she needed right now.

She didn't think, with his history, that he'd be particularly upset.

Mac

OUTSIDE, THE RAIN CONTINUED AS a gentle patter. Mac stood, looking down at her. She looked vulnerable and innocent in sleep, sheets beneath her chin in her fist, one long, pale leg exposed. He wanted to kiss her and tuck her in and make sure her feet were warm enough. Every woman he'd ever known had been very fussy about the temperature of her feet in bed. He rearranged the bedclothes over her, and she gave an annoyed grunt and that leg emerged again. She'd probably bite his nose off if he tried to kiss her.

He retreated into the bathroom, wondering if the sound of running water would wake her, but she was in exactly the same position as before, deeply asleep, when he emerged. Seated at the desk in the room, he drew a sheet of paper toward him and viewed with distaste the quill pen, which had proved a natural enemy when he'd tried it before, scattering random blobs and ripping into the paper. He settled for the rather primitive pencil and scribbled a note.

Lou, bathhouse at 4?

Love,
Mac

Love? Just a figure of speech. His ex-wife Jennifer still signed her emails that way when she reported on Rosie. It was an English thing.

He considered leaving the note on Lou's pillow, but folded it and left it on the table instead. He'd already made one grand romantic gesture of climbing the ivy into her room; two in one night might be setting a precedent he'd find himself unable to fulfill.

With great caution, he sat on the bed and leaned to sniff her sleepy, sweet smell. He didn't think he'd ever met a woman he quite liked smelling as much as this one. Sometimes he felt like a dog sniffing at her, wanting to bury his face in her warm, fragrant spots. He kissed her cheek, the only part of her face visible beneath the bedclothes.

She rolled toward him, the sheet falling away, and smiled. "Julian," she murmured, and her eyes flew open, her expression fading to disappointment when she saw him.

Shit, this wasn't what he wanted to hear or see. What had happened?

Neither of them said anything for a long, awkward moment and he had the sensation of something precious slipping away, leaving him empty and angry.

She had her thinking expression on again. This wasn't good.

"I don't think I'm ready for this," she said finally.

"You've been thinking in your sleep," he said, trying to make a joke of it.

"The sex is great but what I feel—what I *could* feel—for you scares me. I think we should back off." She lay her hand on his arm. "You've been terrific. So generous."

"So terrific and generous I've scared you off?"

She looked away. "Maybe. You've really helped me put things in perspective."

She patted his arm and looked at him with such sweetness and reason he wanted to— Well, he wasn't sure what he wanted. Stomp out in a masculine rage, cry, tell her he wasn't that crazy about her, anyway... Not true and she would know it. Instead, he said, "Glad to have been of service."

"Don't," she said. "I'm sorry. I'm sorry I can't do this, Mac."

He got off the bed fast. "Sorry I can't compete with a dead guy."

He didn't want to look at her face and he wanted to get out before she saw his.

Twelve

Mac

"'Ere, Mr. Salazar. You ain't keepin' up your left like I fuckin' told you."

Mac raised his left arm and tried to focus on Billy Blue the boxing instructor. Billy Blue, where the hell had he got a name like that? The guy looked like a manic leprechaun hopping around in front of him, head bobbing at the level of Mac's shoulder. Half the time, he couldn't understand what the guy was saying, his quick Cockney patter full of glottal stops with *fuck* and *fuckin'* exploding like gunfire.

"Come on, then. Ain't got all fuckin' day, sir." Billy's gloved hands waved around vaguely in the vicinity of Mac's chest. "Give it me."

Mac welcomed the invitation to hit something. He stepped forward, swung a right, missed, lost his balance, staggered. He ducked away from Billy's whirling fists. Billy was the help, though. He wouldn't actually hit guests, would he?

"I gone easy on you up to now," Billy said as though reading his mind. "Keep your fuckin' guard up, Mr. Salazar, or I'll pop you one, innit."

What?

Speak English, you little fucker, or I'll pop you one. Yeah, good idea. 'S'all in the (fucking) footwork (innit) as Billy had said on the first lesson, so he executed a set, or balance, or whatever that dancing step was called (one-two-three) and lunged at Billy, a good, clean fast hook—

Except, Billy wasn't there anymore and something exploded at his temple and against his back.

The ground.

Shit.

"Sorry, Mr. Salazar." Billy leaned over him, hands on knees, contrite and worried. "Never saw you fuckin' comin,' mate, you goes and runs right into my left, innit."

How the hell did anyone understand this guy? "Huh?"

Alan and Ben, who shared the boxing lesson with him, stared down at him. "You're bleeding," Ben said. As usual, he had few words and most of them stated the obvious.

"Blimey, I was fuckin' scared for a minute. Thought I'd really hurt you, innit. You okay, are you?"

People still said *blimey?* Mac sat up, aware that his bare back had come into contact with damp, muddy grass; he and the others were stripped down to breeches and boots. "I'm fine."

He wasn't sure it was true. This day was going to hell in a handbasket.

A woman ran from the house toward them and, for one moment, Mac thought it was Lou and that she would throw herself into his arms. But it was Di, the lady's maid, with a large first-aid box under her arm.

"I did emergency training," she said, and thrust an object under Mac's nose that had him coughing and spluttering.

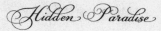

"What the fuck's that?" Mac said.

"Smelling salts. You look a bit pale."

"I *feel* a bit pale now."

"Sorry, Mr. Salazar. Look, this is a cold pack. You'd better put it on your eye, but first…" She rummaged in the box and ripped open a small packet. She pressed the contents onto his eyebrow.

"Shit!" It stung like hell.

"Sorry. It's antibacterial."

"Can I help?" Now it was Rob who joined them—of course, the small grassy area set aside for training was just outside the kitchen area, and probably the entire staff was watching.

Mac turned away, stripping off his gloves, and reached for his shirt, hung over the fence. He raised his voice, a little too loud, the gentleman talking to his underlings. "Thank you for your concern. I'm fine." He shrugged his shirt over his head, aware of tender patches on his back—he must have landed on some stones—and replaced the cold pack on his eye before heading back toward the house.

"Where you goin', Mr. Salazar?"

"I've had enough," Mac said, adding for effect, "innit."

"Mr. Salazar!" Since it wasn't Billy who called, he turned. One of the footmen hurried after him with a small silver tray, which he offered to Mac. A folded and sealed note lay on it.

He nodded his thanks and pocketed the note, waiting until he was out of sight to open it. Apparently, he had a complimentary massage at three—in fifteen minutes—which would fill the time before dinner nicely. And today, everything felt like filling time.

Lou had the ability to turn him inside out and cause him no end of disturbance, and he really didn't like it. He should get over her and have fun. There were plenty of ways, and willing people, around here to have fun with, and there wasn't much to get over, anyway, was there?

After all, she'd used him like some sort of therapeutic fuck machine, and told him his services were no longer needed. The day had started so well, watching her sleep and planning a sexy rendezvous in the bathing pool. He remembered, with some embarrassment, the note he'd left on her table.

He'd looked forward to getting naked in the pool with her and allowing her to use him as much as she wanted. And if he'd had any idea that she was thinking of backing out, he would have dropped the bombshell himself—afterward, of course—and told her it was over. Except, perhaps it wouldn't have been a bombshell for her. She was so cool about everything, maybe she'd just shrug those bony shoulders and agree that it was a sensible and rational decision. He didn't see any way he could extricate himself from the situation without feeling, and probably appearing, dumb. But it was done now. It was over before it had hardly begun.

Besides, in his new identity as a Regency gentleman, he wasn't meant to treat a lady like that, even if he had screwed her ass off.

As he neared the bathhouse and spa, he realized he was striding with clenched fists and muttering to himself, but a good massage would work out the tension in his shoulders and the sore muscles of his back. He removed the cold pack and touched a fingertip to his eyebrow, relieved to find the bleeding had stopped.

He stepped through the doorway into the twenty-first century, the anachronism of a modern spa that Chris and Peter had decided would attract modern women to Paradise Hall. It didn't quite work. The receptionist—or whatever you called her equivalent when she wore a print gown, cap and apron—checked his appointment on her laptop and suggested in a polite English way that possibly he would like to shower first and relax. She snorted back a giggle as she spoke and he wondered if he was catching her in the middle of watching something funny online.

Another staff member, also looking as though she enjoyed some sort of hidden joke, showed him into a room that appeared to be a cross between a brothel and a hospital facility. The shower was stainless steel and powerful, in an alcove decorated with handmade, expensive tiles—his second wife had taught him all about Italian tiles—and a ridiculous assortment of shampoos and soaps. Orchids and ferns stood on ledges and in huge earthenware pots on the floor.

The room was furnished with a chandelier and a red silk couch, which he assumed was merely decorative, since a sturdy modern massage table was also provided. More orchids, quiet piano music playing through invisible speakers, a clean, fresh scent in the air, quite unlike the rusticity of the bathhouse. Wrapped in the bathrobe the facility provided, he settled on the massage table.

Someone tapped on the door and Mac sat bolt upright as it swung open and he saw who it was. "What the hell are you doing here?"

Peter

THEY'D SET UP THEIR DESKS IN the office so they sat back-to-back to avoid distraction. But now the distraction of Chris, even out of his sight line, was more than Peter could bear. He found himself making stupid mistakes on the accounts as he sat, fine-tuned to every breath, sigh and movement Chris made. Now and again he'd receive a gust of Chris's lime-scented aftershave and want to weep with loss and misery.

Why had he done it? Why couldn't he have kept his mouth shut and suffered in silence? His suffering now was overwhelming. He looked back almost with nostalgia at the romantic, sighing yearning he'd had for Rob before he'd spoken and screwed all three of them up. At the time, that was unbearable, too, but in a sort of juvenile, romantic way.

A clatter at the door leading into the yard announced the arrival of the mail. Peter, facing the screen, watched from the corner of his eye as Chris picked up the letters from the mat. He wore those tight, tight trousers hugging waist to ankle that Peter adored—he himself was a little too thick around the middle to carry them off—and a coat of gorgeous dark gray wool that clung to his shoulders and waist, flaring out to brush his knees. He tried not to watch as Chris removed the coat, laying it carefully on a spare chair, and unbuttoned his waistcoat, a lovely dark red-and-gold-silk creation.

Peter ached to touch him. Chris had taken to sleeping on the couch in their living room. Peter, sleepless, in the dark hours of the night, would silently stand in the doorway watching him, hardly daring to breathe. Did Chris really sleep so soundly? How *could* he?

Paper rattled in the recycle box: junk mail.

He cleared his throat. "Anything interesting?"

An annoyed sort of hiss from Chris and an envelope landed on his desk. "I thought you'd set this up as an ebill."

"I did. They said it might take several billing cycles."

"Another Christmas job application." Paper rustled. "A student who wants to work in the kitchen. I'll pass this on unless you'd like to take a look?"

"No, it's okay." He placed the bill in his in-box, something he knew irritated the heck out of Chris. *If it's something to do now, why not just do it?*

Chris didn't say a word.

He'd had enough. This was childish and painful and his fault. All of it. He had to make the first move toward reconciliation.

"Chris, I'm so sorry. I can't bear this silence. Can you forgive me for hurting you?"

Chris, halfway back to his own desk, stopped. "I don't know."

Chris's response catapulted him from anger into fear. "What do you mean, you don't know? What do I have to do to convince you how very sorry I am?"

"I don't know if you can. The damage is done." He sat down and became immersed in whatever was on his computer screen.

"Oh, for God's sake!" Peter stood and thumped his fist on Chris's desk. "Talk to me. Stop—stop fucking sulking!"

"Sulking?" He had Chris's attention now. His face was bright pink.

"Yes, sulking. Try to behave like an adult about this. Let's talk."

"Okay." Chris fumbled at papers on his desk, breaking eye contact with him.

Peter dropped back down into his chair. "Chris, honey?"

Chris dropped his forehead to his hand, elbow on the desk. His shoulders quivered. "I—I always knew this would happen."

"What?" Peter said, thoroughly confused now. "Honey, don't cry, please."

Chris blew his nose and met his gaze. His blue eyes swam with unshed tears. "I knew you were attracted to me because

I was young and pretty. Don't deny it. I know it makes us both sound shallow, but I hoped—I knew—we had something more than that. It's been ten years and I'm not the pretty boy you first met."

Peter nodded, not in agreement, because he was appalled and hurt at what Chris said, but to keep him talking, even though he probably wouldn't want to hear more.

"So I expected it to happen. That you'd pursue another young Adonis. And it has."

"I don't know what to say," Peter said. "I don't know what I can say. I have never expected you to remain a pretty boy. I've loved watching you become your own person—you really were a dreadful, superficial little tart when we first met. I love you for who and what you are. I love watching you flirt with other guys in front of me. I love your energy, your spirit, your enthusiasm and creativity. That's nothing to do with age. You'll always have that." He shrugged. "Look at us. I'm getting grayer and having to watch my carbs. Aging is no fun."

"I'm losing my hair," Chris said in a burst of tearful shame. He pushed his hair back to reveal a minimal amount of exposed temples.

"Honey, it barely shows. And? So what if you are. You can shave it. You'll look really hot. You'll always look really hot to me." He reached for Chris's hand. "You know I've always been afraid you'll leave me for someone more sexy, less staid. Someone more like you. And this thing with Rob. I'm so sorry. I should have just kept my mouth shut. There hasn't been anything between us."

"What difference does that make?" Chris said.

"Not much," Peter said. "I know I don't have the right to ask you for forgiveness, only for patience and time. I try to think of it as some sort of emotional virus. He's straight, he's a fantasy, and one day I'll realize I'm not infatuated with him anymore. That's all. I still love you. You're still part of me, the best part of me, my soul mate."

Chris gave a small smile and squeezed Peter's hand. "I love it when you go all spiritual on me."

"Good." He leaned over the desk and kissed Chris, a small, tentative kiss on the mouth. He hesitated.

Chris looked at him, knowing, ironic. "I have a feeling you want to go all physical on me, too."

"Yes. Yes, I do. I—I've missed you in bed. I miss not being able to have sex anywhere, anytime."

Chris smiled. "Yeah, remember when the Paint Boys walked in on us?"

"And Simon said the only substances he allowed to be spilled on his drop cloth were ones he created?"

They both laughed, a little tentative and shy with each other. Peter leaned to kiss him again, welcoming the flick of his tongue and warmth of his mouth. He came round to Chris's side of the desk and stood looking down at him.

"Well, well," Chris said, and stroked a hand down the front of Peter's breeches.

Peter took the hand and kissed it. "Let me," he said, and dropped to his knees. "Let me do it to you."

He eased open the brass buttons of the fall of Chris's trousers, hearing a moan—his own—as the full beauty of his lover's erect cock sprang forth. A drop of liquid welled already at the slit within the broad, velvety head. He knew he could make Chris come quickly but he wanted to draw out the pleasure, to give as much as he could.

Chris sighed as Peter drew his tongue down, around, nibbling at the shaft. "Hey, big man," Chris whispered. "Want me to do you, too?"

"No. This is all for you. Lie back, enjoy."

Chris's hands caressed his head. "Oh, baby, I've missed you. Missed this. Missed your mouth, your cock, your ass." His hips lifted, pushing his cock deep into Peter's mouth. "You're teasing me. You're going to make me wait."

"I've missed you, too," Peter said. "I love you. I love doing this to you."

He sucked and nibbled and stroked, engulfing Chris's cock completely and then withdrawing to draw his tongue down ridges, around the softness of his balls, with a kiss to the tender skin on the inside of his thighs. Chris moaned and panted, murmuring encouragement and endearments.

Peter buried his nose in the soft nest of Chris's pubic hair, his lover's cock deep in his mouth, swelling and tensing. He marveled at this man's scent, his touch, his helpless groan, the clutch of his hands as Chris gasped, incoherent and lost, and flooded his mouth with his semen.

"Nice one," Chris said, his eyes narrowed in pleasure, sprawled and relaxed in his chair. He leaned to kiss Peter's mouth, lapping at a drop of semen that lay warm on his lip. "Now, how about you? Undo your trousers, lover."

Still kneeling at Chris's feet, Peter unbuttoned his trousers with trembling fingers.

"You're mine," Chris said. He dipped a finger into the semen that oozed still from his cock and held it to Peter's mouth. "Mine. No one else's. Stroke yourself. Make it good. Make it slow."

Peter gazed into Chris's eyes and stroked himself, thrilled at having to obey. Chris sprawled, arrogant and beautiful in his chair, and watched, now and again dropping his hand to pinch and stroke his own awakening cock. "You'd better not come over my trousers, lover. Viv'll be mad at me and I'll make you explain what the stains are. But I want to see come fly out of you. So just you be careful, okay?"

"Yes, Chris." He kept a steady, even stroke, feeling the tension build in his thighs and balls.

"Stop," Chris said. "Stand up." He guided Peter into his mouth, sucked hard and swirled his tongue around the shaft.

Chris released him, lips wet and shiny. "Okay. Finish yourself off."

Peter stood before him, hand pumping hard, hard, and came over Chris's shirt with a helpless whimper.

"What a mess," he said, embarrassed by his copious ejaculation.

"What else is all this linen for?" Chris said, mopping up. "I'd better go and change my shirt."

"Mmm." Peter slid his hands inside Chris's shirt, loving the smooth planes of his chest, the hard nipples. "Thank you, honey."

"Okay, fun and games are over," Chris said. To Peter's disappointment, he tucked his cock away and buttoned up, smoothing his trousers with a flirtatious sideways glance. "Saving it for you for later. And you save it for me, okay? Even if we're half-dead with exhaustion, you know a quickie will help us relax."

"I love you," Peter said. "I can't wait to have you in bed again. I've missed you, missed cuddling."

They kissed, a hard quick embrace before getting on with the day's business, and it was only later that Peter realized Chris had not said he loved him back.

Thirteen

Mac

"I didn't expect to see you here," he said, drawing the bathrobe more firmly around himself at the sight of Sarah in the doorway. Behind her a blonde, horsey Valkyrie grinned at him. "Uh, hi, Annabelle. What are you—"

"Surprise, surprise." Sarah flung off her bathrobe and Mac's jaw dropped. Her body was tight and slender with high, round breasts—his hands curled in anticipation of cupping them—long, slender legs, a manicured strip of pubic hair. Annabelle giggled and untied the sash of her bathrobe, letting it slide from her shoulders.

Oh, God.

"You know, I was really hoping for a massage," he said. "My back's pretty stiff and..."

"Just your back?" Sarah purred. "Oh, poor baby. Don't worry, we'll give you a happy ending, won't we, Annabelle? You won't feel any pain at all."

"I can't fuck a married woman," Mac said, rearranging his bathrobe so that his erection didn't show.

"I'm not married," Annabelle said. She raised her hand to the back of her head and shook out her hair from its usual ponytail. Honey-blond hair cascaded onto her shoulders.

"Yes, but…" He ran out of words as Annabelle and Sarah twisted in a sinuous embrace together, kissing deeply. This was really happening at the wrong time, in the wrong place and with the wrong woman. Women. He should leave.

"Nice to see you, girls," he said, wondering where his clothes had gone. "And, uh, thanks for the show."

He slipped from the table and edged toward the door. He couldn't help it. He looked back and saw Sarah drop her head to suck one of Annabelle's generous breasts.

"Shit."

"That's not very nice, Mac," Annabelle said in the sort of voice she used when she was bullying him during a riding lesson.

"Nothing personal." He took a step away, but somehow his motor skills were confused and he moved in the wrong direction.

"Doesn't Annabelle have lovely breasts?" Sarah said.

He made a strangled noise in his throat and before he knew it he'd taken yet another step toward them both.

They both giggled and stared at the disturbance beneath his bathrobe.

"I told you he had a big one," Annabelle said, elbowing Sarah.

"Why are you doing this?" Mac asked.

"It's for your birthday," Annabelle said.

"My birthday's in October."

"My bad. Wrong date." Sarah cupped her own breasts and that was the end of Mac's good intentions.

His bathrobe dropped to the ground and the red silk couch

creaked as they descended on it, Sarah in his lap, Annabelle kneeling at his feet, her busy tongue lapping like a cat's between Sarah's thighs. His cock pressed up against Sarah's back, her breasts in his hands.

"Stop," he said. "Kiss each other." He dropped his hand to Sarah's little tuft of pubic hair and explored her slick wet folds while she gasped and moaned and fondled Annabelle's breasts.

A loud splintering sound followed by the tearing of fabric came from the couch and it canted slightly to one side, depositing them onto the pile of discarded bathrobes. A stack of condoms fell clear from the robes and Mac grabbed Annabelle's round ass, hauling her to her knees and positioning her the way he wanted.

"Eat her," he said as he rolled a condom on. He watched Annabelle licking at Sarah's pink exposed pussy as he entered her from behind, and for all it was clumsy and ludicrous and though he had only two hands with which to keep his balance and get as many handfuls of breasts (four!) and butt as he could, it was amazing. Just amazing.

"I hope I remember this when I'm ninety," he said. They stopped their licking and gasping and moaning and stared at him. "Never mind, keep licking her. Oh, yeah."

So much to do and watch and stroke and fuck, all this generous female flesh and seemingly endless appetite; the joy of discovering new ways, new angles and positions to pleasure and be pleasured; the glorious slippery mindlessness and freefall into orgasm. And coming back to himself, finally, tangled together with the other two, he heard above the thunder of his heartbeat, the click of the door closing.

"Could you handle another one, Mac?" Annabelle, her

face rosy and sticky, grinned at him. "Don't think so." She squeezed his cock. "Good thing she went away."

"Try some oil," Sarah said. She'd done some miraculous things, miraculous in a very dirty sense, with massage oil and his ass, earlier. She waggled a finger at him.

"Why don't you two carry on," Mac said. "Give me a moment."

He sprawled on the nest of bathrobes, towels and pillows on the floor and watched with the lazy appreciation of a sexual gourmet as Sarah and Annabelle tangled on the massage table, stroking, licking, sucking. It was a beautiful sight. As for him, he was exhausted, sated, played out, screwed out, fucked out, spent. Perhaps he'd never get another erection in his life, but at the moment he didn't care. Much.

But there was one thing he had to know, now that he was regaining some sanity.

"Sarah, Annabelle?"

They looked at him with annoyance, a useless male appendage. "What?" Sarah said.

"Why?" he asked simply.

"I fancy you something rotten," Annabelle said, smirking.

"And I've done everyone else," Sarah said with a shrug.

Their answers left him confused and dissatisfied. It wasn't enough. But he'd fucked women for the same reasons, so why did he feel cheated at being the mark, the target? He contemplated Sarah and Annabelle, shiny with sweat and massage oil, moving softly and rhythmically together. They'd abandoned performing for him. Now they seemed intent only on each other, and he felt a brief stab of envy for women's ability to have orgasm after orgasm. In fact, he was redundant at this point, too depleted to join them on the table—besides which their combined weight had already wrecked one piece of furniture—and suspecting that they'd push him away. He wasn't sure he wanted to join them, anyway.

He stood, wincing, and for one moment regretted he hadn't had a massage where he'd needed it. On weak legs, he made his way to the bathroom, where his clothes lay in a heap on the floor, and dressed.

On his way out, he took a last look at Sarah and Annabelle, who didn't even look up as he left, then gave a friendly nod to the receptionist who was chatting on a cell phone and barely noticed him, either. He glanced at the clock and saw he had over an hour to shower and change for dinner, and— Oh hell, what if Lou had turned up, as he'd asked her to in his note? When he opened the bathhouse door, it was deserted, to his relief. Or his disappointment. He couldn't decide.

HE SAW LOU NEXT BEFORE DINNER as they mingled in the drawing room and his exhausted libido perked up when he saw the impressive cleavage she sported; admirable for a woman with small breasts. She nodded at him, one acquaintance to another, and unfurled her fan, turning away before he could figure if her bodice really was mostly transparent or whether it was just a figment of his overheated if exhausted imagination. As he walked toward Lou, Sarah gave him a small, private smile. She looked as fresh as a daisy.

Viv took his arm. "Quite a shiner you have there, Mac. Should I ask what the other guy looks like?"

"Boxing. You know."

"I hear you're sweet on Lou."

Sweet on Lou. Something struck him in the vicinity of his chest and for one dreadful moment, he thought he was having a heart attack. He waited for pain to radiate down his left arm, realized he was holding his breath and released it in a loud huff. "She's okay," he said.

Viv stared at him, the ostrich feather in her headband nodding against his cheek. "Are you sure you're okay? But anyway, you'd better watch out. The Paint Boys are showing interest."

"Huh?" He followed her gaze to see her arm in arm with them.

"You know what they like," Viv continued.

"Paint?"

"Yes. But they also like doubling up."

"Doubling up?"

"You're pretty dense, tonight, Mac, for a man of letters. They like threesomes and let me tell you, they're pretty good." She gazed at him with concern. "Are you sure you don't have a concussion?"

"I'm fine," he said. "Just tired. It's pretty strenuous being a Regency gentleman."

"That's what I love about it," she said, leading him toward the dining room. "All those manly men. If you want to sit next to Lou— Oh, too late. Paint Boys got there first—and Peter's opposite." Her voice lowered to a sultry growl. "Hi, Rob. I could take those breeches in for you if you like. They look a bit loose."

Rob, holding the door open for them, cast a mute appeal, man to man, to Mac.

"Leave the kid alone," he said to Viv, and pulled her away.

"He's adorable," Viv said, running her fan over her lips. A few days ago, that would have driven him mad with lust. "I think he's a virgin, don't you?"

"I have no idea." He pulled out a chair for her. "I defer to your greater experience."

"But most of the footmen are very yummy." She peeled her gloves off, watching Mac under lowered lashes.

"Give it a rest, Viv."

"Okay," she said with her usual good humor. At that moment, Chris rang the bell and the footmen came in with the first remove, salmon surrounded by shrimps and strewn with fresh herbs, pies and tarts with elaborate golden crusts and bowls of salad that sparkled in the candlelight like green and red jewels.

He tried not to look at Lou, but he couldn't help himself. She was deep in conversation with the Paint Boys, laughing and flirting and working her way through a large plate of food. As he watched, Jon—or was it Simon?—refilled her wineglass. *Easy, Lou. Remember you're a cheap date.*

None of his business, he reminded himself.

She looked down the table, her gaze polite and disinterested, skimming over him as though he was of little more interest than the candelabra.

He'd blown it.

Lou

CHRIS STOOD TO RING THE BELL for the footmen to clear the table, and Lou noticed how Peter gazed at him adoringly. Chris gave him a smile and a wink. So they'd made up. But when Rob came to take away platters from their end of the table, Peter looked away, his mouth tight. Chris, however, made a great show of laying his hand on Rob's sleeve, and engaging him in conversation about something on the table.

What was going on there? She told herself sternly not to get involved. They'd sort it out, and if either of them asked for help she'd do her best. Meanwhile, Alan and Cathy, oblivious to everyone else at the table, sitting next to Peter, giggled and fed each other bits of food. So sweet, Lou thought, and wondered if she'd overdone the wine already. But the footmen were bringing another remove: an oyster stew, platters of vegetables arranged in overlapping layers like works of art, sprinkled with herbs, and small roast fowl.

More wine circulated, and the talk turned to the ball that was to take place in a few days. It was Paradise's first public event, inviting locals, a group of historical reenactors and history and Austen enthusiasts to dance, dine and tour the house. The event would attract media, to give Paradise the buzz Chris and Peter needed. Unfortunately, the current guests at the house had still not mastered many of the dances. "But it doesn't matter," Peter said. "We want everyone to have a good time. Lou, may I request the first two dances with you?"

He raised an eyebrow and looked down the table briefly to where Mac was deep in conversation with Viv.

"I'd be honored," Lou said, tearing her own gaze from Mac. So what if he was flirting with Viv? At least he wasn't glowering at her.

"Excellent." Peter began to talk of the media coverage they expected for the event and Simon and Jon joined in the discussion with their decorating scheme for the evening.

"Do you think we should be masked?" Peter asked. "Chris and I think it would add a lovely touch of glamour. What do you think, Lou?"

"Absolutely," she said. "Although, I think we'll all know who everyone is."

"We can always pretend." Peter winked. "Handsome masked strangers—think of the possibilities. And we do have visitors from the local historical reenactment group attending."

"More women than men, though. Nothing much has changed since Austen's time." Chris spooned oyster stew onto Peter's plate. "And you need to keep your strength up."

Fourteen

Mac

Lou left the dining room arm in arm with the Paint Boys, all three of them deep in conversation. Did she know what she was doing? Surely she wasn't planning a threesome with them? Mac felt a pang of alarm that she was the victim of a pair of sexual predators (because to think she might be a willing participant was unthinkable).

Mac rushed after them and tapped Lou on the shoulder. "Mind if I have a word?"

She turned, eyebrows raised, and the Paint Boys continued forward.

"Well?" she said.

Not good. Downright frosty, in fact.

"I know it's probably none of my business, but I wanted to warn you about those two. They're sort of kinky."

"And?"

"And I wouldn't want to see you get into anything you couldn't handle."

It seemed a perfectly reasonable thing for him to say, but

it didn't improve her attitude. She drew her shawl around herself and glared.

"Anything I couldn't handle?"

"Yes."

"What a hypocrite you are," she said, her voice cold and clear.

Uh-oh.

"You assume, with no justification whatsoever, that I'm *thinking about* screwing two guys, and you advise me against it. Does that seem like a double standard to you, or did you literally screw your brains out this afternoon?"

His heart sank. "That was you, opening the door."

"Yeah, that was me. Doesn't it strike you, Mac, that you're a little possessive for someone who turned me down this afternoon for two of the dumbest women I've ever met?"

"I wasn't interested in their brains." As a joke, it fell flat. "But you dumped me—"

"Yes, I did." She continued to glare at him. "But I found your note and I thought you deserved some sort of explanation. I came looking for you, and you weren't in the bathhouse, so I asked after you at the spa reception desk. Funny how much the woman there giggled. She must have thought you were a real stud. And guess what I found—you healing your broken heart in the way you know best."

"It wasn't like that." He wanted to explain the note—that he'd left it there before she dumped him—but she didn't give him a chance.

"Is it so hard to believe that I might be attracted to guys who are, although you may find it hard to believe, actually good at something and with whom you can hold an interesting conversation? And whether we were intending to screw each other's brains out or talk about Georgian interior design, you know what, Mac? It's got nothing to do with you. Not anymore, not ever."

"Lou, I—"

"Did it ever occur to you that I may have been interested in a threesome?"

"Well, no, I..." He could only stare at her. "I didn't think... I mean, we don't—didn't—really know each other that well. You didn't seem the type. I thought..."

"That I'm not that sort of girl?" She laughed. "Oh, that's rich, Mac. Let's get it quite clear, shall we? What I do is none of your business. I liked you for a time, but now, it's too late. Got it?"

God, what a ballbuster. To think he'd felt sorry for her, or, dumb jerk that he was, that she needed his protection. "I get it, Lou. See you around."

Lou

SHE CAUGHT UP WITH JON AND Simon and linked her arms into theirs.

"Everything okay, dear?"

"Fine."

"Ooh, Mac does have a lovely glower," Simon said.

The two of them exchanged a meaningful glance.

"We've never done a couple, have we?" Simon said. "Do you think Mac would...?"

"I wouldn't want him to. And better not count me in, either," Lou said.

"Oh, dear," Jon said.

Simon clucked his tongue. "Has Mac been a naughty boy?"

She shrugged, proud of her coolness. "There was never much there, I'm afraid."

"And you're absolutely sure we can't help out?"

Maybe it was the wine, maybe it was admiration for their professional skills and the enjoyment she found in their company, but at that moment she felt an enormous affection for them both. But sex with them? No way. For all their naughty perversity, she didn't find them attractive, and the idea of the three of them in bed together made her cringe. "No, thank you, but you're so sweet to offer."

"I understand. It's so difficult to find good help these days," Simon said. She really, really hoped their giggles would give Mac entirely the wrong impression.

BUT LATER, ALONE IN HER ROOM, she wondered why she felt so disappointed and lonely. Maybe Chris and Peter were still up and would tolerate her company, but when she crossed to the door and peered into the gloom of the passage, she changed her mind. She didn't like the feel of that dark, cavernous space—it was altogether a bit too much like a bad Gothic novel. Besides, she had plenty of dark, cavernous feelings at the moment, a huge emptiness that she could attribute only a little of to Julian. It was Mac she'd lost this time, and it hurt, hell, it hurt. But she'd made the right decision, she was sure of it.

She brushed her teeth and retreated into bed, listening to the gentle hiss of rain outside. To hell with him. He was dishonest, greedy, unpredictable, selfish. He was everything she didn't and shouldn't want.

She remembered his hands, his touch. *I'm good at you, Lou. Good in you.*

And today, her shock at opening the door and seeing him rapt, astonished, a participant in some holy rite receiving absolution as the two naked women twined themselves around and over him. Had she ever given him that sort of ecstatic pleasure? Could she? Or, equally important, could she lose herself enough to receive it?

Now she'd never know.

She wanted to persuade herself that she was angry. Maybe she was, but her predominant emotions were abandonment, sorrow, just when she thought she was emerging from that dark tunnel. If that was what he wanted, why hadn't he asked her?

"Really, Mac, your excuses were pathetic," she said as though he was next to her. She turned her face to the pillow to see if any of his scent remained from the previous night.

Nothing.

Good, she tried to convince herself. She didn't need him.

She ran her hand over her breasts and then down her belly. She didn't need anyone but herself. Mac had been a mistake, an aberration—her entry back into the world of relationships and sexuality and some of it she'd enjoyed a lot. But hadn't she known all along he wasn't right for her? It didn't explain why she now felt lonely and abandoned.

Fifteen

Rob

Rob snatched the remote from his dad and clicked off the TV.

"What the fuck—" Mike Temple made a grab for the remote and sank back into his squalid nest of blankets on the sofa. A beer can fell out and rolled onto the floor.

"Can't you get off your arse? Look at you!" Rob gestured at the sofa, the coffee table littered with beer cans, an overflowing ashtray and the crumpled, stained copy of the local paper, open to the jobs page. A few, but only a few, jobs were circled in red pen. "Don't bother with the paper, Dad. All the jobs are online and you need to get out and talk to people."

"Don't you tell me what to do," his dad said. He reached for his cigarettes and lit one.

"You shouldn't smoke in here. It's bad for the baby, right, Sylvia?"

His sister, carrying a tray with mugs of tea and biscuits, shrugged as she made her way across the living room littered with plastic toys. "I tell him all the time."

"See?" Rob took a mug of tea. "Thanks. Getting bigger every day, Syl."

"Okay, okay." His dad lurched up from the couch and took the few steps over to the sliding-glass door that opened onto the patio.

"Don't nag him," Sylvia said. She sank onto the sofa and rubbed her pregnant stomach. "It doesn't do any good."

"Hell with that. Graham!" he shouted. "Graham, get your arse down here and pick up your toys."

A thundering on the stairs announced Graham's arrival. He edged into the living room, clutching something in his hand.

"What's that?" Rob asked, giving him a hug.

"My binky."

"Your—" But before he could say anything, his sister shook her head, warning him not to pursue the matter any further.

"Come on, let's get this stuff picked up and we'll go out and play," Rob said, alarmed that his little brother was reverting to toddlerhood even more. He thought the binky, Graham's tattered scrap of baby blanket, had been safely put to rest a couple of years ago.

As Graham gathered his toys into a plastic crate, Rob cleared off the table. "Want me to hoover, Syl?"

She smiled at him. "No, you don't have to do that."

"I'll go and talk to Dad, then."

"Don't nag him," she said again. "Have you heard from Mum?"

He shook his head, stepped past Graham and his toys and joined his father on the patio. His dad had finished his cigarette and was pulling weeds from between the flagstones.

"Dad, I thought you'd like to see this." He handed his father a piece of paper. "I expect you've seen it already. It went up on the Paradise website yesterday."

His dad took the sheet of paper, glanced at it and handed it back, leaving a grubby thumbprint. "You've got to be joking."

"Why not? Look, it's gardening, repairs and security duties, and you could do that. You like gardening. And it comes with a cottage. It's small but big enough for you and Graham."

His dad grunted and took the paper again. "What about you?"

"What about me? I'm going to Cambridge in a couple of months."

"I don't know if we can afford that."

"Look, I've got an exhibition. It's a full scholarship. You don't have to pay a thing. I'll work in a pub or something for living money."

"Oh, yeah, and leave Graham behind?"

"We'll Skype. It's not like I'm going to another planet."

"Think where your loyalties lie. It's bad enough for Graham that his mum's gone, and now you're leaving us, too? We could use the money if you stay on at Paradise."

"That's your fatherly advice, is it? Then you'd better start acting like a dad. Act like a man. All you do is lie around on that fucking sofa and get drunk. You let Mum take your balls when she left?" He turned away without waiting for an answer and went back into the house. "Graham, let's go. Leave the binky with Syl. Binkies don't like football."

"Yes, they do." Graham clutched the grubby bit of fabric to his chest.

"No, they don't," Rob said. "Give it to Syl and she and

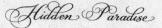

the baby will look after it for you. Get a move on. It's going to rain again soon."

"I'll give it a bit of a wash," Sylvia said. "Make it all nice and clean. It'll like that."

"Okay." Graham uncurled his fingers from the binky. "Don't let *him* get it."

"I won't, love. Get your jacket on." Sylvia whispered as Graham went out to the hall, "Dad tried to throw it out. Graham screamed the place down. Look, Gerry's back in two weeks and the baby will be here in another six. I don't know what we're going to do. There isn't enough room."

"I know." He looked to make sure his dad wasn't watching and handed her an envelope full of money. "Tips for the week. Don't let him know and don't buy him fags."

She giggled. "Thanks, love. Don't they pay you in gold coins, then?"

Graham, wearing his jacket and clutching a football, came back into the room. He cast a longing glance at the binky in his sister's hands. "I'm ready. Come on, Rob."

Bugger, he was late back and soaked to the skin—Graham had thrown a massive tantrum at the sight of the binky swirling around in the washer when they'd got back to his sister's—and after that bit of excitement, Rob's bike had got a flat on the way back and he'd had to walk the last mile in the rain.

Hoping he was out of sight of the office, he hauled his bike across the cobbled yard and opened the door of what had once been the carriage house.

"Rob!"

Too late. Chris stood at the office door, beckoning imperiously.

"Come on in, Rob. No, stay on the doormat please. I don't want the carpet ruined. We need you upstairs."

"I'm on my way," Rob said, and because by now it was automatic, he added, "sir."

"It's raining again, so the ladies can't go out," Chris said. He regarded Rob with a slightly malicious air, or it might have been good-natured teasing. With him, you never really knew. "They need a model for a drawing lesson with Viv."

"A model?"

"Yes. A nude study."

"What! Why me?"

"Drawing was an accomplishment of a well-bred woman. It's quite historically correct."

"Yeah, but…" He unbuttoned his parka, which was dripping wet from the bike ride to the house. "I mean, didn't they draw flowers and things?"

"The beauty of the male body has long been accepted as an aesthetic ideal," Chris said. "Get one of the other footmen to do it if it makes you uncomfortable. I'm sure they'll have no trouble accepting. I imagine the tips will be fantastic. No big deal, but make your mind up. The guests are waiting."

Rob thought of Ivan the permanently erect—absolutely not—and before he could even do a mental inventory of the lads' shortcomings (pimpled bottoms, farting) realized that he'd never live it down if he delegated. After all, didn't they all claim that the female guests were looking for an excuse, any excuse, to rip off the footmen's livery? It would ensure Rob's authority in the house. Decades later, another generation of pimpled, farting footmen with joyfully uncontrolled erections would mention the name of Rob Temple with awe and wonder.

Hell, he had to do it. The leader sacrificed himself for the good of the pack.

"Okay," he said. "Where?"

"The drawing room in ten minutes." Chris gave a thin smile. "Well, don't stand there, dripping. You're on duty as of fifteen minutes ago."

If you hadn't called me into the office for this dumb stunt while I was putting the bike away I'd be there now. "Yes, sir." Rob gave his best insolent sloppy bow, which felt weird in jeans and a sweatshirt. He squelched across the office, but paused in the doorway. It was here that Peter had propositioned him and he was pretty sure Chris knew all about it. "So do I take my kit off in the drawing room, sir?"

Chris sighed and rolled his eyes. "You will present yourself in livery. A screen will be provided behind which you will undress and Viv will provide you with drapery for decency's sake."

"Right, then," Rob said. Well, at least he wouldn't be totally naked. He hoped the drapery wouldn't be inspired to move around too much and that Viv wouldn't get too hands-on about the whole thing. She was okay on her own, all business, but if there were other people around, she was as bad as Chris—when he was in a good mood.

"Good morning, Rob." Peter, carrying a handful of papers, approached from inside the house.

Rob bowed and flattened himself against the wall to let him by, aware that Chris watched them like a hawk.

"We have an applicant for the groundsman position," Peter said. "Mike Temple. A relative of yours, is he, Rob?"

Well, at least the stupid sod had got off his arse and done something. "My dad."

"What an amazing coincidence," Chris said as Rob retreated down the passage, breaking into a run and unbuttoning his shirt as he left.

He changed into his livery, leaving his clothes in a sodden heap on the floor, stopped in at the Servants' Hall to check the bulletin board, and ran upstairs. Viv met him in the hall outside the drawing room.

"You're late," she said.

"Yeah, sorry, ma'am."

"Well, come on in. They're waiting for you."

Oh, shit. Sarah looked rapacious, Cathy giggled and Lou gave him a cool nod. A small dais had been erected (bad word choice) in the center of the room where apparently he was to recline on a heap of pillows, wearing— He looked at it with distaste as Viv handed a piece of drapery to him. Something the size of a small towel.

"Everything off?" he asked in a whisper. "Could I get a pair of boxers or—"

"What do you think?" She raised her eyebrows.

"Okay." Now he was worried that he might have some sort of repulsive flaw he didn't know about.

"And by the way, as I've told you before, and you'd better remind the rest of your gang, boxers are inappropriate. They're not historically correct and they spoil the line of the breeches."

"Yes, ma'am." He resisted the urge to roll his eyes at another bad-tempered overlord. Was it the weather or something? He wasn't exactly all sweetness and light himself, not after that exchange with his father. He could see the old man's point, though. If Rob was the only one with a job in the family, he should hang on to it. Graham would need a new school uniform and other stuff, shoes and so on. Kids always did. He remembered his mum exclaiming over Graham's ability to outgrow shoes in a month, and then sweeping him up into a hug the way she used to do with Rob and Syl.

He didn't want to think about his mum—he didn't feel like bursting into tears.

But if his dad didn't get the groundsman job, or got it and screwed it up or refused to take it as being below him—not that being the owner of a bankrupt chain of tanning salons was particularly high-class—what then? Gerry, who had no great fondness for his father-in-law, would probably demand they all leave before the baby came. Rob just hoped they'd let Graham stay.

He was jolted out of his reverie by Viv tweaking on his sleeve. "I'll let the shoulders out on your coat. Does it pull when you're carrying heavy stuff?"

"A little, yes, ma'am. Thanks."

"You've got some muscle, kid." Her hand lingered.

"Yes, ma'am."

"Stop playing with the help, Viv," Sarah said. "Not unless you're willing to share."

Stupid cow. Yeah, now *you want to share me.* Rob fixed his polite footman smile on his face and escaped behind the screen in the corner of the room, checking first that he wasn't providing a peepshow with the mirrors hung around the wall. Gritting his teeth, he draped the scrap of cloth around his waist.

It either covered his butt or his dick, but not both. He removed the thing and shook it, in the hope of it magically expanding.

"Rob?" Viv's voice came from the other side of the screen. "Here you go."

A tumble of black silk fell into his hands—a robe that might make him look like a Chippendale dancer but at least he wouldn't treat the women to a display of wobbling dick as he crossed the room. He wrapped himself in the robe and grasped his protective cloth in the other, with a sudden burst of sympathy for Graham and his binky, and strode out from behind the screen. Head up, shoulders straight, as he'd been taught in what the lads referred to as footman boot camp. Now the three women were arranged around the room with their easels and he'd have to make a choice—which one to face when he assumed the full monty.

Sarah, her mouth half-open with greed: no. Cathy, pink and giggling: no. And Lou, cool and critical, the lesser of three evils apparently, other than Viv who was busy ripping out the seams of his footman's coat. Lou it was.

He stepped onto the dais and looked her in the eye. He was damned if he was going to look shy, even if he was, and he knew he had nothing to be ashamed of—unless he had some really horrific physical flaw on his back but that wasn't his fault or his problem. He dropped the dressing gown, feeling only slightly like a stripper, and lowered himself to a kneeling position and then onto one elbow, which seemed the most graceful way of getting horizontal. As an afterthought he tossed the minimal piece of fabric over his crotch.

Done.

Lou gave him a small nod and half smile the way she might have done if he'd retrieved her fallen napkin at dinner.

Whew.

"We'll give you a break after twenty minutes, but shout if you need to stretch before then." Viv rearranged him as though he were a piece of furniture, wedging a pillow beneath his arm, straightening out one leg, and he was grateful for her impartiality. He listened as she gave a brief lecture on how they should concentrate on light and shadow and shouldn't be afraid of the pastels and pencils at their disposal or of using color in an imaginative way. Above all, she instructed them, have fun.

They dithered around for a while, Sarah claiming she had to move. Rob was pretty sure she wanted to see if she could get a sighting of his arse. Then they got started and other than a slight giggle or whisper, it was pretty much silent in the room.

Lou's pencil scratched. She shook her head, erased something and stared at his torso. A gentle ripping sound came from behind him—Viv at work on his coat, and then the soft pop of a needle penetrating silk.

"What are the guys doing this morning?" Cathy asked.

"Billiards," Lou said. "Probably getting an early start on the day's drinking. I wish we could have ridden today."

"Can't take the girl out of the cowgirl?" Sarah said in a slightly malicious tone.

"Something like that."

The dining-room door opened.

"Everything okay?" It was Peter, and Rob only just stopped himself grabbing for his dressing gown. "Are your charges behaving, Viv? Good. Let's see. Oh, very nice, Cathy. Lovely line. Did you study art?"

"I liked it at school." Giggle. "We didn't have this, though." She gestured toward Rob.

"And Sarah," Peter went on. "Very unusual. I didn't realize you could see, er, quite so much from where you are."

"I'm using my imagination."

The floor creaked as Peter moved around to Lou and rested a hand on her shoulder. They exchanged a brief, affectionate smile.

"I know. Don't lose my day job," Lou said.

"It's not that bad. So long as you're enjoying yourself."

Rob kept his eyes fixed on the wall above Lou's head. Something had changed—he knew three (possibly four, but Viv was used to people being undressed in her line of work) women were staring at him, but ever since Peter had come into the room, the air had fairly prickled with something more personal, more vivid.

He tried to focus on something else, and sent his mind off for a change of topic.

Lou. Lou in the dark, her breast exposed, rubbing up against him in the dark, her face close to his. His imagination had returned him to the scene again and again, editing out Mac, so it was him alone with Lou in the dark. She didn't shrink from him in alarm, and this time he wasn't embarrassed by the meeting or his obvious erection—had she noticed then? But she'd notice this time and reach down to touch him as he caressed her breast with its lovely hard nipple—

Oh shit, oh shit, there was definite movement beneath the cloth as his cock shifted against his thigh.

She'd see. Peter would see. That bloody silly bit of cloth lay between him and total humiliation, and if he reached down to make sure it covered him he'd draw attention to his state, like a pervert hanging around a kids' playground.

Get down.

That wouldn't work. He forced himself to think of something really awful. He thought about his dad, slumped on the sofa and wallowing in self-pity. No, he absolutely didn't want to think of him. Of Graham running through the mud in the park, kicking his football and shouting, "Look at me, Rob! Watch me!" Poor little fucker. He tried something good

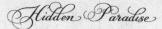

but asexual, Cambridge, the incredible antiquity of those ancient buildings, the place he'd be very soon.

Who'd play footer with Graham then?

Graham would be back at school with his mates. He'd
be okay. Unless he was moved to a different school because
they were kicked out of Sylvia's tiny house. Where would
he end up?

He risked a glance at Lou, who'd bent over to pick up
something from a small table of drawing equipment and was
revealing a lot of cleavage for a skinny woman.

Shit.

All his good negative thoughts undone.

In a panic, he turned his mind to getting a flat tire in the
rain—yes, grabbing the bicycle pump, his chilled hands sliding on the metal, and then that up-down motion—no good.
Think about Graham again. That should shrink things.

Lou raised her head and smiled at him—quite friendly
and matter-of-fact, as if she knew he had a hard-on and it
was no big deal. He shifted his attention to the wall again,
looked away quickly from a portrait of a bosomy Restoration
beauty, and found a safe blank spot on which to concentrate
until they let him take a break.

Sixteen

Lou

After the drawing lesson—which to her surprise she'd quite enjoyed, and not just from seeing Rob's erection, poor kid, he'd looked so embarrassed—there was lunch and then dance practice. The men had divided the morning under cover in the riding arena, shooting period guns or playing billiards inside, with a head start on the alcohol consumption for the day. Mac was at dance practice for once, saying little.

Lou was tempted to quote to him from *Pride and Prejudice* ("It is your turn to say something now, Mr. Darcy") but the time for good-natured teasing had passed.

"Eye contact, Mrs. Connolly!" Becky the dancing mistress bellowed, and Lou locked eyes with Mac as they joined hands and circled, shoulders close together. His gaze didn't falter, but she could read nothing in those dark eyes. Fine. She didn't want to. She hoped her gaze was equally impenetrable.

"And back to your original partner!" Becky gave Lou a friendly shove in the right direction.

Lou returned to Alan, who belched beer fumes in her direction and apologized, red-faced. It was an authentic touch, she told him, and he smiled in relief. She wished now she hadn't seen him and Cathy make love—she felt guilty that she had such intimate knowledge of them. Mac's fault.

The next move put her next to Sarah. "What's his dick like?" she hissed at Lou.

"Whose?"

"Rob's."

"I really didn't notice," she lied. "Sorry."

"Ben wants a threesome with him."

"He does?" She couldn't help glancing at Ben, who was holding Mac's hand and looking almost animated.

"He'd be great. He's used to being told what to do—" Becky advanced on them and they scurried to find the correct place in the dance.

Rob was on duty, in charge of refreshments for the dancers, glasses of lemonade and cakes, standing still at the side of the room. He had a gift for stillness, Lou thought, or maybe it was his training as a footman. Students of his age she'd taught were all restless energy, unable to keep knees or hands still. He'd proved a good model, too, and she was glad she was the only one of the women who'd noticed his errant erection. Peter had noticed it, too, his hands clenching, before he abruptly left the room almost in midsentence. Poor Peter.

She knew how he felt. A sudden gust of desire had swept through her, too, leaving her breathless. His blend of innocence and sweetness was suddenly erotic, straightforward and uncomplicated. Maybe this was what she wanted, what she needed.

The violinist ended his variations on the dance tune with a flourish of his bow, and the dancers bowed and curtsied before crowding around the refreshments table.

Lou took a glass of lemonade and moved over to the window. Outside, rosebushes and trees sparkled with moisture, but the rain had stopped. She drained her glass, and as she did so a footman approached with a silver tray with a note on it.

If it was from Mac, she would decline it, but the handwriting was Viv's, summoning her to a fitting for her ball gown that afternoon. She thanked and tipped the footman with one of the coins in her reticule. He looked down her cleavage as he bowed and she noticed how Rob glared at him.

"Do you need an umbrella, ma'am?" Rob asked.

"How did you know I was going outside?"

"The way you looked out the window. And after you read the note you looked out again."

What a combination, good looks and empathy, and according to Peter, loyalty to his family. Some girl would be lucky to have him. She smiled at him and left to change into her half boots for the walk to the lodge.

She left the house by the front door, taking a moment to gaze at the scenery—the varied and vivid greens of trees and the heavy nod of roses soaked with moisture and spangled with raindrops. She descended the steps and walked along the driveway. Although there was a pleasant, winding footpath that would take her through the trees, she knew how wet she'd get on that route.

From the opened windows of the lodge came a hum of conversation against a backdrop of opera, Viv's music choice of the day. She recognized Mac's voice and was surprised by a sudden homicidal urge at the thought of walking in on him in some sort of sexual situation. But there was no need for bloodshed, to her relief. He sat in his shirtsleeves at a small desk, working on a laptop, while Viv prowled around a dress form, pins in her mouth. Di Brooks, the lady's maid, sat nearby, hemming a garment.

"Welcome back to the twenty-first century," Viv said. "Mac, go upstairs. I need Lou to try on this gown."

"Sure." Mac gathered up his laptop and a small reporter's notebook and headed upstairs.

"It's nice to see him get down to some work," Viv commented, "although our boy seems rather subdued today." She gave Lou a curious glance.

Di laid her sewing aside and stood to help Lou remove her gown.

"Is that mine?" Lou gazed at the deep red gown on the dress form. "I love the color, but it doesn't seem to have a bodice."

"I thought you were woman enough for a bit of titty reveal," Viv said. "You'll have an over gown but you'll have to pull your shift down like this—" She was tugging as she spoke. "Di can help on the night of. And the gown comes with its own petticoat."

Lou looked down at herself, at her breasts pushed up onto a shelf, nipples visible.

"Regency girls really didn't care if a bit of nipple showed," Viv said. "Your areolas are quite light because you're fair skinned, but if you want to be really naughty you can rouge them. So your dance partners will have to look quite hard. So to speak," she added with a dirty cackle.

The petticoat was followed by more tugging of shift and petticoat and stays, and then a slither of satin as the gown was dropped over her head. Di tied the two laces at the back.

As she adjusted the drawstring at the bodice, Mac simultaneously knocked at the door at the bottom of the stairs and entered the room.

"Sorry, I forgot my— Shit, Lou, what are you wearing?"

Lou hastily crossed her arms over her chest. *Don't think you'll sneak a peek, mister.*

"Bugger off," Viv said, throwing a length of fabric around Lou's shoulders.

The door banged behind Mac as he retreated.

"I'm going to have to leave you topless for a bit," Viv said. "Let me just check the hem. Turn, please. Looks okay. Wait, let me adjust here. And here. Good. Now the overdress, which creates the train. You'll have to practice walking in it so you don't tread on it."

The overdress, of dark red gauze embroidered with black and gold, wrapped around her like a shawl, held in place with a paste clasp under her breasts, creating a plunge that emphasized her cleavage and breasts.

"Oh, wow!" Lou stared at her reflection. "That's amazing. Absolutely gorgeous."

"I thought you'd like it," Viv said. "And if you did want to chicken out—which I know you won't—we'll provide an inset you can pin inside the gown. We'll make you up a headdress, quite simple." She nodded at a tangle of overdress fabric and gold cord on the worktable. "They'll be bursting out of their pants, Lou."

"Oh. Good. I guess."

"Yes, we have some nice military men coming from the local reenactment society if Mac lets them get near you."

"I don't think he'll care one way or the other," Lou said.

"Really?" Viv tilted her head to one side like a gossipy bird. "He's such a sensitive soul, isn't he?"

"He is?" Lou said in disbelief. Mac, a sensitive soul?

"Oh, yes, he was on Skype with his daughter earlier. So sweet. Which reminds me, would you like to check your email now you're two centuries ahead? We'll get you changed and you can make yourself at home, have a cup of tea and a gossip if you like." She moved to plug in her electric kettle. "Of course, the problem with Mac is that he needs a really big story to get his career going, but he has to do all these journalistic fluff pieces to pay the bills. Di, let's get the gown off and make Lou decent and then we can have a cuppa."

Back in her everyday cotton gown again, Lou scrolled through her emails. Nothing important—she typed up quick, affectionate responses to her sisters and a noncommittal but friendly progress report to her dissertation advisor. And then a subject line caught her eye and made her gasp in shock: *We have an offer, asking price.*

SHE FOUND HERSELF WANDERING IN the woods, her gown darkened a foot deep with moisture that had seeped into it, bewildered, with only the barest of memories of what she'd done after reading the email. She'd turned down the tea, which was a shame because now she was thirsty, and she'd probably stained her gown and Viv would be furious— she stopped to untangle her skirts from a spray of bramble. She should figure out how to get back to the house, which shouldn't be that complicated, but she had no idea where she was.

She sniffed the air. Someone was burning wood nearby, so she wandered between the trees toward the scent, expecting to come upon one of the grounds staff. Sure enough, a small cottage with an overgrown garden and a decayed gate hanging from a moss-covered stone post lay ahead, a thread of smoke emerging from the chimney.

"Hello?" she called. A flagstone path, overgrown with moss and grass, led to the front door, which stood ajar. She pushed it open. The smell of smoke was much stronger here, billowing out into the room. A footman knelt in front of the fireplace, poking a stick up the flue. "Rob?"

"What?" He turned and scrambled to his feet, removing earplugs. An iPod was lodged in his coat pocket. "Christ, you gave me a scare, ma'am."

"Sorry." She looked around at the one room of the cottage, windows shrouded in cobwebs and a huge black range surrounded by tiles. "What is this place?"

"It's the groundsman's cottage. I came to have a look at it, see if the chimney was okay." He squatted and poked at the flue again and gave a grunt of satisfaction as a mess of twigs and debris fell into the grate. "I'm hoping my dad will get a job at Paradise and he can live here with my brother."

"Oh. I see." To her, it didn't look at all suitable for a small child to live in. "Won't he need a bathroom?"

"There's one through the door there. The water isn't on yet."

She took a quick look through the doorway and saw an ancient rusty toilet with a ceiling-mounted tank and chain, and a claw-footed bathtub.

"It could be really nice once it's cleaned and fixed up," he said.

"So when does he start?"

He looked away and mumbled, "He only just applied. And I'm not sure he'll get it." He straightened up and poked at the fire in the hearth. "The upstairs is cool. Come and look at it. If you want to, that is."

"Okay." She followed him upstairs, where there were two tiny bedrooms right under the roof, and the collapsed remains of an iron bedstead and a few rags lay sadly abandoned on the dusty wooden floor.

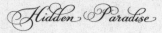

"See?" he said. "Nice, isn't it?"

"Well…yes, I think it has a lot of potential." Her approval seemed so important to him that she found herself agreeing.

"There's no electricity upstairs but Graham can do his homework downstairs, and I'll come over from the house…"

"But you're going to Cambridge. You'd only be here during vacations."

"Yeah." He ran down the stairs ahead of her, saying over his shoulder, "Well, it's not one hundred percent certain."

"What do you mean?" She followed him down the stairs. "I thought you had a really big-shot scholarship. It's a chance in a lifetime. What happened?"

He walked over to the fireplace and kicked the dying embers of the fire. "It's complicated."

She waited, but he didn't seem anxious to elaborate. He unscrewed the top of a bottle of soda that stood on the windowsill, and offered it to her.

She took a gulp, feeling like a junkie. She'd had coffee and tea over the past few days but hadn't realized until now how much she'd missed a cold, sweet and carbonated drink. "Thanks. I'd better get back to the house."

"I'll come with you." He took the bottle back from her and placed it in his coat pocket. "Don't want to get a reputation for skiving off."

"You always seem to work very hard," Lou said.

He shrugged, and ushered her out of the cottage, locking the door behind them. "It's the sort of job where you have to balance what's expected and what you can get away with not doing. Haven't you read Swift? His advice to servants?"

"Tell me about it," she said. She always loved it when one of her students wanted to share a new discovery.

"Well, it's a sort of joke how-to book for servants. I found it online when I was applying for this job. If you're sent out on an errand, you should stay out for hours and have a really good excuse when you come back, like you were saying goodbye to a cousin who was to be hanged, or you'd been to look for your master and had to visit a hundred pubs." He grinned. "It's pretty funny."

"It sounds as though he'd met some very aggravating servants. You might like his poetry. Some of it is very ribald and savage, but others are quite tender and lovely. He was an interesting man. I'm sure there are some of his books in the library at the house." She looked around at the thick growth of trees and bushes. "Which way do we go?"

"This way." He led the way to a break between some bushes that turned out to be a path, taking them to the far side of the lake. The summerhouse stood graceful and shining on the opposite bank.

He went ahead, bending branches back out of the way, while she tried not to get her gown more muddy than it was. As they approached the summerhouse, the light changed from bright to dark and rain came splattering down.

"Run!" He caught her hand and they ran to the comparative shelter, where they watched rain slant and gust over the lake.

Lou laughed, pushing her disordered, wet hair back, and realized she was still hand in hand with Rob. How shocking, holding hands with a servant, and neither of them wearing gloves.

"Rob," she said. "Tell me what's going on with you and university. Can I help?"

Seventeen

Rob

He'd told Di some of it, but not everything. Now words tumbled out of him. He found himself pacing, waving his arms, his fists clenched. At one point, he had to walk away from her and lean his heated face against a pillar, afraid he would cry. He swore a lot, which embarrassed him—after all, Mrs. Connolly was older than him and a teacher and it didn't seem right, and why was he so angry here and now?

Finally, he stumbled to a stop, leaning against a pillar and looking out over the lake. There was a rainbow—Christ, what a cliché—in a steel-gray sky, and the swans floated out onto the water, snaking their necks around. He stopped talking.

"That sucks," she said, and it was so unexpected he wanted to laugh. But he was still afraid of crying and it seemed that a laugh might very well go the wrong way and end up with him bawling his eyes out like Graham.

"So you haven't heard from your mom at all?"

"No. We don't know where she is."

"Shit," she said. Another surprise. "No other family? How about grandparents?"

"She was the one who kept in touch with everyone, because most of them don't like my dad. So we didn't see much of them. And she took the address book with her."

She snorted. "I don't much like the sound of your dad."

"He's not that bad. I mean, he's a stupid wanker, but he's my dad."

She came over to him and laid her hand on his sleeve. "If I may step out of line here, Rob, you do realize that just because they're your parents doesn't mean they'll never fuck up. It sounds to me like she left her husband, not her children."

"But she did leave us," he said, sounding like Graham at his whiniest.

"Yeah. It sucks. But what makes me really mad, Rob, is your dad manipulating you and trying to get you to drop your place at Cambridge. Don't do it. You obviously love your brother a lot and that's admirable, but don't sacrifice yourself for him. It won't help anyone in the long run. Think he'll care in ten years' time? He won't. But you will."

"But—" Wow, she looked great when she was worked up and wet, with her dress sticking to her and her hair going all wild around her face. He promptly forgot what he was going to say.

"I see kids going to college for all the wrong reasons," she said. "I get to grade their shitty papers. I'd hate to see a smart, nice kid like you screw up."

"You think I'm nice," he said. He was coming to the boil again, but in a different way this time. "I'm not nice, Lou. Not if you knew what I was thinking." He was about to do something that was not at all smart and was definitely not the action of a kid.

Her eyes seemed to go wide and she swallowed hard. "And what's that?"

He pushed her against one of the columns and bent his head to hers; her breasts and the hard ridges of her corset pushed into his chest, and she gave a small gasp of surprise. He swooped his mouth onto her open lips—they were soft and sweet—and her body seemed to change, becoming more pliant, yielding to him, inviting him. He cupped her face with his hand, her skin smooth and delicate against his palm, her pulse beating against his fingertips.

She made a sound he couldn't really interpret but one of her hands latched on to his arse, pulling him against her. If she'd had any doubt how randy he was before, she knew now, with his hard-on pressed between them, driving against her.

Her tongue slithered against his, explored his lips, and then her head tipped back to allow him to suck and nibble at the pale skin of her throat and shoulders.

She pushed him away as his hands curled around her breasts, laughing. "You're absolutely right. You're not nice. Nice young men don't kiss like that."

Eighteen

Lou

"What?" He stared at her, dazed, and then laughed. He backed off and sat down on one of the stone benches at the base of a pillar, and she could tell he was embarrassed by his erection.

"Look," she said, "we're both in a state of turmoil at the moment and, if you like, we can just forget this and move on. I'm too old for you, and—"

"Wait." He held up a hand, grinning. She'd never seen him smile so broadly. "There's only one direction I want to move in, and that's into bed with you. How old are you, anyway? And, shit, this is all coming out wrongly, but what's your state of turmoil? You've been listening to me rant and I didn't even notice you were upset."

"Oh." She flapped her hands at him. "My ranch—well, that's a bit grandiose, it's more of a small farm but it's in Montana—I put it on the market, not even expecting it would sell and not even knowing whether I wanted to sell. It's complicated. I found out today there's been an offer, the asking price, and now I don't know what to do. And I'm twenty-seven."

"I'm nineteen. Eight years. Is it that big a deal?"

"Actually, yes. I teach kids—sorry, young adults—your age. You're taboo."

"You perv, Mrs. Connolly. Doesn't that give you a tingle?"

"*You* give me a tingle. And you're nice—no, really, you are. You're kind. You're a decent sort of guy. You helped me upstairs when I was drunk as a skunk, and didn't even grope me. I don't want to be a corrupter of youth but you're obviously not that innocent. And I certainly don't want to play the cougar."

"Yeah. Well. I wouldn't worry about that too much. I don't think an eight-year difference qualifies you as a cougar. You're not my idea of a cougar." He studied his feet, crossed at the ankle, as though finding something fascinating there. "So what's the deal with the ranch? Do you think you'll sell it?"

She was surprised at his thoughtfulness. "Do you really want to know?"

He nodded, so she continued, "I've lived there for just over a year. I have about ten acres, a few head of cattle, a horse and a couple of dogs. It's very small, but it's in a beautiful setting. I was married there. My husband's ashes are scattered there. I don't know if I can bear to leave, but I don't think I can bear to stay, either."

"Do you have to tell them yes or no right away?"

"I emailed that I was thinking about it. With the way the market is right now, I thought I could wait months for an offer, let alone one where they agreed to my asking price. My sister wants me to move back to Boston—most of my family is on the East Coast—but it's hard to get a teaching job anywhere. My job is pretty crappy but it grounds me."

He nodded. "But you're out in the middle of nowhere, right? Don't you get lonely?"

"Yes. It's a two-hour drive to the campus. My nearest neighbor is five miles away, and that's considered virtually in each other's backyards." She hesitated, thinking again of his situation. "Would you like me to talk to Peter and Chris about your dad? It's okay, I know about Peter's indiscretion."

He snorted and stood up, swinging his arms. "Indiscretion. Yeah, that's one way of putting it."

"He said you were very mature about it," Lou said.

"It happens. You fancy the wrong people. You get over it. There's no need for you to talk to them on my behalf, but thanks for offering."

"Okay," she said, thinking a quick word with Chris might not be a bad idea, and Rob hadn't actually told her not to. She suspected he was smart enough to know she'd do it anyway. "I'd better get back to the house."

"Me, too. I need to get things going for dinner." He took her hand as though it was the most natural thing in the world and they started walking toward the house.

"Do you like being a footman?" she asked.

"It has its moments. We get to laugh at the guests. It's funny how they forget we're around. I suppose it means we're doing our job well. We have a lot of inside jokes, and nicknames for the guests, and so on."

"Really? What's mine?"

"Schoolmarm."

"Oh, come on. For real?"

He stood aside to let her bypass a puddle in the path. "Absolutely. Sarah's Most Likely. It's short for Most Likely To

Put Out. Ben's Vegetable Love, because he's so thick. And Mr. Salazar... Are you and him, uh..."

"No. What's his nickname?"

"You came up with it— Mr. Darcy. Remember, the first night you were here? It stuck. And you know about the Paint Boys. They're rather creepy, aren't they? We call Viv the Jam Tart. She found out and pretended to be mad but I think she likes it."

"How about Dave and Cathy?"

"Ruggerbugger and Giggles."

"That's appalling," Lou said, laughing despite herself.

They walked in silence together. Rob picked, or rather, tore off a rhododendron blossom as big as his fist in a great spray of raindrops and presented it to her with a bow. She tucked the dark pink flower behind her ear.

"Well," Rob said, "we're nearly at the house and..." He looked shy. "Look, Lou, was that it? A quick snog?"

"You know where my room is." The words tumbled out of her mouth before she could stop herself. It all seemed so uncomplicated, all of a sudden—she liked him, she desired him, and in a week or so she'd go back to the States and he'd go to Cambridge at the end of the summer. They might email for a few weeks or months, she might advise him on girlfriends or his studies, they'd follow each other on Facebook, and then gradually their correspondence would fade.

"Oh. Yeah, yeah, I do." He shoved his hands into his coat pockets and retrieved his iPod. "Tonight, right?"

"Sure." She gave him a quick kiss on the cheek. He didn't respond and she wondered if he regretted their sudden intimacy. So maybe he wouldn't show. No big deal.

"Okay, then." He plugged his earbuds in and headed for the back of the house.

Lou shook her head as he walked away. Men, sometimes even the most straightforward of them, were at heart creatures of mystery.

"You look lovely, dear. I can't wait to see your ball gown. I hear it's rather daring." Chris handed Lou a glass of something garnished with mint and laden with slices of fruit as the guests mingled in the drawing room before dinner.

"Chris, is this some sort of lethally alcoholic and historically inaccurate cocktail?"

"No, dear, it's sangria. Drink it slowly."

She raised the glass and sipped. "Peter and I had a chat the other day."

"That must have been nice for you, Loulou."

"Stop it." She put her arm around his waist and squeezed. "Come out onto the terrace with me. I need to talk to you."

He accompanied her, but looked apprehensive. "I can deny you nothing, my dear, but I fear you're poking your nose where it doesn't belong."

"Probably. You know you and Peter are my best and dearest friends. Do something for me."

"If it involves that little tart of a footman—"

"Oh, please, Chris. That's grossly unfair. He's a nice kid."

"Really? How do you know? Uh-oh, Loulou. You haven't been messing with the help, have you? Bad, bad girl. Did you have fun?"

She rested her glass on the stone balustrade and looked out over the lawn. A herd of deer moved like delicate ghosts from the shelter of the trees. "You're not getting any lurid details."

Chris moved to stand beside her. "What do you want, Lou?"

She gave him a brief version of the Temple family's predicament. Chris raised his eyebrows. "She left her kids?"

"Two of those kids are grown up and are intensely loyal and loving to their little brother. Their father needs to get his act together, and he's applied for the groundsman position."

"So have twenty-three others, most of whom seem nuts, including an Australian who expects us to fly him in for an interview and at least two Wiccans. Your Mike Temple likes gardening, he knows one end of a hammer from the other and, most importantly, he's local, and all of that definitely puts him on the shortlist. But I'm not making any promises, love."

"I understand." She hesitated. "I don't even know the guy. I suspect he's a total jerk. He's trying to make Rob feel guilty about going to Cambridge, which of course he absolutely has to do—it's the only chance he'll get. But maybe if Mike gets his own life together, he'll lay off his son and Rob won't deny himself the education he deserves." She took his arm. "I know you'll do the right thing."

He started as though he'd forgotten she was there. "I love seeing those deer," he said, nodding toward the herd. "It gives me such a lord-of-the-manor feeling. If only they didn't want to eat the roses. But that's life, isn't it? Let's go into dinner, Lou. You know that whenever I get philosophical it's because I'm hungry."

SHE BARELY NOTICED WHAT SHE ate, because Rob was there, moving around the room, handing dishes, organizing the other footmen. He paused, one hand on the back of Mac's chair, to have a short conversation, giving Lou the opportunity to compare the two of them: Mac's dark, saturnine looks and strong profile; Rob's fair skin and the copper glow of his hair by candlelight. Opposites, but both men she desired—and to her regret she still desired Mac. She sighed as she saw them together: innocence and experience, light and shadow, a sun god and a prince of darkness.

She smiled at her own fancy, and Peter next to her tut-tutted and moved the wine bottle away from her.

"Apparently, I have quite a reputation as a lush," she commented.

"I'm hardly one to preach the virtues of a clear head," he said. "Drink or love, they make fools of us all. But at least Chris and I are talking to each other now." He raised his wineglass to Chris at the other end of the table. Did Lou imagine it, or was there a slight hesitation before Chris responded?

"I'm glad," she said.

"And you and our Mr. Darcy?"

"Not a chance." She tossed back the remains of her glass of water, thinking that the same gesture with wine would have so much more significance.

"A pity," he said. "Viv speaks very highly of him."

"Even if he does come with references, I'm unimpressed."

"Okay. Let's change the subject. We have one room that's completely unrestored, stripped down to lathe and plaster, and I wanted to ask your advice. Do you think we should leave it as is—with its underpinnings on view, so to speak—and make an exhibit area?"

"I think that's a good idea. Or you could have the Paint Boys restore sections of it to various periods. After all, the same family lived in this house for over two hundred years and you've got lots of examples of different paints and wallpapers."

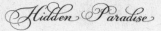

"Let's look at it together soon." Peter stared at a dish laid before them. "What on earth is this, Rob?"

"Beef tongue, sir. Looks gross, tastes good."

"Go on. Try it." Lou seized the carving knife that lay on the dish, pushed aside a careful garnish of herbs and marigold blossoms and sawed Peter a slice.

He poked at it with his fork, took a bite, and nodded in appreciation. "Not bad, but I see you're not partaking."

"Oh, my plate's full." She smiled at him in all innocence. "Besides, I own cattle. It's too personal for my tastes. What if I was eating the tongue of a cow I knew?"

He shook his head. "And what do you plan to do with your best friends, the cows? Have you made any decisions?"

"Not yet," she said, not wanting to tell him or even think about the offer. A week, that's what she'd told her agent. She'd make up her mind in a week. "It's too soon."

Rob's arm brushed against her shoulder as he reached for an empty dish near her and she almost jumped out of her skin. She hoped Peter hadn't noticed. But he had such lovely manners, he wouldn't say anything even if he did. At that moment, she wanted to ask his advice as though he was some sort of genial father figure.

Looks like I have the hots for Rob, too. I'm not in love with him or anything, but he's so sexy and nice, and he kisses like a dream. And I invited him to my room tonight and now I don't know whether he's going to show or not and it's driving me insane.

The third remove was cleared away. Lou, as the most senior lady present, gathered gloves and fan and stood, and by some miracle all the men at the table remembered to stand, too. "Ladies, we should leave the men to their port." She tapped Peter on the shoulder with her fan. "Sir, I trust you won't leave us pining for you too long."

As she led the ladies out, Rob bowed and opened the door. His gaze locked with hers for a second before he lowered his eyes and a jolt of lust shot through her.

If he showed up, things might be very interesting tonight.

To HER RELIEF, IT WAS ROB WHO choreographed their assignation. There was no music tonight, but a couple of raucous card games, with Sarah, to everyone's amusement, offering Ben as a stake.

After a cup of green tea and at the end of a round of whist, Lou stood and announced that she was having an early night. Rob opened the drawing-room door and told the nearest footman to take over for the evening—and that was it.

In the hall, he plucked one of the fake candles from a tray. "Light you upstairs, ma'am?"

"Certainly." There was no one else around, as far as she could tell, but other staff members might lurk in the shadows and she waited until they were halfway up the stairs before dropping the formality. "What will the other footman think? The one you asked to take over?"

"Oh, they're convinced I get more than them all put together. They think it goes along with being head footman." She could hear the laughter in his voice.

"And do you?"

"I think they're all lying through their teeth about what they get up to."

Well, that was an ambiguous answer, confirming her suspicion that despite the expertise of his kiss, he was relatively inexperienced. She'd find out soon enough.

They entered her room and he placed his candle on the bedside table. She switched on another candle on the mantelpiece and wondered what she should do to put him at ease.

But he advanced on her, pushing his coat off and onto the floor, and she met him halfway, thrilled at his ardor.

"You're so lovely," he said, reaching for the bodice of her gown. "How do I get this off— Ouch!"

"Sorry. Let me unpin it. Don't—if you bleed over it, the Jam Tart will get mad at me. Okay. Everything else unties."

"Your tits are amazing." He blushed.

"Once the corset's off they're not nearly as impressive." She made a start on the buttons of his waistcoat and he unknotted his neckcloth as he bent to kiss her. Her petticoat dropped away, joining her gown and his shoes on the floor, and he managed to get his breeches off and his shirt over his head. He wasn't shy. He was in a hurry, and she found his excitement infectious, unlacing her corset as fast as she could and stripping off her shift.

"You're wrong. Your tits are still amazing." He cupped them in his hands and bent to kiss her.

She let her hands savor and sample him, the strong muscles and smooth skin with only a dusting of hair on his chest. His cock hard and eager, pushed against her belly, but when she ran a finger down its length he gasped and moved away. Later, she promised herself, later she'd touch and play and tease, but now his tongue did just that in her mouth and her nipples rubbed against his chest and she wanted him in her. Now.

She let him take the lead, let him guide her onto the bed and continue to kiss and caress her. When he slipped a hand between her thighs and touched her, sure and deft, she trembled and arched and came, fast, so fast it almost hurt.

And he stopped. "Lou?"

She opened her eyes. "Mmm?"

"This is sort of embarrassing."

She touched his face. "What's wrong?"

"This is as far as I've got before."

"Rob, honey, you're doing very well. You made me come."

"Oh. Good." He rubbed his face with the palm of his hand. "I, um, thought you did. But I haven't actually, you know, fucked anyone yet."

She was touched and charmed by his admission. "Now's your chance. If you want to."

"Oh, yes. Please. But I don't want to fuck it up."

"You won't." She reached into the bedside drawer and prepared to sheathe him. "How would you like to do it?"

"Very competently." He gasped as she rolled the condom onto his cock. "But—"

"Rob, just fuck me, okay? I'm not going to grade your performance." She pulled him onto her and he slid inside her and his face held a look of awe and wonder that disarmed her. A tear slid from her eye into her hair and she hoped he hadn't noticed, but he was caught up entirely in his own pleasure and she watched as his face changed and his jaw tightened. His eyes darkened and fixed and he shuddered against her and groaned.

"Sorry, sorry," he said. "I couldn't hold back."

She ran her hands over the muscles of his back. "Hey, no need to apologize."

"That was amazing. Absolutely amazing." He smiled at her, shy and proud at the same time. "I don't think it did anything for you."

"You will. We'll make sure of that."

"I'm not a virgin anymore," he said with a grin.

"I don't think you were much of a virgin before."

"Okay, a technical virgin." He eased himself off her and became absorbed in kissing and fondling her breasts. "What would you like me to do?"

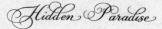

"Keep doing that. What would you like to do?"

"I'd like to look at your cunt," he said. "Is it okay to call it that? I've only ever done it—or as much as I've done—in the dark, and she was shy, and, well, I'd like to have a look."

"Okay, but it probably won't look like anything you've seen on the internet." As he swooped down between her thighs to begin a thorough investigation by the light of one of the LED candles, she added, "Rob, I'm so glad that isn't a real flame."

"Here," he said. His finger played and caressed. "Is that it? Can I make you come again? Can I make you come all night, Lou?"

She was quite sure Rob could make her come all night with his tender, careful touch, but she found herself greedy for his body, eager to make him tremble and cry out and arch beneath her.

"Let me touch you," she said, and he abandoned himself to her. He shuddered when she scraped her nails across his scrotum and groaned in pleasure when she took him in her mouth. She explored him, found his preferences, what pleased him, what sent him into a frenzy, and in so doing rediscovered simple pleasure herself, becoming Eve to his Adam.

It was all so easy, so uncomplicated. She loved kissing him, loved the sound he made when she took his cock in her hand and stroked him, circling his shaft with thumb and forefinger, fast and rough, or slowing to a teasing, sensual slide. He was embarrassed, at first, by the ease with which she made him come, apologizing after he spilled in her hand. But he surprised her, seconds later, by laughing and stretching out against her, murmuring how sexy she was, and asking what she'd like next.

"Would you be disappointed if I said I wanted to sleep?"

"No, that's okay. We can do it in the morning. If it's okay for me to stay."

"Sure." She turned in his arms, burying her face against his chest, smooth except for a few silky hairs. "I'd like you to stay."

It was he who fell asleep first, his face nuzzled against her neck, his breath soft and even. She switched off the bedside light and lay awake for some time, having doubts about what she'd done, and if tomorrow would be awkward. And the day after that? And at some point, she'd have to return to the ranch. It struck her that sex with Rob had been an effective means of escaping that reality. And quite likely he was using sex to escape his problems, too, as well as fulfilling the strong sexual urges of a young male. But to her relief their coupling didn't exclude tenderness and kindness.

Rob

HE AWOKE AFTER A COUPLE OF hours and listened to a clock somewhere, probably the big grandfather clock in the foyer, strike the hour. Three o'clock. He pressed against Lou, resting his face in the sweet fragrance of the nape of her neck, rubbing his hard-on against her. He could fuck her just as they were. He wasn't sure if she was awake or not, but he'd have to fumble around for a condom, and he wanted her absolutely conscious of what he was doing. He wanted to do it right. He still couldn't figure out exactly how to make her come without using his fingers. She seemed to do okay on top of him. His cock stiffened a little more as he remembered the way she fluttered inside against him.

She sighed and slipped her own hand between her legs, turning slightly so that her uppermost leg twisted over his. "Fuck me," she whispered.

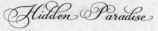

Bloody hell. Definitely awake.

He turned the light on and reached for a condom.

She blinked at him.

"I want to see what you do," he said.

She grinned. "Okay."

He slid into her with a little help from her—it was an unaccustomed angle for him—and then watched as she rubbed her clit, hoping he'd last out, amazed at her ability to draw out her own pleasure and his, too. He had to slow down a couple of times and ask her not to move. He discovered that she whimpered in pleasure when he put both hands on her breasts and thumbed the nipples.

"Clit and nipples," she said drowsily, drunk with pleasure. "They work together. But I guess you knew that? That's so nice, Rob."

She didn't have to say a word when she came. Her whole body told him; the way she arched and tensed, her hand moving faster and then slowing to the barest touch, her lips parted, and moaning as he thrust hard. Inside there was an unmistakable clench and pulse on his cock and he gritted his teeth, staying with her, letting her ride out her orgasm before she relaxed and it was his turn to tense, approach the brink and go over.

Bliss.

She fell asleep almost immediately, her hand still between her legs. He disentangled himself from her and went to take care of the condom. When he came back, he slid beneath the sheets, debating whether he should get some sleep or start again. He smiled at the thought of her touching herself. His cock rose again.

Shit. He could jerk off, he supposed. There was something very sexy about the idea of masturbating next to someone you'd fucked and who didn't know—or maybe she did—what you were doing.

He slid his hand up his shaft. He told himself he'd stroke enough to calm but not excite. Maybe. Then he'd stop. But not just yet. A little more.

She stirred. "Rob?"

He froze.

"It's okay. Keep going if you want."

"Oh. Okay."

"Sorry." She propped herself up on one elbow. "Did I take the fun out of it?"

"I don't know. I've fucked you and I've got another hard-on and I didn't want to disturb you…" He found himself babbling.

She ran her fingertip around his nipple.

He shuddered. He'd never had anyone touch him like that before, looking into his eyes in the near darkness, daring him to continue, while his hand slid helplessly on his cock.

"Do you like that?"

"I don't know."

"Were you hoping I'd wake up? What would happen when you came? You'd have to be very quiet."

He understood now. She was playing with him, pretending to be shocked. "I wanted to come on your tits."

"That's pretty perverted, Rob." She smiled. "But if you insist…" She stretched out and touched her own nipples.

"Christ, Lou."

"Do you like the idea of being discovered when you jerk off? Who do you think is going to walk in on you?"

"You," he said. "Viv. My maths teacher from primary school. She was really hot. My sister's best friend, Shannon, she has a huge bum. Sarah, though I can't stand her—"

"Okay," she said, and he could tell she was trying not to laugh. "So I discover you jerking off. You're so excited. You can't help yourself. You can't stop even though I'm looking at you as though I can't take my eyes off you. And you can't tell whether I'm disgusted or turned on or whether I'm thinking of punishing you, but it doesn't make any difference, because you're going to come. You can't help it."

"Lou," he groaned, and came copiously—he felt like some sort of sperm machine. He'd lost count of how many times he'd come tonight.

"Wow," he said. "Sorry."

"Don't be sorry," she said. "You liked it, didn't you?"

"Yes, but it was…I didn't know people did that."

"It's a common enough fantasy."

"Do you… Have you…?"

"Oh, sure. I used to let Julian, my husband, catch me all the time."

"What did he do?"

"He'd pretend to be very stern and order me to come. Or he'd take over. Or…" She heard from her voice that she was smiling. "Sometimes he'd pretend he had a whole bunch of guys with him and that I was the floor show. I liked that. Or he'd tell me my mother was about to walk in and that always did the trick. Apparently a lot of women find that sexy, although the idea always made me uncomfortable after."

"Jesus," he said.

"But I think that's part of it. Knowing you're going to push yourself, reveal something potentially shameful to yourself and your partner. You make yourself vulnerable and get beyond it. It's all about trust—love maybe—but absolutely trust."

"What else do you fantasize about?" he asked.

She reached for a tissue and dabbed at the semen drying on her chest. "Oh, having two guys. That's something I've always wanted to try. I thought this evening about you and Mac."

"I didn't think you and he were still..."

"We're not. Don't get all bent out of shape. We're talking fantasy, remember? I'd like to see you two together."

He frowned. "Together? You mean, jerking each other off or something?"

"If you felt like it. I'd like to watch you but if you just wanted to concentrate on me that would be fine, too."

"Yeah, well, that's nice, but I don't think it's going to happen. And I don't know if I'd want anyone up my bum."

"I'm quite shocked you take it so lightly." She ruffled his hair. "Even though I robbed you of your technical virginity a few fucks ago."

"It's a fantasy, you said."

"Well, we're in Paradise Hall, where anything goes. This is a fantasy experience."

"I think that meant dressing up and stuff, not kink."

"It seems to me there's not much difference between kink and dressing up. They're very much related. Peter and Chris definitely had sexual adventures in mind when they went ahead with this, just one step beyond the sensual experiences of food and drink and clothes in this gorgeous historical setting."

"Mmm." She could argue rings around him and he was too sated and sleepy to argue back.

"So what if I wanted to be with you and someone else at the same time, Rob? Would you be okay with it?"

"So long as it's not Ben. He's an arse. People talk about

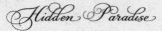

having threesomes all the time, so I guess it's not that weird. If it's what you want."

Her arms were around him, his face in the fragrance of her hair. It was almost as good as fucking, and his cock twitched in anticipation. But he was tired, far too tired, safe and comfortable. Falling asleep was like a homecoming.

Nineteen

Peter

Mike Temple was unnervingly an older version of Rob, but not quite as handsome and with dull brown hair instead of Rob's lovely coppery sheen. He had the appearance of someone who'd made an effort, a cut on his jaw from shaving, although his suit was a little too loose as though depression had made him lose weight. A man who had hit rock bottom, he had dragged himself into a semblance of self-respect and energy, attempting to show himself as a serious candidate for the job.

He sat in the office with a briefcase that Peter suspected was empty except for the résumé he had handed over, a duplicate of the one sent by email.

"Rob thinks the world of this place. It's nice to see it fixed up."

"We couldn't have done it without the help of the village," Peter responded. "And Rob is a tremendous asset. You must be very proud of him."

"He does okay."

Peter bit back a sarcastic rejoinder. "You'll miss him when he goes to Cambridge."

Mike made no reply, and Peter gazed at the résumé. His current occupation was unclear—read unemployed—and his last job had been as owner of a line of tanning salons. "This position is quite a bit different from your previous employment."

"I need a change. I'm good with my hands. I like the outdoors." This from someone whose pallor suggested he'd barely set foot outside for weeks.

"Your first job would be to renovate the cottage that comes along with the job. It's nothing fancy but it's structurally sound, and big enough for one."

Mike nodded. "Sounds good," he said with an effort.

"Any questions?" Peter asked, fighting back an urge to grab Mike Temple by the shoulders and shake some life into him. It was like dealing with a zombie. Thank goodness, the door opened and Chris came in. "Ah, here's my partner."

He introduced them and let Chris take over the questions. Then he wished he hadn't.

"It doesn't say here you declared bankruptcy," Chris said, pushing the résumé across the desk with a look of disgust.

"It's nothing to do with my abilities," Mike said.

"But it might be something to do with this job. It's quite likely we'd be entrusting some financial dealings to you— ordering supplies, for instance—and we'd need to know whether you were capable of handling it correctly."

"I'm not a crook," Mike said with a very slight flash of animation.

"Why did your business fail?" Chris said.

"Supply and demand. People are scared of sun damage now."

Chris said nothing.

Peter gathered his wits—he'd known Chris to be bitchy but never outright rude—and prepared a polite, noncommittal statement to usher Mike from the office with the promise of a decision within a few days.

But Mike came to life. He rose, his briefcase sliding to the floor. "Who the fuck do you think you are?" His fists clenched. "You come to this village with your money and think you can treat us like shit. I need this job, you bastards. I've lost everything. I've lost my house, my wife and my kids hardly give me the time of day. I've fallen about as low as I can but I won't take this crap from you or anyone. You can take this job and your fucking cottage and shove it up your feudal arse." He pounded on the desk, leaning forward, his face darkened with rage. "It could be you, you arseholes. People stop coming to this fancy knocking-shop, and then what? You might be begging me for a job."

He turned and blundered toward the door. Chris, without a word, handed him the briefcase as he passed.

After he left, Peter turned to Chris, shocked. "What's got into you?"

"He's trying to ruin the life of his own son," Chris snapped. "Lou talked to me. He should bloody well feel bad. He's a ringer for my old man."

Chris rarely talked of his family and Peter had learned not to ask.

"I thought you didn't like Rob," he said feebly.

"It's nothing to do with whether I like him or not. Give Temple the job if you like."

"I don't know whether I should," Peter said. "He doesn't make a great first impression. But hell, how many of us take the opportunity to stand up and shout abuse at a job interview? I know I've wanted to. Even if he felt he had nothing to lose, he has some guts."

He went outside to the yard and through the archway to the parking lot, not expecting Mike to still be around, but his car was still there. Mike sat at the wheel, engine running, and Peter was horribly afraid for a moment that he might have run a hose from the tailpipe. But Mike's face was in his hands, his shoulders moving.

Oh, jeez. Peter gave him a moment, but Mike continued to sob, so he walked forward and tapped on the glass.

Mike looked up, smearing his face with his hands, and glared at Peter with embarrassment and rage, but he lowered the window. "What the hell do you want?"

"The job's yours if you want it," Peter said.

"You've got to be joking." Mike fished a rather grubby-looking tissue from the car and blew his nose.

"I'm not. Take it or leave it, but please let me know." Exasperated, Peter started to walk away, but heard the car door open and close.

"Yes, of course I'll take it." He appeared at Peter's side, holding out a hand. "Sorry about all the yelling back there."

"No problem," Peter said, shaking his hand with some reluctance. "You'd better take a look at the cottage."

"I'm bringing my youngest to live there," Mike said with a challenge in his eye.

"I'm afraid we don't provide child care," Peter said, thinking he'd better check out the insurance policy.

"That's okay. Rob'll help out."

"Until he goes to Cambridge," Peter said. "And he does have other duties here."

"Right."

This had all the makings of a disaster.

Mike peered over Peter's shoulder. "Oh, hi there, Rob. God, you look a right fairy."

"It's livery. Get over it," Rob replied.

"Bloody hell, I won't have to dress up like that, will I?" Mike looked horrified.

"The position doesn't require livery," Peter said, but couldn't resist adding, "unless we call you into the house for additional duties. Mike, please call me to arrange when you'd like to move in, and I'd suggest without your child until you've got it fixed up. It's a bit primitive. Rob, why don't you show your father the cottage?"

Rob scowled. "Okay."

Father and son moved off together through the woodland, Rob's shoulders rigid, Mike strolling, hands in pockets and whistling, as though five minutes ago he hadn't been sobbing his heart out in despair and rage.

Hoping he hadn't made a terrible mistake, Peter returned to the office.

Chris, at his laptop, sent him a bright smile. "What happened? I sent Rob out to find you. I thought he should have advance warning that his old man was on the premises."

"Oh, dear God." Peter sank into his chair. "I sometimes feel as if I'm in a soap opera."

"Just wait until the ball tonight. Fresh meat for Sarah, some sort of showdown between Mac and Lou and Rob—"

"What? What have Rob and Lou been up to? Oh, shit. It's three o'clock. Are the caterers and florists here?"

"All here and all under control. Calm down, lover. The only thing we can't control is the volatility of our guests. You're supposed to meet Lou and the Paint Boys about two minutes ago for a discussion of the mystery room of the fancy knocking-shop."

"Oh, lord, so I am," said Peter, checking his watch. "Give me a kiss."

Chris reached for him and the kiss turned into something far sexier and intense than a peck on the cheek.

"Wow," Peter said when he came up for air. "What was all that about?"

"I behaved like an arse," Chris said. "It's an apology. A promise. I love you, and later tonight, when we get the chance to catch our breath, I'll show you how much."

"I love you, too," Peter said.

He passed through the foyer, which would combine with the drawing room and dining room, connected doors fully open, to form the ballroom. The caterers were at work, assisted by the footmen and others recruited from the staff of the agricultural college a dozen miles away, unloading glasses and tables and chairs to take to the terrace where supper would be served. Others arranged furniture and assembled a dais for the musicians. The florists hung swags of flowers on the staircase and twined them around the pillars, and a dozen or so huge vases of flowers stood in the center of the foyer to be arranged around the rooms.

Di the lady's maid wove her way toward the staircase, a pile of shimmering gowns in her arms. She gave him a clumsy sort of curtsy as she passed, and hoisted the hem of her own gown to ascend the stairs.

Already some media had arrived, with video cameras and microphones and those fluffy sound things that looked like bottle brushes. One of the footmen, that boy Ivan who always seemed to have such a bulge in his breeches (well, Peter couldn't help noticing these things) was keeping an eye on them. Later Peter would give interviews and Chris would direct their own videographer… He let his mind wander to

the terrifying list of responsibilities connected with this evening. They really needed someone with solid media experience to run that side of things for them, someone who truly
understood what Paradise Hall was about and could put the
right sort of spin on stories.

The noise subsided as he walked through to the wing
where the Paint Boys were set up. The room they were concerned with opened from their workroom/lab, a smaller and
indeterminate room built onto the back of the house. Until
recently, paint and ladders and other supplies had been stored
there, since it had a door that opened to the outside and a
ponderous Victorian sink with hefty iron faucets. The walls
were covered with unpleasant green paint and a single light-
bulb hung from the ceiling.

Outside in the small meadow next to the kitchen garden,
a couple of guys sparred, wearing boxing gloves and stripped
to the waist. Out of force of habit, Peter paused to check out
their physiques and admire the contrast between Billy Blue
the boxing instructor and his pupil, Mac. Very nice.

Lou stood at the doorway, checking them out, too, but
she pretended she wasn't, which made him smile.

"It's a bit of a problem," Jon was saying. "Oh, hi, Peter.
We can't date this room. We've uncovered an older fireplace,
which is probably original, but it's not very impressive, is it?
Rather small and messy. We could get the linoleum off the
floor—although it's pretty much off in so many places—
and pull up the floorboards and see if anything interesting
turns up."

"According to the house plan," Simon said, gesturing at a
facsimile of the oldest plan they possessed, "in 1841 this was
the housekeeper's room, and plumbing wasn't put in until
the early twentieth century. It's a rubbish room, my dears.

Let's tart it up and do an exhibit here and you can charge the great unwashed a quid a head to come in."

"Absolutely not," Peter said. "Free admission for all. We're giving back to the community, remember. At least, if the grant comes through so we can actually afford the money to do it and hire a curator, we'll be giving back to the community. Why, we might even offer you the job, Lou, my dear."

She was staring at the wall. "You're all wrong," she said. "This isn't a nothing room. Look at that doorway. It has an arch above it, bricked in."

"We know, dear," Simon said.

"Okay. Imagine, oh, I'd think three such doors. Only, they aren't doors, they're triple-hung arched windows. I bet if you got that plumbing and plaster off, you'd find them underneath. What's outside?" She opened the door and they saw her outside, pacing, and examining the wall and ground.

"Southern elevation!" Jon cried. He and Simon exchanged a significant look and rushed outside to join Lou. A lot of gesturing and exclamations of excitement followed.

"What's going on here?" Peter asked, bewildered by the historians' antics as they came back in.

"As I suspected, you have a layer of late-nineteenth-century brick on the outside but a nice big dressed stone ledge at the bottom of the wall," Lou said.

"Tell him, dear," Simon said.

"You have a hidden Georgian conservatory," she said. "That's why the fireplace is so small, because you'd probably have a stove in this room. You should restore it, Peter."

"Oh, absolutely," he said. "And we can still use it as part of the exhibit area—whenever we get the funding. How wonderful! Do you think we could get it done by Christmas? Think how marvelous it would look with banks of poinsettias and narcissi."

"Make it into a gift shop," Lou said.

Jon and Simon were having one of their shorthand conversations from which Peter gathered they were thinking of sacrificing dinner and some of the evening's festivities to knock down plaster. He turned to Lou and wondered whether he, too, was beaming with excitement. "I guess we'll have to use the other room as an exhibit room now. I do like your idea of different styles and wallpapers. Could you work me up a proposal?"

"Look, that's really sweet of you, Peter, but I'm not a historian. Not really. I'm an Austen scholar. Get the Paint Boys to do it."

"You could write your dissertation here," he wheedled.

She made a face. "I don't even want to think about my dissertation."

"So come here and write something else then."

"I would if I could think of something original to say and if I were able to leave the ranch and if you had funding." She sighed. "Too many *ifs*. I'm filthy from poking around in that fireplace. I'd better go and change for the ball."

Peter had always thought that Julian would be here for the opening ball, with Lou radiant on his arm, his best friends and the most handsome couple there. He wondered, from the look of sadness on her face, whether she was thinking of that, too. But she leaned to kiss his cheek, reminded him that he'd engaged her for the first two dances, and went off to get ready.

Twenty

Lou

"I need more silk flowers! Are you going to use those, Lou?"

"Oh, hi, Sarah. Come on in. Make yourself at home."

Lou stared at Sarah in astonishment as the other woman rummaged on her dressing table. Obviously Sarah wasn't going to respond to any sort of subtlety or sarcasm.

So it was true; they *were* the Bennet sisters before a ball. Women ran in and out of each other's bedchambers, trading finery, admiring each other's gowns and generally behaving like teenagers. Possibly the Bennet sisters didn't room hop as Sarah did, wearing only a thong and a pair of historically incorrect thigh-highs, and transforming the atmosphere of the room to the set of a sleazy porno movie.

A middle-aged woman wearing modern clothes and carrying a Regency gown swathed in plastic, entered the room and apologized profusely at the sight of Sarah. "Oh, goodness, I am so sorry. I was looking for— We had a room assigned to us and I saw the open door and thought this must be it, but—"

Lou, fully dressed, or the nearest she could get to it in her new nipple-revealing gown, threw a robe in Sarah's direction and escorted the woman from the room. "I'm so sorry, that was our resident nymphomaniac. You must be with the reenactment society. I believe you're changing in the blue room. Let me show you where it is."

Lou accompanied the woman to the door of the blue room, chatting about the ball and the house, the older woman in a fit of giddy excitement at the prospect of dressing up and parading around with her husband, in his militia uniform, on her arm. She declined Lou's help with lacing. Sure enough, the room was full of women changing into their Regency gear, with Di helping out and making necessary last-minute repairs.

"Will you get to dance?" Lou asked Di. The young woman glowed in a low-cut white gown, ribbons threaded through her hair.

"No, I'm dressed up to represent the status of the household. Rob said we should have a servants' ball another night." She plucked a threaded needle from her bodice. "Do you mind if I put an extra stitch on your sleeve, Mrs. Connolly? I'm not quite happy with the way it sits."

She stood still as Di made a few quick deft stitches at her shoulder, snipping off the thread with a pair of tiny scissors from a chatelaine at her waist. As Lou left the room, Di waded back into the crowd of women who needed corsets laced, hems repaired, lost items to be improvised.

When she returned to her room, Sarah was gone and Lou took a deep breath, enjoying the solitude and silence. She took inventory of her outfit and gathered her fan, gloves and fancy red-and-black reticule. Her remaining silk flowers wouldn't work with this gown, or the headdress Di and

Viv had created, a small turban which was little more than a twist of the same fabric sewn into a circlet. But she needed some sort of adornment, some bling. She looked at her meager collection of jewelry and picked out the ruby on a fine gold chain that Julian had given her for their wedding. When was the last time she had worn this? At his funeral?

For you, Julian, she thought. *You should have been here tonight. This should have been our moment, and you would have loved the discovery of the conservatory. You'd be out there with the Paint Boys, bashing off plaster, given half the chance.*

She threaded the necklace carefully around the turban, adding a few clumsy stitches to secure it with the sewing kit the room provided. By candlelight, her inadequate housewifery would pass and the ruby, a large square-cut stone, glistened. Perfect.

A touch of glossy red on her lips and she was ready, and only just in time. She joined a flow of guests down the stairs, where women in gorgeous gowns and men in Regency evening wear or military uniforms mingled. Footmen passed through the crowd with trays of champagne. There was a little more light than usual in the foyer and she guessed the floral arrangements concealed hidden lights. A few flashbulbs exploded as they descended the steps, members of the media incongruous in modern clothing, and a couple of camera crews.

A man stepped forward and bowed, dressed in a severe black swallowtail coat and snowy-white linen. His evening trousers were black knit that shone with the luster of silk and clung to his beautiful physique, a lock of dark hair tumbled over his forehead. He extended a gloved hand to her.

"Mr. Darcy, I presume," she said.

His gaze met hers. "May I claim the first dance, Mrs. Connolly?"

"I regret I am engaged, sir. The third may be yours."

He raised her hand to his lips. A few more flashes fired off. She tucked her other hand into his arm and before she could stop herself, blurted out, "Mac, I have something wonderful to show you."

"You certainly do," he said with a wolfish grin of appreciation as he stared at her bodice.

"No, it's something you haven't seen before. Something no one has seen before. We'll have to wait till after dinner, but it's simply amazing."

"Well, now I'm really interested." He looked at her with uncharacteristic hesitancy. "Does this mean we're friends again?"

Did it? She had come straight to him to share her excitement about the latest solved mystery of the house. What had begun as a little harmless role-playing for the sake of the camera had turned into a moment of intimacy, a sudden sharp yearning for what might have been.

"I've missed you," he said as she made no reply.

"I've missed you, too," she said, "Or at least, the potential of you."

"I'm sorry. I behaved like a jerk."

"You did."

"Is that forgiveness?"

"I'm not sure." They walked through the first set of double doors, flanked by two motionless and immaculate footmen, into the drawing room. "I think it's an acknowledgment of imperfection. And an admission that I believe time is too short to hold a grudge."

"Ah." He shot her a glance of sudden understanding. "I'm

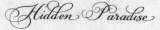

glad we're talking again, Lou. And may I tell you that you look stunning? Especially the tits."

"Thank you. So do you, but not so much in the tits department."

"New coat," he said, rolling his shoulders. "Tailored to an inch by the lovely Viv."

"Did you know she's called the Jam Tart downstairs?"

He snorted with laughter. "Been fraternizing with the help, Lou?"

They passed Rob, who stood straight and still, eyes ahead like a soldier on guard.

Mac looked at her with sudden understanding and regret. "Okay. None of my business, I know."

Had she been so obvious, given some sort of physical signal that indicated her desire for Rob? She thought, with pleasurable anticipation, of how she'd teach him all about oral sex later.

"Wow," Mac said, snapping her back to the present. "It looks pretty good in here, doesn't it, Lou?"

Pretty good was an understatement. The dining room was breathtaking. Although dinner was light, by Regency standards, the first of two removes were already on the table, a glorious symphony of color and texture. Platters of oysters on ice stood side by side with arrangements of sliced cold meats garnished with herbs and flowers, salads studded with nasturtiums and squash blossoms, and delicately swirled fruit fools in sparkling crystal dishes. The table was set with infinite care; Lou knew Rob had checked and double-checked the symmetry of the place settings, each piece of cutlery laid at a precise distance from the edge of the table. In the center of the feast, a massive sugar sculpture representing Paradise Hall rested on a lawn of green marzipan.

The visitors plucked cameras and cell phones from reticules and coat pockets and flashes filled the room. The footmen circulated with bottles of wine and pitchers of lemonade. Rob's lads were all on their best behavior, very few leers down the fronts of gowns, hardly a drop of wine spilled. Rob stood watchful at the sideboard, now and again indicating with a discreet nod that a guest needed help or a plate should be removed, or receiving some sort of signal from Peter or Chris.

Lou found herself sitting next to one of the local landowners who regaled her with stories about the family who had owned the house, finally abandoning it to ruin twenty years earlier, until it had risen to its current glory under the loving care of Peter and Chris. The man had introduced himself as Stote, which at first she thought might be a nickname but realized somewhat belatedly that he was in fact Lord Stote, a neighbor Peter had mentioned.

"What do you think of the theory that Austen stayed here?" she asked.

"Oh, supposedly she stayed with us, too," he said. "So my good lady says." He gestured down the table at a solidly built, gray-haired woman working her way through a plate of oysters. "Truth is, m'dear, Jane's brother Edward knew the families of both houses. He knew a lot of people. She could have visited, you know, in the period between her father's death and Chawton, when she and her mother and sister were wandering around like gypsies and when there were gaps in the letters. Frankly I've always thought Edward was a bit of a rotter not getting them settled somewhere before."

"I've wondered about that, too," Lou said. "But as for whether Jane Austen was at this house or yours…I think everyone dreams about finding one of her letters in the attic, or a fragment of an unfinished manuscript. But it's unlikely, isn't it? I don't think we'll ever know."

"Lots of rubbish in my attic," Stote said. "You should come over, m'dear. Have a cup of tea, look at our little place. Stay for a weekend if you like. We don't get many young people in our house these days. Bring that young man, too."

Which one? she wondered.

"He's quite a decent chap for a Yank," Stote added. Probably he'd be shocked that she was fooling around with downstairs. "And I'll claim a dance with you later, Mrs. Connolly, if I may."

She thanked him and let him commiserate with the guest on his other side on their mutual dry rot and deathwatch beetle infestations, while she amicably shared the nearest plate of oysters with Mac.

The footmen removed plates and platters, placed ice in crystal glasses before each guest and poured a light, sparkling wine.

After this, Lou knew, the footmen would clear the table and the rooms would be opened up for dancing, sets of doors opened and folded back. The musicians were set up at the other end of the linked rooms in the foyer, and refreshments would be served outside on the terrace beneath the light of the moon and some lanterns. She intended to dance all night and then exhaust Rob.

This was as good a time as any to show Mac her discovery.

She swallowed her last mouthful of ice cream. "Come with me, Mac."

Twenty-One

Mac

Come with me, Mac. What a wonderfully suggestive choice of words. He arranged himself as discreetly as he could beneath his linen napkin and then stood to hand her from the table. Couples were rising now, the men—or at least those who knew the correct etiquette, which was most of them—leaping to their feet if any woman nearby looked as though she was going to stand.

He abandoned the relative safety of the linen napkin and the cover of the tablecloth, swirled the tails of his coat as he stood—he rather liked dressing this way although it embarrassed him that he did—and did his best to ignore Chris's lewd wink. The guests had about fifteen minutes to get out of the footmen's way as they cleared and disassembled the huge table and transferred the sugar sculpture to the sideboard. Chris and Peter ushered the crowd to the other side of the house, where the musicians were now set up on a dais, and let the guests admire the decorations and the restoration work.

"I should be honest with you," Lou said as they strolled

through the gathering. "I'm planning to sleep with someone else tonight."

"Words an Austen heroine probably never spoke," he said, trying to make a joke of it and not let his disappointment show. Well, he'd blown it, he knew that. It was too late. But it didn't mean he couldn't enjoy her company. And he was touched by how excited she was about this recent discovery, whatever it was, probably something entirely geeky about the history of the house.

They headed away from the crowd and into the east wing of the house, toward Paint Boys territory. "They're not here," she said as they came to a padlocked door. "But they won't mind."

She twirled the combination lock and pushed the door open, flipping on a light switch. The room was part office, part laboratory; he'd interviewed them a few days ago here, and found a solid core of knowledge beneath Simon and Jon's silly, flitty exteriors. Now paint cans, ladders, drop cloths and other equipment were stacked neatly in one corner and a door stood open to an adjoining room.

She grabbed his hand. "Look what we found!"

He, busy staring at her breasts in the first decent light he'd encountered so far this evening, said, "Are those your nipples?"

"Who else's do you think they'd be? Look, Mac. They got some of the plaster down. Do you see?"

The small room was a horrible mess, a great pile of plaster and rubble on a drop cloth over a sink, unpleasant-looking iron pipes exposed. In the stone walls, three arched doorways were revealed, bricked in. "Uh, very nice. Sorry, Lou, I'm not a historian."

"It's a conservatory," she said with great patience. "These

were probably triple hung windows that reached all the way to the floor. You'd have plants in pots in here, jasmine or orange and lemon trees, maybe, and when the weather was warm you could put them outside to catch the sun. Beneath this flooring there are probably flagstones. And that fireplace behind you was a stove. Isn't it gorgeous!"

"It's great," he said, moved by her excitement. "Will Peter and Chris restore it?"

"Absolutely. They're after funding for an initiative to make this wing of Paradise an educational center and hire some staff." She ran her fingertips through the pile of debris over the sink, coming up with a small white object. "Part of a clay pipe. We're pretty sure the rebuild happened by the time our only house map was drawn up in 1841 and this pipe can date it fairly accurately. I'll bag it up and then we can get back to the ball."

She led the way back into the other room where she plucked a plastic baggie from a box and stowed the pipe inside. She marked the outside of the bag with the name of the room—the disaster area was already named the Conservatory, he noted—and wrote a quick note on a small sheet of paper, which she explained was acid free, with her name and the date, and which wall the item had come from. The folded note inside the sealed bag, she placed it in a large plastic tray that already held other treasures (even if they looked like garbage) from the wall—some bits of corroded metal and a fragment of blue-and-white china.

He didn't care if she was fucking someone else tonight. They wouldn't see her like this, thrilled by the fabric of the house, brushing dust from her fingers and gazing at the artifacts as though they were a golden treasure trove.

"Lou," he said. "I have to kiss you."

"Oh, Mac," she said, and came into his arms in a rush, knocking her headdress slightly askew, her hands coming up to his face. Maybe it was excitement over this discovery and she was kissing him because she couldn't kiss what looked like a demolition zone, but he'd take what he could get.

He had missed her, he'd missed her feel and taste and scent, and she held his jaw, fingertips directing his mouth to hers, her lips soft against his. Her tongue touched his and he hardened immediately, wanting her skirts up—and her breasts, how could he forget those? He pressed a nipple against his palm, so hard and sweet. She wore nothing under that damned sexy gown, and he had a finger up her leg and inside her—real crass, but her excited whimper and wetness told him she didn't mind a bit.

But then she slapped at him, pushing him away, one hand grabbing at her head. "No! Oh, no! Stop!"

"What?"

She fell to her knees on the wooden floor, clawing at the floorboard like a madwoman. "Oh, no!" she said again.

"Honey, tell me what's wrong."

"My necklace!"

"I didn't think you were wearing one."

"On my headdress. I put my necklace on it and it's fallen off. It's gone between the floorboards. Julian gave it to me." She looked around wildly and wiped her face with her hand, leaving a smear of plaster dust. "Get me the crowbar."

Get me the crowbar. Not the most romantic words ever spoken to him, and his iron-hard erection would probably serve just as well, but he grabbed a crowbar from the tools hung on the wall. He offered to help, but she waved him away, and set to prying up the wooden floorboard. "The Paint Boys will be mad at me," she said, heaving at it with a screech of nails. "I should have asked them to do this."

He watched her, rather enjoying the sight of a Regency lady wielding a crowbar—nicely toned arms, he noted— and bent to help lift the floorboard aside. "Wait," he said, and spread his handkerchief on the floor for her to kneel on.

"Thanks." She was already delving into the dark space and let out a sneeze. "Centuries of dust." Her hand emerged with a handful of garbage, the gold chain and ruby shining in its midst.

"What the hell's that?" he said.

She backed off his handkerchief, still on her knees, and spread the trash over the clean white linen. "Probably a rat's nest."

His first reaction was to say "yuk," but she looked as though she'd found the Holy Grail. She touched the stuff with her fingertips, very delicately, and his hard-on, which had subsided a little, surprised him by coming back full force.

"Look," she said.

He looked. A tangle of hair or straw, a scrap of fabric, something black and wrinkled he couldn't identify, and a scrap of paper with writing on it.

"What's the black thing?" he said.

"Probably a piece of mummified fruit, like a piece of orange peel. Something organic, it might even be leather. Look, Mac. Just look."

"I'm looking," he said, but wondering why she found it so exciting. It must be something like the bricked-in arches that he just didn't have an instinct for.

Still gazing at her prize, she said, "On the table to your left. White cotton gloves. And one of those plastic bags with a side pocket."

He handed her all she asked for. She slipped on the gloves and pushed the hair, or whatever the fibrous stuff was, aside with one finger to reveal the piece of paper. "Don't you recognize this, Mac?"

He reached out to touch it, but she snapped, "No! Get some gloves on!"

As he slipped on a pair of gloves—best to humor the lady under the circumstances—she carefully lifted the handkerchief and its gruesome contents onto the table. She picked her necklace clear and fastened it around her neck. "Look," she said, her voice full of awe. She was crying, not as she had before when she thought she'd lost her necklace, but as though intensely moved. "Don't you recognize that writing?"

He squinted at the few words in black ink—hardly faded, he thought, probably since it had been hidden in the dark so long—and it did look vaguely familiar.

"There's a signature," she said. "Initials."

JA

"You're kidding," he said.

"It's hers," she said. "It's how she signed her letters."

He broke the silence by reading the writing. "'Passion I bear for you'—at least, I guess it's *you* even though the *U* is missing. And 'inconstancy you have.' Strong words."

"I think there's an *E* before it. 'The inconstancy,' maybe? A handwriting expert would be able to tell. And of course whatever the full sentence was depends on the size of the piece of paper she used, and...so many things."

She prodded at the piece of fabric, mustard-yellow-and-blue pattern on a buff background. "Probably an Indian cotton block print. Someone should be able to date that. Look how fresh the colors are. It's amazing, Mac. It's a time capsule. This could change everything we know about Austen."

He couldn't resist his own growing excitement. "Give me an exclusive, Lou," he blurted.

"What? Oh, yes. Sure. Sorry, I forgot you're a journalist. It could be years. Paper, ink, handwriting analysis will have to be done, DNA testing—"

"DNA?" he said. But then he realized the stuff he'd thought was straw was tied with a blackened ribbon.

"The dye from the ribbon has deteriorated, and it or something else has altered the chemical structure, but I'm fairly sure this is human hair. Her hair. Or maybe his—she was returning her unfaithful lover's lock of hair." She shook her head. "Okay, let's think, Mac. We can't tell anyone about this. Not even Peter and Chris, for the moment. I need to call my dissertation advisor. She's the best person I can think of to talk about it, figure out how to move forward. But let's get it bagged up first."

She slid everything into the plastic bag and frowned in annoyance. "They don't even have a tray for the underfloor of this room." She slipped off her gloves and reached for one of the sheets of acid-free paper. "We'll measure where it lay from the southeast corner of the room. But first let's get this floorboard back."

Since he seemed to have been delegated to her assistant, he quite happily hammered the floorboard home while she crawled around with a tape measure, getting her beautiful gown quite dusty in the process. She wrote a huge amount of notes on the paper before sealing it into the pouch on the side of the bag and then placed it into a cardboard box. The box, with her name written on it, went into a file cabinet.

She kicked dust over the floorboard, treading it in so that it looked indistinguishable from the rest of the floor.

"Okay," she said, brushing at her skirts. "You're pretty

dirty, too. We'd better get ourselves cleaned up, and, oh goodness, I think I've stood Peter up for the first dance." She shook her head. "Oh, what the hell. This is huge, Mac. Just huge. It's going to change everything. For you, for me—"

He loved her like this, the ardent scholar, the seeker of truth.

Hell, he loved her.

"For us?" he couldn't resist but ask.

"We'll be colleagues," she said, looking at him hesitantly. "We'll see."

It was better than *absolutely not,* so he'd take it.

She glanced at the file cabinet. "I think it should be safe here."

"Why shouldn't it?"

"Press. They're all over the house and I don't want the Paint Boys finding it if they do any tours or interviews on the restoration. It should be kept stable, but it's fine for now." She closed the file cabinet door. "You've hardly said a word. Are you okay?"

"I love you," he said. He didn't mean to tell her, not here, like this. Not after he'd screwed things up with her and she'd gone and fucked Rob—he was pretty sure that was who it was, unless she was planning to cavort with the Paint Boys. But she had said she was sleeping with "someone else," singular. But anyway... "I love you, Lou."

Her usual worried expression returned. "I can't—"

"No," he hurried to say, before she could go on, "it's not fair of me, not after this. It's the wrong time." He picked up the handkerchief, shaking it out, not really wanting to fold it back into his pockets after it had housed a rat's nest, even one with possible major literary associations. "Just know that whoever this other guy is, I'll beat the shit out of him if he hurts you or doesn't treat you right. Turn around, and I'll swipe the dust off you."

She was the one who fell silent now, other than directing him to a box of wipes which they used to clean their faces—she had a smear of plaster dust on her nose and a gray smudge of dirt on her chin and he wasn't much better.

"I'm sorry," he said. "I don't want to rain on your parade."

"You're not. I'm just sorry I can't— Well, that things went wrong for us."

"Me, too."

They inspected each other under the harsh fluorescent light. She insisted they give their hands a final cleansing with the wipes, and then they agreed they were clean enough for candlelight.

Lou gave one more longing glance at the file cabinet and they left the room, clicking the lock closed.

"So," he said as they walked back toward the ball, "Rob's a bit young for you, isn't he?"

"I like him. He's smart, kind and sexy."

So am I. "Well, if that's what you want."

"It is."

Back off, Salazar. He tried to turn his thoughts to the story, when he could break it, how, who he could offer it to. He should talk to Peter and Chris, when Lou was okay with sharing this with them, persuade them to put the money up to rush the DNA tests. *This is huge.* He could probably get a job anywhere after this if he handled it right. He and Lou, they'd make a good team.

"Who do you think Jane's guy was?" he asked her.

"Shh!" she looked around as though paparazzi lurked in the paneling. "There must be some sort of documentation from local diaries or collections of letters, who was visiting whom at the time. On the other hand, those have never come up to confirm any of the traditional beliefs that Austen stayed here, either. If she was writing to him, he might have had no connections with the area. I'm pretty sure it wasn't any of the usual candidates, certainly not Tom Lefroy who was too early. I think pop culture has blown that flirtation way out of proportion."

"Except that Lefroy said he was in love with her."

"Sure, years later when she was a famous authoress. Wouldn't you have claimed you were in love with her? And I don't think it was the Reverend Blackall, the clergyman she may have fallen in love with in Devon, for instance, when she was in her late twenties."

"Why not?"

"Gut instinct. I know clergymen were very worldly, but 'passion' and 'inconstancy'—as you said, strong language. It suggests something bad, a betrayal, like Marianne and Willoughby. And it may have been the sort of letter you write and then tear up. Or a false start—the back was blank. Paper was very expensive then. You filled every scrap when you wrote."

"Why did it survive, then?"

She shrugged and looked troubled for a moment. "I guess she tore it up and threw it into a fireplace that was unlit. But the rat got there before the housemaid. Mac, you're a pretty tough guy, aren't you?"

"Yeah. Why?"

She grinned, wicked and disarming. "Well, you may have noticed I was rather insistent about using those antibacterial wipes."

"So?"

"The black thing I told you might be orange peel or leather had a tail. It was probably a dead baby rat."

His stomach turned. "Oh, my God. I think I'm going to throw up." He tore the handkerchief from his pocket and threw it away as far as he could. "You knew that all along?"

"Sure. I didn't want to gross you out."

"You've grossed me out now. That's disgusting."

They could hear the musicians now and see the dancers, most of whom were following the steps far better than they ever did.

She was laughing like a fool.

"Okay," he said. "You're absolutely certain you're going to sleep with Rob tonight?"

She smiled up at him and nodded. "I promised to teach him all about oral sex."

"Oh, my God. First the rat and now this. This is going beyond normal revenge." He shook his head and took a deep breath. "Lou, I'm about to say something to you that no Austen hero ever said."

"Yeah?"

"You said you were interested in a threesome."

"I don't know if *interested* is the right word."

"Oh, what the fuck. Let me join you and Rob, Lou. Have both of us, and to hell with it."

Twenty-Two

Lou

"Faithless jade!" Peter said at the sight of Lou, who entered as the dance ended and the participants dispersed. "So I was thrown over for a heterosexual."

"More or less," she said. "Sorry, honey, Mac and I had something to do. But I'm here for the second dance, so please forgive me."

"Of course. But, really, are you two on again?"

"Absolutely not." She grinned at him. *Oh, Peter, I have such a surprise for you.* "I just missed a dance. Even Austen's gossipy neighbors wouldn't have inferred anything from just one dance."

He kissed her forehead, to her surprise. "It's nice to see you so happy."

She gulped down a glass of lemonade. "I am happy. I'm sad, too, because Julian should be here."

"Me, too." He touched the ruby at her throat. "I remember this from the wedding. Such a lovely day."

She longed to tell someone about her other momentous

discovery, that she and Mac had rekindled something, or possibly made a new start. Elation and anticipation of the night ahead were enough to make her giddy; it might not be love, but it was something. Maybe after a night with two lovers, she'd know how she really felt about Mac, her complicated, troubling man.

She placed her glass on a tray held by one of Rob's footmen. The musicians hefted their instruments and Becky the dance mistress moved into position, microphone at the ready, and curtsied.

Lou and Peter joined the dance, greeting the couple next to them. She looked down the line of people wearing beautiful costumes, some of which she knew were more historically accurate than others, but the soft golden glow of the careful lighting lent them harmony and authenticity. Peonies, honeysuckle and jasmine, forced open by the heat of the room, spread their intoxicating perfume.

"It's perfect," she said to Peter. "The stuff of fantasy. All we need now is Darcy in a wet shirt."

After a brief walk-through led by Becky, the dance began, slow and stately, the couples weaving in and out of the set, turning, changing direction, changing places. As she and Peter progressed up the set, they met Viv and Mac, she splendid in her favorite peacock feathers and a matching bright emerald gown, tamed by candlelight to a subtle glow.

"Very nice, Lou."

Naturally, Viv was looking right at Lou's nipples. So was Mac. So, now that she thought about it, had almost every man she'd encountered in the dance. Except for Peter, who was far too gentlemanly and not particularly interested in female anatomy.

"Strange how this light plays tricks on the eyes," Mac

said, smiling at her. "I hope you're not making anyone forget the steps."

"With our level of competency, I can hardly be blamed for that," Lou said.

Mac took her hand. They circled, close together, gazing into each other's eyes.

"Well, Ratlady?"

"That's a truly hideous nickname."

"What did he say?"

"I haven't asked him. Yet."

They changed hands and changed directions.

"If he isn't man enough…" Mac said.

"Oh, I think he is."

"Another poor bastard whose balls you keep in your reticule."

"The spoils of love."

"I'd say of war." He swung away to rejoin Viv and turned a smoldering gaze on her that made first Lou and then Viv giggle.

"Oh, dear, you girls," Peter said. "What shall we do with you?"

Mac took his hand, looked into his eyes and said, "I don't think you need to concern yourself."

Lou and Viv, hand in hand, giggled again, lost direction, and were gently directed by other dancers back into position.

"This is serious pleasure," Peter said to Lou, "and you must concentrate. You're amusing the footmen."

So she was. Rob stood at the side of the room, smiling at her with delight.

She smiled back.

"Really, dear, I hope you're not distracting the staff."

"Heavens, no," Lou said.

The next dance, the one she had promised Mac, was in a much more uninhibited style with clapping and vigorous movements that several of the men, and some of the women, interpreted as jumps or steps with fancy, improvised foot-work. Lou knew it was more historically correct than the previous dance, which dated from more than a century before their period, but she regretted the lack of excuses to gaze into Mac's eyes.

"Your fine eyes," she whispered, as he picked her up by the waist and swung her around.

"When will you ask him?"

"Later."

He set her onto her feet again and they joined hands with the couple next to them.

"So how soon can we get out of here, Lou?" he asked as they met again.

"To hell with that. He's working and I aim to dance until I drop."

"I'll make you pay."

"I look forward to it."

Rob

THIS WAS BLOODY AMAZING. IT looked like one of those Austen movies his mum liked so much; everything looked… right. It wasn't just a bunch of people dressed up pretending to be something else, it was like being there, as you might imagine it. He'd pretty much got used to the fact that the guests were all gorgeous, but tonight's greatly expanded crowd represented all sorts of ages and body types, a few teenagers, but a lot of them quite old, about the age of his Gran. Like the old guy who'd sat next to Lou at dinner; apparently he was some sort of lord. But a couple of blokes he knew from the pub, an electrician and a school-bus driver were there, too, half throttled in their high collars. And somehow this mix of people lent the occasion veracity and truth. This was something you could believe in, not just a fantasy.

Only the frequent flash of cameras and the occasional sighting of a cell phone broke the illusion. They were on to the fourth dance, and this time Lou was dancing with Lord Stoat (surely he didn't spell it that way). Something was going on between her and Mac, he was pretty sure, but then she looked amazing. Who wouldn't want to get off with her?

But she was getting off with Rob tonight. Of all the guys here, she wanted him.

He thought he'd feel different after last night, and for a time he did—*I got laid, I made her come!*—but then the day was pretty much normal, other than it being the day of the ball, which meant a lot of work, along with the surprise appearance of his dad. Maybe he was different, though, because instead of the usual insults he and his dad exchanged when forced together, they had something approaching a conversation. And while it was about doing work on the cottage, he felt that it represented a change toward each other. He hoped he could remember in future that his dad was damaged goods and not be so hard on him; and maybe his dad would stop messing him around about Cambridge.

He took another look at Lou. He was pretty sure he could see nipples there, but it was maybe only the pattern of the fabric. He did the math again. At eleven, his second shift would come in, and he could leave someone—maybe Ivan, if he wasn't too drunk—in charge and then he could go and receive his oral-sex lesson (fucking a teacher was bloody miraculous). He'd have to be back on duty at five, if not earlier, so the sooner they got out of there the better. She, however, seemed to be having a great time dancing, and she looked wonderful tonight. Beautiful. Sexy. Those gloves up over her elbows were hot, rather like stockings—real ones, not those stupid Regency ones. Maybe she'd keep them on.

The dance ended, leaving the room smelling slightly less of flowers and more of overheated people, and he straightened up, hands clasped behind his back, striving for that balance of official dignity and friendliness. He nodded to Dejan to take the band's drinks over now they were taking a break, and people surged toward the refreshments on the terrace.

To stop it being too much of a mob scene, he had the lads waiting to intercept them with trays of drinks, lemonade, wine and cider. No one was really rowdily drunk yet, but he knew it was only a matter of time. Some people would drink, dance out the alcohol and keep a balance. Others, like the guys who'd parked themselves in one of the downstairs rooms, would just drink. He had several of the lads keeping an eye on them.

Lou unfolded her fan and lifted it so only her eyes were visible. She nodded her head toward the front of the house; smart move, if everyone was heading for the back. He followed her, keeping an eye out for glasses that might need to be picked up on the way back.

Outside, the air was cool and fresh, the night clear. One of the band members was outside, talking on his mobile, pacing up and down, his feet crunching on the gravel. Lou was there, the stone on her necklace dark against her pale skin, and he reached her in a few long strides, crushing her to him. She was warm and flushed and ripe.

"I've wanted to touch you all day," he said, kissing her randomly, face, lips, neck.

She returned his kisses, the fan on her wrist bumping against his shoulder as she cupped the back of his head.

"Wait. I want to get my wig off." He took it off and shook his head. "God, that's hot. Hot warm, I mean. Are you having fun? You look great." He peered at her gown, perplexed. He could have sworn… "I can see your nipples. Bloody hell."

"Glad you like it." She grinned.

He couldn't resist ducking his head to kiss first one, then the other nipple. "Mmm, they're hard, Lou. Want to get behind a bush?"

"I've created a monster." She laughed and pushed him away, but only a little. "I want to dance a bit more, then we can leave whenever you're ready."

"Great." He nuzzled her neck.

"Just one thing." She raised herself on her toes to whisper in his ear.

"What! You're joking." He took a step back, astonished and a little apprehensive.

"Look, if you don't want to, it's okay. I'll tell him no."

He scratched his head, something that was particularly satisfying after taking off his wig. "I'm sort of surprised. It doesn't seem like him."

"And does it seem like you?" she asked.

He shrugged. "It's pretty normal now, threesomes, isn't it? I'm just starting out. I'll take anything I can get. No, that sounds wrong. I'm cool with it, Lou." He grinned, triumphant. "He must be really desperate to get your knickers off again."

"If I were wearing any," she whispered in his ear, giving it a little bite.

"Oh, shit, Lou, I have a massive erection now."

Her hand slid down, cupping him. "Sorry. I didn't realize you'd get so turned on by the idea."

He couldn't resist shoving against her hand although he knew that would make things worse. "I'm turned on by the idea of you, Mrs. Connolly, and if there's someone else around I might learn something new. See how the experts do it. Just one question." He cleared his throat. This was important. He was doing it for her (mostly; he found it pretty exciting himself) but he really needed to know in advance. He put his wig on again as though it gave him authority. "Is his dick bigger than mine?"

She slapped his arse. "You'll find out soon enough."

Mac

GROUPS OF PEOPLE LINGERED ON the terrace; half a dozen young women and a couple of guys in military uniforms, the girls giggling and the guys not sure of what to do with their swords. In a corner a couple sat kissing passionately—Cathy and Alan, of course. Ben sat nearby, watching them with a hunger that made Mac uncomfortable. That was the trouble with three people; whatever you were doing, one tended to get left out. It was an odd sort of dynamic. On the other hand, he didn't think Ben had been invited to Cathy and Alan's party. Ben just showed up and watched or, Mac's own theory, did whatever Sarah told him to.

The terrace was transformed by lanterns strung overhead and tables decorated with centerpieces of flowers and sugar constructions, temples and depictions of gods and goddesses. Some guests had already nibbled at the edible works of art and a couple of them had collapsed into sugary ruin. Waiters came to and fro with trays of desserts, things dipped in chocolate, cupcakes with gilded or sugared flowers, coffee, tea, slices of orange, glasses of wine. A table of cheeses and bread stood at one end of the terrace for those who fancied something more substantial.

Mac, nursing a cup of coffee—after his ridiculous suggestion earlier, he had decided he wanted to be awake and alert—waited for Lou.

Finally, she emerged, smiling, and despite himself he smiled back and rose to his feet. "Well?" he said.

"Oh, I'm hungry." She sat at the table.

"Again? Didn't we only just have dinner?"

"All that dancing. And I'm thirsty." A couple of footmen rushed over—either Rob had arranged for VIP treatment or they just wanted to get an eyeful of her nipples—and she loaded a plate with dessert and chose a cup of coffee.

Let her try to keep him in suspense; he'd show her. He faked a yawn.

She removed gold flowers from the top of a tiny chocolate cupcake, cut it into four pieces with her fork and ate the first with excruciating slowness. Then the second.

"Lou!" he leaned over the table. "For God's sake, stop driving me crazy."

She made a questioning sound and fed a sliver of orange into her mouth. Slowly. She licked her lips and started on the next piece of cake.

Mac leaned over the table, scooped up the remains of the cake with his finger and swallowed it.

"I was looking forward to eating that," she said.

"Too bad. Have you asked him?"

"Oh, yes." She peered into the tiny silver pitcher that accompanied her coffee, looked around for a footman and beckoned. "Do you think I could have some milk for my coffee? I really prefer it over cream."

"The lady will have cream and like it," Mac barked, and waited for the footman to leave. "Well?"

She smiled. "He was quite intrigued that it was your idea."

"It wasn't."

"Yes, it was. I quote, 'Have both of us, and to hell with it.'"

He groaned. "You're right. It was a moment of desperation and insanity. And what did he say?"

Her smile broadened.

He knew what that meant. "So we're on. Okay, Lou. Now this is serious." He looked around to make sure no one was within range. "Just out of curiosity."

She began dissecting another dessert. "Yes?"

"This is awkward."

She patted his hand. "It's okay. You can ask me anything you want."

"I have to know..." His mouth went dry.

"Is his bigger than yours?" She popped a strawberry into her mouth and chewed for what seemed a long time. "As I told him—you'll find out soon enough."

Twenty-Three

Lou

When the next dance ended, Lou curtsied to Chris, her partner, who made an elaborate, flourishing bow in return. From farther down the set, Mac watched her.

"Turning in already?" Chris asked as she retrieved her fan, reticule and gloves from a chair at the side of the room. The fan and reticule had become a nuisance, bouncing around on her wrist, and the gloves, although she liked the soft cream kidskin, made her too hot.

"I think so. Thanks for the dance." She was so tempted to tell him about the big discovery, but of course she couldn't. Instead, she kissed his cheek.

"It's been an honor to see you get your groove back, Mrs. Connolly," Chris said, "even though I expected you to dance until dawn. It's only midnight. But I daresay you have other fish to fry."

"I wouldn't put it quite that way." She smiled and looked around for Peter, but he was deep in conversation with a group of people she didn't know. "Say good-night to Peter for me and I'll see you at a more civilized hour tomorrow. Tonight has been a triumph. You're both brilliant."

She spent a little time chatting to people she knew and others she had met that night, declining offers of another dance. When the music started, she went in search of Rob and found him on the terrace, hand in hand with Di, executing a mock country dance.

She stood and watched, remembering how only a few days ago she had seen Mac dance here alone. Rob and Di stepped in time to the music, then broke away into their own rhythm, he furling her into his side and then out again, turning her under his arm. They were well matched; both of them knew how to move. Di gyrated around him in a Bollywood-inspired, hip-swaying move, arms arched overhead. He copied the move back to her. They laughed, joined face-to-face, arms around each other's waists, and then picked up the country dance steps again.

Rob knew Lou was there; they exchanged a brief glance of understanding. She liked that he kept dancing and admired the deft, graceful way he partnered Di, deferring to her when she wanted to attempt a fancy dance move—a bit of hip-hop now, sexy, brash—and making a response that was all masculine, all his own.

Their audience, some of the waiters and kitchen staff, clapped in time and called encouragement. The scent of marijuana was strong on the air.

Lou smiled and left them to it. He'd arrive in her room when he was ready, and she felt for the first time that she was not altogether welcome there—Upstairs eavesdropping on Downstairs' amusements.

A footman stood guard at the bottom of the stairs to dissuade the curious from exploring upstairs where the guests stayed. He bowed and unhooked the silken rope at the bottom of the stairs to admit her.

It was a matter of discomfort to her that she still had trouble distinguishing the footmen from each other, but that was the point, wasn't it? The matched set of handsome young men, so enthusiastically selected by Peter, their wigs making them look even more alike to the modern eye.

In her room, she took a shower and considered how to put her nervous gentlemen callers at ease. The Regency wardrobe did not extend to sexy negligees. It was an era when women looked sexier dressed than undressed, except for the floating draperies of classical figures. She had nothing that approximated floating draperies or the zephyrs necessary to keep them afloat.

Clad in a towel, she debated putting on rosewater or lavender perfume, both of which she now associated with wholesome clean white linen.

The tap at the servants' door made her jump out of her skin. "Who's there?" she asked. She had no doubt that later in the night as the company became drunker there would be some rowdy explorations of the house.

"It's me," Mac replied.

"Not coming through the window tonight?" she asked as she let him in.

"That was my grand romantic gesture. It seemed to work. For the moment, anyway." He sprawled on one elbow on the bed, very obviously wearing only his silk dressing gown.

"It did. It was very clever of you to arrange the thunderstorm, too."

"You look very...clean." He chose the word carefully.

She sighed. "What do you suggest?"

"The top part of your gown," he said with a leer. "The lace thing."

"It might be a bit sweaty." She picked up the gown, which she'd folded and laid over a chair.

"We won't mind."

She went into the bathroom with the overdress and slipped it over her head. "I don't know, Mac," she said. "It looks a bit slutty."

"Great."

"I mean, real slutty. Adult triple-X slutty."

"Even better. Come on out, honey, show me what you've got."

She took another look at herself in the mirror. The overdress didn't even fit properly without her corset, but hung with the clasp at breast level, and it certainly didn't cover anything. If anything it framed her pubic hair, but that, she decided, was appropriate for Oral Sex 101.

She emerged from the bathroom.

"Fantastic," Mac said. "Do you think he'll mind if we start without him?"

"I don't think it would be polite," she said.

They both burst out laughing. It was nice to laugh with him, relieving the tension they both felt.

"We could play chess," she suggested. "I have a chessboard."

"With you dressed like that? I won't even remember the moves."

She sat on the bed beside him. "I wish I could call the States now."

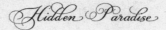

"Me, too. I'm so grateful you came up with this to distract us, Lou, because I won't get a wink of sleep."

"My pleasure."

Another nervous burst of laughter.

"He's probably late because he's jerking off in the shower to give himself some staying power," Mac suggested.

"There you go, ruining my fantasy," she said. "Don't be mean to him, Mac. He's probably just as nervous as you are."

"Hell, I'm not nervous."

A tap at the servants' door, and Lou noticed how Mac, who wasn't at all nervous, sat up straighter and pulled his dressing gown closed.

She opened the door. Rob, wearing boxers and an unbuttoned long-sleeved shirt, a bottle of champagne in one hand and wineglasses in the other, gaped at her.

"Uh," he said.

She caught the bottle before it crashed to the floor and pulled him inside. "Great to see you, too."

"Sorry," he said. He bent to kiss her cheek. "All the blood suddenly rushed from my head. Oh, hi, Mac."

"Let's have a drink," she said, leading Rob to the bed. "Look, guys, I haven't done this before, so let's try and relax."

Rob looked at her, then at Mac, as he eased off the champagne cork, catching the foamy liquid into a glass that he handed to Lou.

"Thanks." She patted his thigh as he poured two more glassfuls.

He shifted at her touch. She glanced down at a very impressive erection, then sideways to another. Two very impressive erections. Now what?

She put her glass aside, having taken one sip. Champagne,

for all its innocuous bubbly silliness, was an unreliable friend for her. She sat demurely—or as demurely as her ridiculously revealing outfit allowed—legs tucked to one side. She needed to get them past this initial awkwardness, do something to release the heat and tension that built in the room.

She rolled onto her knees and kissed Rob, hard and open-mouthed, trailing one hand down to his crotch. Then Mac, scraping her hard nipples over the roughness of his chest as she pulled his dressing gown open. The bed moved as Rob leaned in and took her breasts in his hands. His lips nuzzled her neck, finding a spot that sent shivers down her body. Mac's mouth opened to hers, dark, delicious, and that must surely be his hand stroking the inside of her thigh, flirting with her pubic hair. His finger dipped briefly to her clit.

An image popped into her mind of an old circus photo that had fascinated her as a child—a woman in jodhpurs and with a Clara Bow mouth and rigidly waved platinum hair wielding a whip and chair to control two enormous tigers. These were her tigers, her two huge wild beasts, hers to tame, whose purrs might turn to snarls in a heartbeat.

Mac released her mouth. "I hear you want to learn about oral," he said to Rob. "Okay, kid, watch this. Then you can take a turn."

Lou scooted up to the head of the bed, spreading her legs wide.

Rob had shucked his boxers. He stared at her, his cock dark and rigid, a drop of liquid at the tip, as he knelt beside her. She drew his hands back to her breasts and watched his fingers circle and squeeze her nipples.

Mac moved between her legs. "See here." His voice was a low, sexy rumble. His thumb pushed her apart, revealed her folds. "This is her clit, this cute little pink ridge. I could make her come pretty fast, but I think we should keep her on the edge for a bit." He lowered his head. His tongue rasped, rough, exciting on the sensitive head of her clit. Her legs jerked involuntarily at the pressure.

"Or like this." He lapped at her like a cat with a saucer of cream, swift delicate strokes, building a rhythm. She reached to caress the rough silk of his head and with the other hand ran a finger slowly up the length of Rob's cock.

He gasped and moved away. "Too much, Lou."

Mac's hand slid casually on his own cock. He gestured to Rob and moved to Lou's other side. "Here, your turn."

Rob slid between Lou's legs, gazing at her exposed sex. He lowered his head to kiss her thighs and work his way upward and inward. His tongue was warm and gentle, a silken swirl, a persistent thrum.

Mac shifted and laid a hand above Lou's pubis, fingers spread, pulling her open. "Is that good, Lou?"

"Yes," she breathed.

Mac's mouth landed on hers, licked at her lips and descended to kiss and suck one nipple, then the other. "You want Rob to make you come, honey?"

She wanted to close her eyes and roll her head back and let the impending orgasm crash over her, engulf her. At the same time, she wanted to watch everything they did, Mac's dark head at her breast, Rob's between her thighs, Mac's spread-eagled hand, pulling her taut, the glimpses of wet pink skin below Rob's lapping tongue.

"He's a natural," Mac murmured against her breast. "Come for us, Lou."

Yes, she was almost there, her breath coming short, legs

rising, and she reached to clutch Rob's head, greedy, frantic, and then, oh, yes, she was there, *there,* now.

She floated back to earth.

"Was that okay?" Rob said.

"Amazing." She beckoned. "Come here."

Still on his elbows, he blushed. "Um, actually it was good for me, too. I, um, when you came…"

She smiled when he raised himself to a kneeling position. "It's okay. I'm very flattered. You know, Rob, I think it's the first time I've seen you without an erection."

"Make the most of it. It won't last for long." He leaned to kiss her and she reached down to receive his swelling cock in her hand.

"Do I get some of the action?" Mac pushed him aside. He turned Lou's face to his and touched his lips to hers. His kiss was slow and tentative. He sighed and rested his face against her neck.

"What is it?"

"I didn't know how jealous I'd feel," he muttered.

"Look, mate." Rob put a hand on his shoulder. "I'm jealous of you because you got there first—sorry, Lou, that sounds bad, but you know what I mean—and at a guess, I'd say you're jealous of me because she fancies me and I get perpetual hard-ons. That's just biology. It's my age, so I'm informed."

"The gospel according to Rob," Mac said.

"If you like," Rob said. His hand lay on Mac's shoulder still. They were touching each other, not in a sexual way, but at least in acknowledgment of each other's presence.

"Want a fucking lesson?" Mac asked.

"It's okay, I think I know how to do that," Rob said with great politeness.

Lou smothered a giggle.

"We'll ask the lady what she wants," Mac said. "Lou?"

"I think I want to do this," she said. She gave Rob a quick kiss on the lips and pushed Mac against the head of the bed. His erection lay dark and heavy against his belly; a shining thread of translucency hung at the tip. She reached her tongue out to lap at it and Mac groaned.

"Rob," she said, "you know where the condoms are."

She ran her tongue up and down the ridges of Mac's erection and saw his belly tauten as he sucked in a deep breath. He raised a hand and caressed her head, smiling into her eyes. "Whatever you want, Lou, but let me come soon. I'm dying here."

A shy cough from behind her. "Lou, who gets the condom?"

"You do, sweetie. This may take some coordination." She positioned herself on her knees, butt raised, hands on either side of Mac's hips, and smiled encouragement over her shoulder at Rob, who knelt, rolling the condom over his new erection. He grinned back, excited and flushed.

"You're looking worried, Lou," Mac said.

"Just thinking, Mac."

"Probably not the best thing to do under the circumstances. It's probably going to be clumsy, but I can guarantee at least two of us will get off. You, Mrs. Connolly, may have to wait your turn."

She lay a finger over Mac's lips as, behind her, Rob fumbled and pushed, finally sliding home. She let out a moan—he felt even bigger than usual.

"Okay, Lou?" Rob asked.

"Oh, yes. Absolutely." She smiled into Mac's eyes, to reassure herself as much as him, and bent her head to his cock again, taking him deep into her mouth with as much care and love as she could give. He gave a great groan of appreciation. Now, this wasn't tiger taming, this was a trapeze act, maintaining an awareness of Rob thrusting into her while attending to Mac, who moaned and writhed beneath her. She braced one arm against the bed, balanced, and caressed Mac's tightening balls, her finger probing beyond. He was so close, his torso arching, hips rising to meet her caress.

"Coming," he gasped.

Inside her, Rob swelled, hesitated, drew back, plunged.

Mac made that soft sound she knew so well as he fell helpless into his orgasm. She choked a little, ungraceful, at the sudden rush, his cock jerking again and again in her mouth. He murmured her name, hands relaxing on her head, stroking her hair back.

She raised her head to smile at him, and he swiped his thumb at the side of her mouth where semen had dribbled out. "Messy girl."

"That was really hot." Rob, panting, collapsed sideways across Mac's calves.

"Get the hell off me," Mac said in a friendly way. He reached for a pillow and tossed it to Rob before pulling Lou into his arms and kissing her. "You okay?"

"Yes. You are, too, I guess?"

He smiled back at her, lazy, sated, loving.

Rob yawned. "Do I get a kiss, too?"

"Sure." Lou reached for him and, to her delight, Mac threw his arm over Rob's shoulders, drawing him close to them.

Rob tilted her head to his, his kiss sweet and tender, then turned his mouth to Mac's. A moment of hesitation, then their lips met in a kiss that surprised Lou both by its duration and its masculine tenderness.

"You little perv," Mac said with affection, ruffling Rob's hair.

Twenty-Four

Lou

"This isn't quite what I expected," Mac said a few minutes later. "It's like having a large dog in bed."

Rob lay between them, curled around his pillow, fast asleep and occupying half the bed and most of the covers. After that wonderfully sexy kiss, he'd smiled in a goofy, sated way, slid down Mac's shoulder and fallen asleep like... Well, Lou had to admit Mac was right—like a puppy.

"And he's got a hard-on again," he added in disgust. "He's like the Energizer Bunny. I should have jerked him off before he fell asleep on us. Or do you think he wants a teddy bear?"

"Stop grumbling," Lou said. "I loved seeing you kiss him. Thank you for that."

He rubbed his face, yawning. "I've got to admit, I did it for your benefit, but I felt, I don't know, tender toward him. I don't think it's turned me gay. At least, so far I don't feel like listening to Judy Garland or discussing window treatments."

"He's exhausted," Lou said, "and he has to get up in a couple of hours, so be quiet and let him sleep. And while you're at it, stop being such a crass homophobe."

"Me, a homophobe? I'm in bed with you both, aren't I?" He lay a hand on Lou's hip, his arm across Rob's shoulders. "I guess we should try to sleep."

"I guess so. Big day tomorrow—I'll have to get to Viv's later in the afternoon to call my advisor right when the sun rises in the States. She's on the East Coast and gets up early."

"You could call from the office here, couldn't you?"

"No, my advisor's vacation phone number is in my bag at Viv's. I don't have the number memorized."

His thumb caressed her hip. "At least I get you to myself when our personal footman leaves. My demoralized, shocked penis might be brave enough to come out of hiding by then."

A FLASHING LIGHT AND A TINNY ringtone a couple of hours later catapulted Rob out of bed, and he swore copiously as he groped for his cell phone in the dark. More swearing and rustling sounds followed as he retrieved his boxers and shirt. The servants' door clicked shut behind him.

Lou regarded Mac with envy. He was fast asleep, hands peacefully crossed on his chest, the sheet covering him up to his navel. And below that... Delightful. And she didn't have to share or worry about circus acts.

She kissed him. His lips moved a little. "You awake?" she whispered.

No response.

She slipped her hand beneath the sheet and stroked, marveling at the satiny skin, even more tender than her kidskin gloves, stretched taut over the ridged power and strength. Strength and sweetness, such a wonderful combination. And the head, as smooth as velvet with its surprising ridge, all those textures and shapes within a wonderful few inches.

Her mind wandered. She could get a condom and slide herself onto him, waking him in the best way possible. Or not waking him, pleasure herself with slow, subtle movements.

A hand shot up and grabbed her wrist. "Just what the hell do you think you're doing?" he growled. "Having lascivious thoughts about me again, Lou?"

"Yes. Feel how hard my nipples are." She guided his hand. "And here, I'm wet."

"Has the kid gone?"

"Yes."

His fingers fluttered against her clit and withdrew. "Good. Get a condom and slake your lust on me." A yawn. "Just keep the help out, okay? I want you to myself. And you can damned well do all the work."

She took her time with him, leaning to graze her nipples against his chest, watching his face as the room lightened with the dawn, revealing dark stubble on his cheeks and chin, the handsome jut of his cheekbones, his lips puffy still from kissing. He abandoned himself to her desire, lying so still that at one point she wondered if he was asleep, but his eyes opened, drowsy and mischievous. He tried to control his excitement, but she knew the signs now, and slowed deliberately if his hips lifted or his breathing quickened.

So sweet. She shuddered against him, her nipples scraping against his stubble, her hair falling around his face.

"Thank you," she whispered.

His eyes flickered open. "You're welcome, honey."

"Thank you for this, and for Rob. For being so sweet to him."

"Glad to have been of service, ma'am."

She stroked his face. "You were wonderful. I know you were out of your comfort zone."

"I sure was. I did it for you."

"I know. I love you for it."

"You do?"

"Yes, I do. I love you, Mac." It was both painful and liberating to admit it.

"Good. I love you, too, but you know that, right? And now..."

He came to life with a lusty roar, tumbling her from his cock, turning her and slapping her butt. "You've had your fun! On your hands and knees now. You're going to get fucked within an inch of your life."

She caught her breath as he pushed into her, hard and powerful, his hand raking from her nipples to her clit, his mouth sucking hot at her neck.

"Like this?" he growled. "Hard enough for you?"

A few strokes, that was all it took, hammering into her, flesh slapping against flesh. She took care of her clit when he gripped her hips to pump harder into her, filling her. An orgasm wrenched her seconds before he cried out and slowed, sweat dripping from his forehead to her shoulders.

She collapsed beneath him.

"What the hell was that?" he said in a whisper, and stroked her back tenderly. "That wasn't sex, it was some sort of seismic event. You okay?"

"Great," she mumbled, wishing she had words or energy to tell him more as he rolled off her and enfolded her in his arms. But there were three words that expressed her feelings, and she had to say them, now before she fell asleep: "I love you."

A TAP AT THE DOOR WOKE HER next. She snatched Mac's dressing gown and went to answer it. She'd overslept. The light outside told her it must be late morning. Mac rolled over, pulling the sheets over himself and a pillow onto his head.

Di was outside with a tray of tea. "Sorry, I'm late, ma'am. We're all a mess after last night. There's an extra cup here if you need it. Do you need any help with your gown this morning?"

She was relieved Di hadn't brought two extra cups. "No, I'm fine, thanks." The young woman looked exhausted, shadows beneath her red-rimmed eyes. "Are you okay?"

Di nodded, a tear sliding from one eye. She shoved the tray at Lou, stepping away. "I'm fine."

"You're not. Come on inside," Lou said. "Mac's here, but he's asleep. I'll draw the bed curtains. Have a cup of tea with me."

Lou poured them both tea at the table by the window.

"Sorry, I've got a bit of a hangover," Di said. "It doesn't help. My boyfriend broke up with me this morning. Well, last night. He texted me, but I didn't get it until this morning."

"That's horrible," Lou said, and remembered Di and Rob together last night.

But Di continued, "He said he was fed up with never seeing me and he'd found someone else." She blew her nose on a well-used tissue from her apron pocket. "I was having such a great time here with Rob and Viv and everyone. Now everything sucks."

"I'm so sorry," Lou said. She put her hand over Di's. "Had you been together a long time?"

"About a year. I know, it's not long but I loved him. I

thought he loved me. And now I don't know what to do. I don't want to stay here but I can't go back to London."

Lou said, "If I were to offer you some advice, I'd suggest you stay here. For now, anyway. People like you, and you have friends here. It's a safe place to be sad, if that makes sense."

Di sniffed and wiped her eyes. "Yeah, that does make sense. Thanks." She drained her tea and stood, offering Lou a weak smile. "I'd better get going. You have anything to go back to Viv?"

"Only last night's gown. I'll take it back later."

"Okay. Mind out, though, Viv'll be like a bear with a sore head. She was really putting it away last night and she may have company. I'm keeping out of her way today."

MAC WAS STILL ASLEEP WHEN LOU, showered and dressed, her ball gown over her arm, left the room. It was late morning, about 5:00 a.m. on the East Coast, and while her advisor was a notorious early riser, Lou thought breakfast and a quiet stroll over to Viv's would take care of another hour. The house was quiet, a few footmen, yawning and with aprons over their livery, taking down last night's wilted garlands from the pillars and staircase.

She stopped by the breakfast room, where another couple of footmen, tired and unshaven, slouched against the wall. It appeared few guests were awake and nearly everyone had been up until dawn. Helping herself to a roll and butter to eat on her walk across the grounds, she drank some more tea and suggested the footmen sit, since no other guests were present. They collapsed onto chairs like rag dolls. One of them rested his head on the table and fell asleep.

The grounds were even quieter, not a soul around. Her

discovery yesterday now seemed almost like a dream. What was the story behind those few words? What other treasures might they yet find in those two, last unexplored rooms or in other houses in the neighborhood?

She reached the lodge and tapped on the door, remembering Di's warning about Viv's state of mind. After a few minutes, the door dragged open to reveal Viv with mascara-ringed eyes, her spiky hair on end, a cigarette hanging from her mouth.

Viv removed the cigarette and coughed for a good thirty seconds. "Oh, it's you. Come on in."

Lou followed her flapping kimono into the lodge. One of the footmen—Ivan, Lou thought—sat at the table, smoking and reading a newspaper.

"You," Viv said to him, "out."

"Don't I get a cup of tea, then?"

"No, you bloody don't. Sod off."

"Okay," the footman said, not sounding too upset about it. "Bye."

"It's always a mistake to let them stay over, even when they have a cock that huge," Viv said, running water into her electric kettle. "Throw the gown into the hamper. I thought it looked good, if I say so myself."

Lou explained that she needed access to her bag.

"Sure. I'll make tea and get back to bed if you don't mind. Take as long as you need."

Lou thanked Viv as she directed her to the storage area where guests' bags resided in wire cages, each with a padlock, and reminded Lou what her combination was. Then, yawning, Viv left to return to bed.

Ever since she'd known Julian, he'd had this bag. It was entirely impractical for travel, the leather making it too heavy, and it had no wheels. In addition, she now found, there was a new tear in the lining. She scrabbled around in the dark before taking the entire bag into the kitchen and wishing her notebook was not small and black and almost impossible to find. Her hand closed on something within the lining, her fingertips brushing the leather seam, a bundle of papers wrapped around something that, from its size, had to be her notebook. She placed it on the counter and unfolded the papers that she saw now were email correspondence.

Oh, Julian. The whole point of email is that you don't print everything out. Isn't the house full enough of your printouts and notes and lists, and none of them any good to me?

At first, she thought they weren't his emails, since the one she chose at random was sent to an account unknown to her, not the university email he used for everything. She was about to throw them away, but she saw his name on them and picked a random page.

Julian, I can't wait until I see you again. I'm lying here, thinking of you and how much I love you....

Love letters. She was reading love letters to her husband, some of which included his passionate responses. In growing disbelief, she looked at the dates. They were in order, starting the semester after she and Julian had married, and the first ones did use his university email account. He wrote to welcome someone called Christine to the campus and thank her for finding and returning his appointment book.

Christine.

Did Lou know her? She couldn't recall anyone on campus called Christine.

A week or so later, the other email address was in use and

the messages were about when they could meet. Some emails referenced attachments, which thank God he had not printed out, the very special photos Christine had taken with her cell. He'd written after one of these: "You excite me so much. I can't wait to see you. I've told my wife the Wednesday-night committee meeting is still on, so usual place? I can't wait."

The lying bastard. She remembered the Wednesday-night committee meetings, but she also remembered a lot of sex with him, loving, inventive, frenzied sex. And all that time....

She read on. More meetings, more photos, more references to sex—in his truck at the side of the road, in his office.

And Christine's contributions—short, sexy messages full of abbreviations and exclamation points. Christine used *c*ck* and *c*m* and *f*ck* as if the full words were too weighty for her smartphone or her intellect. She frequently forgot to put on underwear—"LOL." And her spelling was bad, her grammar worse.

Sex standing up, sex on his desk, sex in Christine's dorm room.

Her *dorm room?*

A student. No wonder students had played such a large part in Julian's fantasies and Lou was suddenly overcome with guilt that she had encouraged them. She thought of those dirty games with a shudder of horror now.

Julian wrote, "Even though you're not my student, we have to be careful because of campus ethics. My wife doesn't suspect anything, but when I'm with her it makes me miss you even more and think about you all the time."

Lou's stomach lurched.

Some angry emails a little later on when Christine demanded more of his time and attention, and insisted that he get a smartphone so they could email each other at any time. Julian, technophobe that he was, had refused.

A series of messages, building in intensity, were about going away together to a conference.

Then a panic. "Don't order your plane ticket. Lou says she might want to come with me. I'm doing my best to dissuade her. More later."

Lou remembered that. Julian told her she'd be bored and that the conference location was not that great; but she'd welcomed a chance to write, order room service and test the capacity of the hotel bed with him. Christine apparently wanted those last two items, too. But their neighbor's wife went into the hospital for surgery and Lou found herself helping with chores and cooking for them, so she'd stayed home. She and Julian were inexplicably short of money the following month and now she knew why—Christine's airfare.

The next email detailed a pregnancy scare, and Lou decided she had read enough.

Her marriage had been a lie. All of it, a lie. And today, of all days, she'd learned the truth.

Passion...inconstancy.

She knew what she must do now.

Twenty-Five

Rob

He and Di sat on the front steps of the house, throwing pieces of gravel back into the driveway, an easy pastime since there were always pieces of gravel on the steps, a seemingly infinite amount. This was a sloppy, lazy sort of day, nearly everyone hungover and short of sleep, standards relaxed. In the two hours he'd been off duty last night, there had been no terrible disasters—nearly everyone was drunk, someone had vomited in the rosebushes, and one of the cooks had gone crazy and waved a knife around, insisting someone had stolen his stash of marijuana.

And Di had been dumped by her worthless boyfriend, which made Rob feel bad for her—he hated to see her weepy and sad—but also vaguely hopeful about his chances, because he liked her. He really did. They got on, and she'd come to him first with the bad news—or nearly first. She'd talked to Lou.

"I thought she was standoffish, you know?" Di said to him now. "But she's okay. Nice. She said I should stay on here, because I wasn't alone here, even though I feel like flushing my head down the toilet." She sniffed, her needle darting in and out of a bunch of cloth on her lap. "I don't know. I might take a few days off. How about you?"

"I don't know." He yawned and apologized.

He threw a piece of gravel and watched it skip and sparkle in the sunlight. He hated the idea of offering himself to Di as some sort of first reserve—*boyfriend dumped you? Never mind! Here I am, infinitely shaggable good old Rob*—but he also didn't want to find she was going out with someone else because he'd misjudged the timing. Neither did he make the mistake of saying Di's boyfriend must be a real jerk, because what did that say about Di?

"Rob?" He turned to see Ivan at the front door. "They want you in the office."

Oh, shit. Maybe there'd been some almighty cock-up last night and he was about to get a bollocking. He stood up, brushed off his breeches, and Di reached up to tug his coat straight. He ran through his mind what could have been left undone from last night or today, but everything had gone well, even though very few people had shown up for breakfast or nuncheon. Dinner, in an hour or so, might be better attended, as it should be, since it was the farewell dinner for this particular group of guests.

He went round the outside of the house to the office. Peter and Chris were there, their faces serious, with a tall slender woman in jeans and T-shirt. She looked familiar and the sight of a woman's legs made him a little lightheaded.

"Lou?" he said in surprise. "Mrs. Connolly, I mean."

She nodded. Her face was tight and strained, her arms crossed tight over her front as if to protect herself. She propped herself on the edge of Peter's desk. Shit, he thought. What had happened?

"I'm leaving this afternoon, Rob," she said. "I've got a flight out early tomorrow."

What the hell? "I'm sorry to see you go," he said politely, since they weren't alone.

She nodded. "Yes, originally my plan was to stay on and do a little work here for Peter and Chris, but I've accepted an offer on the ranch, so I need to go home and attend to it."

Was it his imagination or was there the slightest pause before she said the word *home?*

"We were wondering," Peter said, "what your plans for the next few weeks are. Our next trial run is in mid-August and we hope Lou will be back by then, and as you know there's plenty of work to be done around the place. But in the meantime..." He looked at Lou.

"I need someone to help me clear out the ranch, sort things, put stuff into storage and so on, within the next month. You can come over on a tourist visa—I'll pay your fare and a small stipend for a couple of weeks. Peter and Chris have very kindly agreed to spare you if you're interested."

"Wow. The States!" he blurted out.

"It's Montana. Beautiful and isolated, very rural, but there's certainly no reason why you shouldn't travel for a bit while you're over."

He had the distinct impression he wasn't being invited for a two-week bonk fest, but he saw a sudden appeal in her eyes—*help me, help me.* Naturally, like the sucker he was, he prepared to saddle up his white charger.

"Think it over. Let Peter and Chris know in the next couple of days, please." She held out her hand, the ice queen bidding her subject to depart. "You've been terrific, Rob. Thanks."

He shook hands with her, but something felt off. This was wrong, all terribly wrong.

The office door closed behind her. He looked at Peter and Chris, whose faces both held stunned, resigned expressions. "What is going on?"

"We don't know," Peter said. "But we think it may be Mac."

Rob ran out after her. "Lou! Wait."

She stopped, turned and ran into his arms, pushing her face against his shoulder. "I can't talk about it, Rob. I'll tell you one day. But not now. I'm sorry."

"What did he do to you?" *The bastard, the bastard.*

"Who?" She looked up at him. She wasn't crying, as he thought she might be, but she looked vulnerable and shaken.

"Mac. I'll kill him if—"

"He didn't do anything. It has nothing to do with him."

He believed her, sort of. But what else could it be?

"I don't get it, Lou."

She sighed. "I don't expect you to, but trust me. Please come over. I won't be a mess then, I promise. I need a bit of time alone." She put her arms around him and hugged him. "You've been great, Rob."

"Don't go," he said, his voice going all wobbly and strange.

"I'm sorry." She kissed him and he watched her walk away.

Another woman walking out of his life for no reason he could understand. He swore and kicked the paneling—it was okay, it wasn't original—and gave himself a satisfying stubbed toe. But it didn't help.

Mac

THE DIMNESS OF THE DRAWN BED curtains made him sleep until well into the afternoon and Lou, of course, had wandered off somewhere. He considered lounging around sexily to wait in the bed that smelled of her, but really more of him and Rob.

He considered. Did he feel gay today? Not particularly. Horny yes, but only where Lou was concerned.

And then it came back in a rush of excitement, the scrap of paper with its familiar signature, the implications of what they'd found, what it would do for Paradise Hall and all of the people he cared about here. Particularly Lou, his lovely Lou, who'd achieve fame, if not fortune, who'd establish herself as an unmatched Austen scholar with the discovery.

Hardly anyone was around, and he remembered the current crop of guests would disperse within the next few days, but the house was pretty much deserted. Nuncheon had come and gone, and the kitchen staff was more surly than usual, telling him they were tired of him begging for food at odd hours, which meant they'd eaten all the leftovers. One of the cooks relented and fried him a couple of eggs. Mac had to listen to his long, bloodthirsty monologue of what he'd do to the villain who'd had stolen his stash, which didn't improve Mac's appetite.

Wandering around the house, he came across footmen taking naps in odd corners, but no Lou. He was on his way to the lodge to see if she was still at Viv's when he saw someone sitting on a bench, staring out over the lake. He had to look twice; he wasn't used to seeing women in pants anymore.

"Lou!" he waved at her.

She raised one arm about halfway and gave a restrained wave.

He strode along the path, expecting her to run to meet him, but she simply stood up and waited, aloof and unmoving.

When he moved to take her in his arms, she held up one hand to stop him. "I can't do it, Mac."

"Can't do what?"

"I can't break the story. I'm leaving now. There's a car coming for me any minute."

"Lou, honey, what's wrong?"

"I can't do it," she repeated. "It's a violation. It was her life, Mac. Something terrible happened to her, a betrayal of trust. Let someone else do it. I won't."

"Don't you think you're being a bit melodramatic? You're jumping to a lot of conclusions from those few words."

"What else could they mean?"

Out on the lake, the swans floated into view, followed by four small gray blobs. He hadn't even known they had eggs hatching.

She dabbed at her eyes. "You said it yourself—strong language. *Passion, inconstancy.* Don't make this harder for me than it is."

"Harder for you! You said it yourself—this is huge. We'll handle it with tact. What the hell did your advisor say?" He stared at her in disbelief. Was she out of her mind?

She shook her head. "It doesn't matter. I have to go back to Montana. There's an offer on the ranch. Look, you don't understand the implications of this. Millions of people would have their illusions of Austen destroyed. They don't want to think of her as a woman who's wrecked by passion. They want her to be the epitome of happy endings and true love."

"So? A few old biddies might reach for the smelling salts, but—"

"Austen lovers are not old biddies!" She glared at him. "What about your mom?"

"Oh, she wouldn't mind being called an old biddy," he lied. He took a step toward her and seized her hand. "For Christ's sake, Lou, run away back to the cows if you want, but this story will break whether you want it to or not. You should take credit for it, whatever the truth of the matter is. You know there's going to be an immense amount of scholarly interest—you could make your career with this."

"I know." Her hand was like ice.

"So? Come on, Lou. You and me, as soon as you come back. Otherwise I'll break it on my own. I'll tell Peter and Chris today. They should know. I'll show them the rat's nest. We'll work out a media plan—"

She took her hand from his. "My car's here. I have to go."

She walked past him toward the lodge where a car had pulled up. The driver got out, popping the trunk open.

"I'm sorry, Mac."

She walked away from him. He followed, and even at this moment he couldn't bear to see her go. Even now, when he hated her for what she was doing. She disappeared into the lodge and he watched as she came out with a purse on a strap over her shoulder and a battered leather bag that the driver put in the car. Viv stood in the doorway, waving goodbye as the car drove off.

To hell with her and her scruples. What was wrong with her?

He marched back to the house, sick at heart, and went to the east wing. The Paint Boys, uncharacteristically languid, lounged at the tables, Jon doing a crossword puzzle, Simon staring at a computer screen. The trays filled with plastic bags were now empty.

He headed for the filing cabinet. "Can we help you?" Simon asked.

The shelf where Lou had left her box was empty except for boxes of pens and staples.

"Lou left me a box with her name on it."

"In there?"

"Yes. It's a box about this big." He measured with his hands. "Like the empty ones on the shelf there."

"Oh, a large artifact box." Jon yawned and stretched and laid his crossword puzzle aside. "You're sure it was in there? We don't use the filing cabinet for artifact storage. What was in it?"

He improvised. "She brought me here last night to see the conservatory and her necklace broke. So she put it in a box to pick up later and she asked me to get it for her before she left this afternoon."

They looked at each other and shook their heads.

"Can you think where it might have gone? If someone had picked it up, say, and thought it was one of yours, and figured it was in the wrong place?"

"The only people who would have done so would have been me or Simon," Jon said.

"Where do you keep stuff if it isn't in this room? Could you have moved it?"

"Nothing here, I'm afraid. We take sorted and classified artifacts to a museum storage facility. In fact, I'm just back from a delivery."

"Where is it?"

Simon smiled maliciously. "That information is not divulged to the public or the media. And even if someone did discover its whereabouts, they would have to deal with a very sophisticated security system."

"We have over five thousand pieces in storage there," Jon said.

"Many of which are stored in artifact boxes of many sizes."

"Fragments of china, scraps of cloth, coins, nails…"

"Pieces of wallpaper, the occasional earring, pins, beads, the ever popular unidentified metal object…"

"Okay, okay, I get it." He left them, wondering if they would continue their litany whether he was there or not.

Maybe she'd hidden the box somewhere else in the house.

Or maybe she'd taken it back to the States with her.

But more likely, and far worse, she'd destroyed it and everything else that they'd planned, including their future together.

DINNER THAT EVENING WAS A subdued affair, guests picking at their food, footmen yawning and spilling sauce. Even Rob was off his game, responsible for dropping and breaking a platter in a spray of gravy and shattered china.

"You may have noticed, Mac," Peter said, carving hefty slices from a huge cut of beef, "our handling of media is a little haphazard. We are in dire need of someone to handle press for us, write some white papers and so on, do clever things on the website."

"I'll see if I can come up with some names for you."

"Forgive me for being obtuse. We were thinking of you." A large slice of beef, bleeding slightly, thudded onto his plate.

"Well, I don't know. It's real good of you to consider me."

"On the contrary, I think you'd be very good for Paradise Hall. Do think it over, Mac. I know you're pining for our Loulou, but she'll come around. After all, she's going to curate our education center."

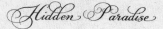

"When we get the funding and when she's recovered from her sulk," Chris said.

"Well, there's a reason she's not herself today," Peter said. "I thought it was you, Mac—that you'd committed some dreadful act of depravity on her person—but of course I realized too late, after she'd gone, why she was out of sorts."

"You did?" Mac said.

"It was her wedding anniversary, poor darling. I wish she hadn't rushed off, but she is rather a private person. But you'll let us know soon, won't you, Mac, about the job?"

"Think it over," Chris said.

"Sure," Mac said. "Thank you for thinking of me. I appreciate it." *Of course you want me as a press officer. I'm the ideal candidate. I've been complicit in losing you the story of the century.*

Ten days later

Rob

"Remember," Mac said as he turned the Land Rover into the airport entrance, "rubbers are erasers. Maryland doesn't rhyme with fairyland. If they've never been here, they're convinced this is a country of warm beer and London fogs. And don't forget to ask Lou about the box."

"What's in that box anyway?" Rob asked. Why the hell did Mac have to make everything so complicated and mysterious? He had a suspicion that the box was a code word between Lou and Mac that would result either in her shrieking with laughter or banishing him from her house, leaving him alone in the wilds of Montana.

"Nothing much."

It was what he said every time the issue of the mysterious box came up.

"Feeling gay today?" Mac asked.

Rob pretended to consider the question. It had become a running joke between them. "Not particularly. How about you?"

"About the same as yesterday. Your dad asked me what color he should paint the cottage downstairs and I told him camouflage green. Something very butch." Mac glanced at him. "I don't know about the stubble on you, though. You still look too damn pretty."

Rob fingered his chin. "Shit. I thought I'd better try and look older in case Lou, well, you know, I mean, she may have puritanical Midwest neighbors."

The traffic slowed as they entered the passenger drop-off area. "They're five miles away, so unless they have radio surveillance on her house and can read the date of birth on your passport, you're safe," Mac said.

And, Rob thought gloomily, she might not want to have sex with him anymore. Perhaps it had been the livery, or the whole playacting thing that turned her on, and back home she might just regard him as the equivalent of one of her students and consider him off-limits.

"What are you going to do now?" he asked Mac.

"I turned the piece on Paradise in to my editor this morning, so I'm off the hook and free to scrape around for more freelance assignments. I'll go to London and visit my kid. She's the same age as Graham, but she likes pink things and ballet, not football." He cleared his throat. "Have you heard from Lou?"

Poor bastard, he asked every day. Viv had threatened to ban him from the lodge, he lurked around there so much asking to check his email.

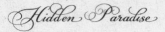

"No. Only through Chris and Peter and only stuff about travel."

A car pulled out in front of them with a screech of tires and Mac steered into its vacated space. "Okay, this is it. Have a good flight." He popped the boot. "Email if you want, let me know how everything goes."

Rob nodded. "Yeah. Thanks for the ride."

Rob went round to the back of the car and grabbed his bag. He ran a mental checklist—passport, iPod, mobile—and Mac appeared at his side and swung him around, enveloping him in his arms.

"What the fuck if it does look gay?" he said. "I'll miss you, kid. Keep in touch."

They lurched together in a clumsy, affectionate hug. Rob let Mac go, giddy with excitement again at the thought of going to the States, hefted his backpack onto his shoulder and headed for the automatic doors. He looked back and waved and Mac, grinning and looking like anyone else in jeans and a regular shirt, waved back. He wasn't Mr. Darcy anymore. He was a friend.

Twenty-Six

Lou

Lou had cried for an entire transatlantic flight, throughout the domestic flights for the final leg of her journey and during the expensive cab drive back to the ranch. She was too demoralized and exhausted to ask any friends to pick her up. The next morning, heavy-eyed, congested and aching, she called her neighbors to let them know she was home, and retired to bed with the worst summer cold of her life. She called her neighbors again, this time for help.

"You should have let us know you were coming home before." Bea Reynolds, a motherly woman in her sixties, unloaded containers of chicken soup and brownies into Lou's refrigerator. The dogs gamboled around Lou, wanting her to go outside and play with them, delighted at her return.

"I lost track of things," Lou said. Boy, had she ever lost track of things.

Leo pushed his nose into her hand and whined. She bent to kiss his head and he panted enthusiastically. "Sorry, baby,

I can't play with you today. Bea, I think I'd better go back to bed. I'm sorry."

Bea brought in a tray of soup and ginger ale and cold medicine and shooed the dogs out. "You don't want to let the dogs on the bed," she said.

"Why not?" She didn't think she was ever going to sleep with anyone again. She might as well let the dogs keep her company. She craved their easy affection, the thumps of their tails on the covers.

"They're farm dogs. They should be outside. Now you get some rest. Colds from overseas are always the worst. We'll check in on you tomorrow and Bob will look after the livestock until you're better." She looked out of the bedroom window and shook her head. "Too late to put in a garden this year. It's a pity."

Lou was mildly entertained at the thought of vicious overseas viruses striking down innocent Americans; Henry James would probably have approved. She thanked Bea and gazed at the view. It was so unlike England, hard and bright and dry. She'd woken this morning, sick and disoriented, not knowing where she was, finding her bedroom and the harsh glare of the summer intimidating.

"This fell off your bed stand," Bea said, replacing a framed photograph of Lou and Julian on their wedding day. "Such a dear man. You were married around this time last year, weren't you, honey?"

Lou blew her nose in response and as soon as Bea left, turned the photograph over.

After several days of being cosseted and fussed over, she woke up feeling guilty over the amount of time and care her neighbors spent on her, and with a hankering to go outside. She stumbled out into the sunlight, blinking at the unaccustomed brightness, and decided her recovery had begun. Hard work was the answer, and she went into a whirlwind of activity, collecting boxes, and starting the arrangements for Rob's arrival.

Peter and Chris emailed gossip about the house and its employees and the restoration work, and reminded her that they'd like her to return. She wrote an occasional affection-ate, noncommittal reply.

It might have been a mistake to invite Rob. At the time, she had felt someone uncomplicated, kind and efficient was the answer, and in addition he could bring her news of Par-adise Hall. She wasn't sure if she wanted to have sex with him. She wasn't sure she wanted to have sex with anyone ever again, not after her discovery about Julian. Maybe it was the effect of returning to the ranch, once the happiest place in the world for her, but which now represented a dull despair.

Now, with time to think, she realized the flaw in her logic. She couldn't continue this way indefinitely—it was unfair to Peter and Chris, her friends. And to Mac.

She didn't want to think about Mac, although memories of their time together haunted her. She wished she hadn't hurt him at their last meeting beside the lake. How cold she'd been, and how she'd steeled herself to ignore the pain in his eyes.

SOMETHING HAPPENED TO HER AS she waited for Rob's plane to discharge its passengers. Her breasts tingled, the touch of her cotton dress on her thighs seemed unbearable and her body was light with desire. Here, in the airport, she had gone into heat because a man was coming to see her and she couldn't wait to touch him, slide her hand into his shirt and onto the warm skin of his back, press herself against his erection.

So much for her original plan to work him so hard all he would be able to do at the end of the day was collapse into a chaste bed.

The first burst of people came through the gate, and a woman with a small child ran into the arms of a guy in a business suit. Two guys hugged and slapped each other on the shoulders. Ah, there Rob was, backpack slung over one shoulder. He raised an arm and waved to her and she had to stop herself rushing to him and running her hands over him, to seek his mouth with hers. She wasn't even sure her legs were up to any sort of rush. She moved at a sedate walk instead.

"Hi, Lou." He looked a little apprehensive, as well he might, summoned from half a world away to help an un-predictable woman shove things into boxes, as though there was no closer source of labor.

She came to her senses and asked how his flight was and if he had luggage, the usual sort of airport-pickup conversation. He handed her a bag of English chocolate from duty-free with a shy smile.

She couldn't take her eyes off him. He'd grown some fashionable stubble that gleamed coppery gold and gave him a little edge. His lips were slightly chapped, dehydrated from the long flight. She couldn't help imagining both lips and stubble on her breasts, her thighs, but she pushed such thoughts aside and offered him a drink from her water bottle. Later, she would have the secret pleasure of placing her lips where his had been.

"No luggage?" she asked again. She couldn't remember what he'd said.

"No, just this."

They stood looking at each other. "Like the boots," he said.

"Thanks." She wore her cowboy boots and her cotton dress fell to just above her knees.

"I've never seen your legs before. I mean, you know, in a dress." He grinned. "Okay, um, I'm ready."

So was she, weak with desire. How embarrassing. They spent some time wandering around the parking garage before she realized she'd brought them to the wrong level, and then there was a clumsy, silly moment when they both headed for the same side of the car. Their elbows brushed and she stumbled, her knees weak.

He laughed, apologized and climbed in the passenger side of the car.

"You okay, Lou?"

"Yeah, fine, just dropped the keys. Excuse me—" She fumbled on the floor, her face perilously close to his thighs. How easy it would be to reach for his zipper.

Her fingers closed on the keys before she embarrassed herself further and she concentrated on getting in Reverse, steering and getting them safely out of the airport.

"How are Peter and Chris?"

"Doing well. They're getting a bit of a break from guests. They say hi and ask that you take a look at your email. The Paint Boys send their love. They went off to do a short job on an Italian contessa—that's what they said. I think there's a villa involved."

"Not necessarily," she said. "How's your family?"

He shrugged. "Okay. Dad's in the cottage. We—Mac and I—worked on it, doing it up with him, though I think Mac was using it as an excuse to procrastinate on his deadline."

Lou tried to ignore the jolt she felt at the mention of Mac. "Graham's at my sister's—she's going to have the baby around the time I get back. She's huge and complaining all the time."

So his mother was still in hiding. Lou suspected she'd be back for the birth of the grandchild and wondered if Rob had thought of that, too.

"What's Mac doing now?" she said, eyes fixed on the road.

"He went to London to see his little girl. He didn't say what he'd do next." He peered out of the window into the dark. "Are those mountains?"

"Yes."

"Cool." He yawned and rested his head against the glass.

"Take a nap if you like."

"I'm okay."

But the next time she glanced over, he was asleep. She allowed herself one self-indulgent lustful gaze at his sprawled thighs. His hands, curled and relaxed in sleep, still bore newly healed scars from his time downstairs at Paradise Hall.

She made a deal with herself. If he wasn't interested, they'd be fine together, just being friends. But if he was interested... her mind wandered into some tantalizing possibilities. He'd checked her legs out pretty thoroughly. Of course he'd seen her bare legs—and much more—before, but it was different when she was wearing a dress with the mystery of what she wore underneath. What sort of panties was she wearing today, anyway? She vaguely remembered picking out her Walmart specials, colorful cotton in a pattern of stylized flowers more suited to an eight-year-old than a grown woman. First thing to do when she got home was change those panties or abandon them altogether.

She sighed. Here she was acting like a teenager, while the real teenager in the car slept. She couldn't predict what would happen and she wouldn't fantasize. Not while she was driving. Maybe later, alone, in bed, where she could take the fantasy to a satisfying end. Maybe she'd think through, and in much greater detail, the possibility of pulling over and unzipping him, tangling in the backseat, or taking him in her mouth while he gasped and twisted beneath her. Or his fingers, busy between her legs—she squeezed her thighs together—and…

Flashing lights and the blare of a horn warned her that she was wandering into the path of oncoming traffic, and she got herself back into her lane and back into a rational frame of mind. She should enjoy this time with Rob, whatever the outcome, and make saying farewell to the ranch as happy a time as it could be.

Meanwhile, there was something satisfying and tranquil about this silent drive in the dark, the bulk of the mountains on the horizon blotting out the stars, with only the occasional headlights of a passing car to remind her that others existed outside their little world. Rob slept on, peaceful.

WHEN THEY ARRIVED AT THE HOUSE she tried not to check out his butt as he hauled the backpack out of the car. He tipped his head back and looked at the stars, much clearer and brighter than any night skies she'd seen in England. The dogs bounded up to them in the house, sniffed at Rob and decided he was their newest and dearest friend, bumping against his legs and demanding attention.

"Nice place," he said politely, a hand on each dog's head.

"Push them off if they're a nuisance. Leo is the brown one, Saturn is the border mix."

"Why did you name a dog after a car?"

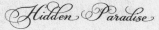

"After the planet. I have English tea. Would you like some?"

"I'd rather have a beer, if you don't mind."

She passed him a bottle. "I should warn you that the legal drinking age in this state is twenty-one."

"Bloody hell." He twisted off the bottle cap.

She fixed him eggs. It was odd to have him in her kitchen, and the awkwardness of showing him the bed in the study— or not—lay ahead.

"What's going to happen to the animals?"

"I'm leaving them here, except for Maisie, my horse. I sold her to a friend whose daughter used to come over to ride her. So she's in good hands."

"You're leaving your *dogs?*"

"They're farm dogs. They like people but they're attached to the territory and to each other. They're friends with my neighbors' dogs. They quite often go visit and hang out. And my buyers really like them."

"They're getting the cows, too?"

"Oh, yes. They love the idea of being gentleman farmers, just like Julian. They plan to get goats and chickens, too."

"Yeah, that sounds nice. My mum had chickens."

"My neighbors sell me eggs. We do a lot of trading and bartering here. I used to trade eggplants for eggs."

He laughed and got up to put his cleaned-off plate and cutlery in the dishwasher. Nice, a well-trained man, rinsing them off first, too. "Where are you going anyway, Lou?"

Wasn't that the big question? "It's not certain."

"Back to Paradise?"

"Possibly. A friend in the town has offered me space in her house. I have to write my dissertation, you see, and I

can teach a few classes at the university. I haven't really decided yet."

"I know, it's none of my business." He ambled into the
adjoining room. "Okay if I watch TV?"

The dogs accompanied him. She heard him click from
channel to channel before settling on something with a lot
of gunfire, typical male. She spent a lot of time wiping off
the counter and range and table, not that they needed them,
and retrieved her voicemail messages, which included the
daily exasperated, affectionate call from Peter.

"Loulou, are you out communing with the cows again?
Give us a call, dear, or email or something. We miss you.
Bye."

When she went to join Rob, he was fast asleep, shoes off,
stretched out on the couch. Saturn and Leo were snuggled
up to him. They gave Lou guilty, challenging looks.

When she turned the television off, Rob didn't stir.

"Down!"

Both dogs slunk off the couch. After letting them outside,
she told them to go to their own beds, although she doubted
they'd stay there. She laid a throw over Rob and opened the
door to the study at the far end of the room, where the bed
was made up, since she'd decided that was the path of lesser
embarrassment. He already knew where the bathroom was
and by default where her bedroom was. It was hard to get
lost in a house of less than a thousand square feet. Her buyers
planned to build an extension, just as she and Julian once had.

The first items she had packed to go into storage were
photographs of Julian.

IT WASN'T THAT LATE, BUT SHE went to bed anyway. A few
feet away, a distance she could cross in a matter of seconds,

Rob slept. The house was quiet. She opened her laptop and looked at the growing list of unread emails, many from Paradise Hall, from Viv and Peter and Chris. The sender address of *msalazar* leaped out at her. She knew that sooner or later he'd get her email address. He was a reporter; he knew how to figure things out.

She closed the laptop without opening the email, laid it aside and switched off the lamp. Although she intended to indulge in a little fantasy and touch herself to a satisfying climax, she found herself suddenly inhibited. Perhaps it was the presence of Rob in her house. What if he heard, even with the door closed? She couldn't guarantee she'd be quiet. She hadn't had to stifle her orgasm sound effects for years, not since sharing a dorm room as an undergraduate. If necessary, Julian's tongue or hand had muffled her cries during family visits.

But she wouldn't think about that.

She tried to find a comfortable position and fell into a light, restless sleep.

Dreams came—light, sexy touches on her legs, her thighs through the sheets, an enthusiastic panting and hot, vile breath in her face.

She sat up and switched on the light, revealing Rob and a couple of companions. "Did you have to bring the dogs with you?"

"Sorry, I must have left the door open." He knelt beside the bed, wearing only boxers, which, she smiled at seeing, were distended by his erection. "I was planning to crawl under here and, um, do things to you. If it's okay."

If it's okay? "Oh, Rob, honey." Breathless with desire and relief, she lunged forward to kiss him. He tasted of toothpaste. His stubble grazed her cheek.

The dogs whined, tails wagging, wanting to join in the fun. "Out!" she said to them. "Go to your beds."

They slunk off.

"I've been inconsistent with them. They're confused. Could you shut the door, please?"

She moved over in the bed and he discarded his boxers, kicking them away as he walked back to her, erection swaying. He stripped her nightshirt off over her head with brisk practicality.

"I didn't know whether you wanted me," he said in between kisses as he got onto the bed. "I thought you might set the dogs on me."

"They'd slobber you to death." She was embarrassed that he was the one who had the courage to attempt a seduction. "I'm sorry if I was weird."

"I was so sad when you left."

"I'm sorry," she said again, her breath catching as his mouth moved down her neck.

"I wanked myself stupid."

She giggled. "Too much information, Rob."

"I thought about doing this. Kissing your nipples. I love it when they go hard in my mouth. Did you know they swell just before you come?"

That scrape of unshaven cheek, just as she'd imagined it, on her breasts and belly, and now on her thighs as he eased her legs apart. "I thought about doing this, too."

His tongue flicked and circled, teasing and probing before settling into a rhythm that she adjusted with small movements of her hips, her hand on his head to guide him. She cried out as her orgasm hit, wrenching and tumbling her, and in its wake he slid into her, keeping her aloft and aiding her descent to earth even as he came.

"Brilliant," he said. He rolled off her, chest heaving, and gathered her to him, his arm around her shoulders. "Can we do this a lot?"

"Absolutely. In between clearing things up."

"The house doesn't look so bad, except for the books."

"You haven't seen the barn yet."

Twenty-Seven

Lou showed Rob the barn the next morning.

"Bloody hell," he said, staring at the dusty interior crammed with broken farm implements and pieces of furniture and things Lou had never dared examine.

"This stuff has been here for years," she said. "The buyers need the space for their goats and chickens so I offered to clear it out, since they gave me such a good price."

They hitched up the trailer and truck and Lou backed them up to the barn door. Rob was already dragging rusty items out. "What if I find something that might be valuable?"

"I doubt you will, but leave it aside. I'll offer it to the antiques dealer in town. Be careful. Drink lots of water. You're at a higher altitude than you're used to and you don't want to get dehydrated."

"Yes, ma'am."

She went back to sorting and boxing books. So many books, so many memories. She resisted the impulse to leaf through favorites and read them; she knew nothing would get done if she let herself be distracted. Julian's books would be offered to his colleagues. Most of hers would go into storage, the remainder would go with her wherever she went.

She slapped a red label on a box to designate it for storage and decided to check on Rob.

His shirt hung on a nail near the entrance and she paused to admire the sight of him wearing only a pair of shorts. For the first time since Julian's death, she'd gone into his side of the closet where his clothes had hung undisturbed, and found work boots and work gloves for Rob to wear. To her relief the clothes had felt impersonal, those of a stranger.

Rob saw her approach, waved and removed the earbuds of his iPod and then his work gloves.

"Find anything good?" she asked.

"Only some ancient porn. I thought you'd like to see it." He nodded toward a pile of magazines. "Those girls' tits are amazing, like tactical weapons or something. But it's pretty tame stuff."

Lou looked at the magazines that did indeed feature pouting women with conical breasts and laughed. "I guess the farmer came out here for a bit of solo relaxation." She tossed them onto the trailer. "You're doing great. We can take a trip out to the dump this afternoon, meet the neighbors."

He brushed off some of the dirt and kissed her. "How are the books coming along?"

"I think they're breeding. My efforts don't make any difference." She could smell his sweat, earthy and delicious. She pressed him up against the side of the trailer. "You remember your oral sex lessons? We forgot something rather important."

She ran her hands down his bare chest.

He tugged at her T-shirt but she brushed his hands away. "Observation only this time."

She found the fastening to his shorts and pressed her palm

against the swell behind his zipper. He sucked his breath in as she unfastened and unzipped, stroking. His cock was hard and smooth and warm, springing into her hand.

She murmured against his lips, "I'm going to suck it, Rob. Think you'd like that?"

He made a sound, half gasp, half groan.

She played with him a little, stroking and pinching while he pressed hot and eager into her hand. By the time she slid to her knees before him, his eyes were closed as if in pain, but he opened them wide when she blew gently on his cock. His scent, fresh male sweat, balanced with an earthiness, a little pungent, rose to her nostrils.

"That feels good," he said.

Oh, she had much more to show him. She darted out her tongue and wove a seductive, wet pattern around the tip. In response, a bead of liquid welled from the coral-colored slit. She swiped it up with her finger and sucked the salty sweetness into her mouth.

He sighed and shuddered as she returned her mouth to his cock, sucking him in deep, tonguing him hard and then with a featherlight touch, and adding in the occasional tender scrape of teeth.

"How's that?" she said, lifting her head.

"Brilliant. Could you do it some more?"

She did, this time stroking his balls and the tender skin on the inside of his thighs, enjoying the way his entire body tensed, the small, involuntary movements of his hips, and his murmurs and sighs of appreciation.

"Lou," he said, his voice urgent, "oh, Lou, I'm going to come. In your mouth." He tensed, head thrown back, hands gripping the side of the trailer, and thrust into her mouth, shaking, crying out. His semen filled her mouth. She swallowed, choked a little at another spasm and another, warm and copious.

He sighed. "That was incredible. Sorry there was so much. Did you enjoy it?"

She wiped her mouth and gave his softening cock a kiss. "Yes, I did. It's very gratifying to give pleasure, and to reduce your lover to quivering helplessness."

"Did I taste okay?" He cleared his throat and said, "I mean, it's sort of personal, isn't it?"

"In the best possible way." She rose to her feet. "Taste yourself."

He shuddered as he kissed her, groaning as he had when he came. With her mouth on his, he undid her jeans, pushing them down, burying his fingers inside her. "I don't have a condom on me," he said against her mouth. "Didn't think I'd need one out here. But I'm going to make you come, Lou."

She kicked away one flip-flop and extricated a leg from her jeans, raising it to his waist as he touched and rubbed. His tongue silenced her, filled her, and only after she'd come did he release her.

She dropped her head onto his shoulder. His cock, hardening again, pressed between them. "We'll never get any work done if we keep doing this," she said.

"Okay." Laughing, he pulled his shorts up from where they'd fallen around his ankles. "We'll save this one for later."

"I was thinking you might be hungry," she said, getting back into her jeans. "It's getting pretty hot in this barn, too. Maybe we could take a nap after lunch."

"Great idea." Hand in hand, they strolled back to the house.

SHE LIKED HAVING A MAN IN THE house again, but she also found Rob's presence annoying. It drove her insane when he was plugged into his iPod and she found herself shouting and waving to get his attention. He could spend hours channel surfing or tapping messages on his smartphone.

But he made up for it in bed, tender, affectionate and considerate. She found his enthusiasm for the ranch touching. She even gave him a riding lesson on Maisie, which he claimed to enjoy.

She couldn't explain that her time here had been the happiest in her life. That when she found out about Julian's betrayal and infidelity, those memories became tainted, ugly. You couldn't stay in paradise once your innocence was destroyed.

It was the one topic she and Rob argued about.

"This has to be the most beautiful place in the world," he said, gesturing at the mountains as they sat on the porch one evening. "I can't believe you're leaving it."

"There are other places," she said, "and yes, it is beautiful, but it's hard here. The winters are awful if you live alone. This was Julian's place. I followed along."

"I think you're nuts," he said.

She drained her beer and placed the bottle on the deck. "You may be right, Rob, I may be nuts. But there's also a lot you don't know about me and what I want."

He stood and glared at her, then marched back into the house.

It was almost dark. She sat looking out at the indigo sky, the moon rising above the mountains, sorry that she had offended him.

She gave him a little time, and then followed him back into the kitchen. His back to her, he paid a great deal of attention to unloading the dishwasher, placing plates carefully onto a shelf.

"Sorry," she said, putting her arms around his waist.

"It's okay. I'm sorry. I was being presumptuous." He turned and took her in his arms. "I know you're unhappy. I want to help."

"You do help." She rested her face against his shoulder, allowing herself to find solace, however temporary, in his arms.

He would, and should, leave her soon. They might maintain some sort of friendship but at the moment she was still too much the elder, he the acolyte. The eight years' difference might not be so divisive in five or ten years' time. It would be interesting to find out what sort of man he became, where his curiosity and smarts and generosity would take him. Almost certainly he'd find a girlfriend once he started college, and she envied him the adventures ahead.

He knew where he was going, at least. She didn't, only that she was leaving the ranch.

OVER THE NEXT FEW DAYS, THEY worked well together, carrying boxes and loading and unloading. Down to only the bare necessities in the house, Lou had hired a van to take a few pieces of furniture, her personal possessions and her books to a friend's house in town.

Rob, cross-legged on the floor between boxes, looked up from his phone. "Lou, we're nearly done here, right?"

"Just about. Would you like to take off soon?"

"Well, yeah. I mean, it's been great and I've loved hanging out with you, but you don't need me anymore."

"You're right. I think you should go have adventures. It's beautiful here but we're too far from anything for you to have any real fun."

"I've had real fun with you, Lou." He grinned. "But see, if I change my flights and leave the day after tomorrow, I can meet up with some people in New York. Di's at her cousin's on Long Island and she invited me to stay."

Ah. Di. He'd mentioned her quite often. "That sounds like a great idea," Lou said. "You'll love New York."

"But I don't want to leave you alone. You've got to get the truck loaded when you move out. And, you know, in case you get sad."

"It's okay. My neighbors can help." She smiled. "My ghosts are laid to rest. And a lot of that is due to you."

"Aw shucks, ma'am," he said in a terrible American accent and clicked away at lightning speed on his phone. "Okay. I'm set. The plane leaves at ten-thirty, day after tomorrow. You sure that's okay?"

"Absolutely. I'll make you pay in bed."

"Brilliant."

Mac, two days later

HE DIDN'T TRUST THE GPS IN this wild country but it was all he had to go on, since maps showed only a series of roads running in straight lines. He'd never been out West before; to the West Coast plenty of times, but this was something different, cowboy country. Wolf country. The Wild West.

It was a far cry from being a Regency gentleman.

Lou wouldn't answer his emails, or Peter's. Thank God he had a spy in the camp, the ever-efficient Rob.

His GPS told him to turn in one mile. Since he'd been on this highway for over fifty miles, the prospect of turning the steering wheel was quite thrilling.

At the turn, a mailbox marked Connolly told him he was close to his destination. He drove carefully down a dirt road and arrived in front of a small ranch house and a couple of outbuildings; but the view, sloping up to the mountains, was spectacular.

Someone was leaving, driving a truck up another dirt road that wound away from the house toward the mountains. He got out of the car and stretched. No one around, just a couple of dogs lounging on the porch. They sprang to their feet and barked loudly, tails wagging, and then came over to investigate him. He must have looked fairly harmless because seconds after their initial ferocity one rolled over to have its belly tickled, while the other one pranced around in an invitation to play.

"Anyone home?" he shouted, in case the barking hadn't succeeded in announcing his arrival. You never knew on farms; people might be walking around naked. He'd be quite happy to see Lou naked, or even fully clothed at this point.

A cloud of dust disappeared around a bend in the dirt road—probably trailing a vehicle that had left the farm and gone that way. He got back in the car and followed. He didn't have far to go. After a few minutes, the dirt road petered out into a few ruts and he found a truck parked on the verge of a meadow of long golden grass, dotted with scrub oak and sage, and with a few grazing cattle.

Lou, wearing a pair of jeans and a shirt, was absorbed in placing stones in a circle about a foot in diameter. Apparently she hadn't heard him drive up. She stood, brushing off her hands, and reached to throw a few pieces of dry vegetation into the circle of stones. Reaching into the front pocket of her jeans, she pulled out a lighter and with the other hand, a bundle of paper from her back pocket. This didn't look good.

"Lou!" he shouted.

She looked up with what looked like annoyance on her face as the papers flared into flame. But then her face softened as he approached. "I'm not burning *it*," she said, even though he already knew that. Then, "How did you find me?"

"Our mutual friend Rob."

"I'm surprised it took you so long." She gave him a grin.

"How are you doing?"

"I'm good," she said and added, "pretty much."

They both watched the paper burn.

"What is it?" he asked.

The paper blackened, curled, fell into ash. She watched it turn gray and then stamped on it, making sure that no live sparks remained.

"Julian and I were married here," she said. "I scattered his ashes here." She poked a foot at the embers. "And I just burned the evidence of his affair here. The whole time we were married. I never knew. He was in love with hard copy, you see. He never met an email he wouldn't print out and leave somewhere. I found it in the lining of my bag the day when I went to the lodge to use the phone."

"Passion and inconstancy," Mac said, understanding why she had been so distraught, why she had run.

"Exactly," she said. "I'm guessing you found it."

"Yes, after a lot of raging and wild speculation. At first, I was ready to accuse you of destroying a historical artifact, breaking my heart, ruining my career, the works."

"I don't blame you."

Uncertain, he reached into his pocket. "I don't know if you want this back." He handed her the ruby on a gold chain.

She took it, gazing at it. "It's a beautiful stone but I don't know if I'll ever want to wear it again. Would you like to give it to your little girl when she's grown up? If you don't mind her having a stone with unhappy connotations, that is."

"I think the connotations would depend on who wore it."

He hesitated, afraid she'd refuse, and said, "Why don't you give it to her when you meet her? If you'd like to, that is."

She smiled, looking thoughtfully up at him. "Thank you. I'd like that very much." She dropped the pendant into her shirt pocket and finally, thank God, took his hand. "How long did it take you to figure out where it was?"

He clasped her hand against his chest, drawing her closer. "I knew you were upset, but I couldn't bring myself to believe that you would destroy anything related to Austen, not when I could think about it rationally. I also knew you'd only tell Peter and Chris about it, if you told anyone, and you obviously hadn't. I nearly went off on a wild-goose chase trying to find the storage facility of some museum that was protected like the Pentagon, according to the Paint Boys. But the more I thought about it, the more I became convinced that you would protect the rat's nest—"

"Oh, don't call it that."

"Okay, the Austen rat's nest. The possible Austen rat's nest. And what better place for it than where it was first found. Sooner or later someone would get to it legitimately. If it had been safe there for two centuries, it would surely be safe there now."

She nodded. "I put it back with the pendant after I found out about Julian. Everyone was asleep and the Paint Boys were out."

"It's still there, still safe," he said. "So...what now, Lou? Peter and Chris are fairly sure they have the funding for the education center. You have a job offer in your email."

"Oh." She didn't sound nearly as excited as he thought she might.

"Uh-oh, you have that expression on your face again."

"I know, I'm thinking." She looked at him with some

trepidation. "I guess I just want to know what…all my options are. The sort of options even Peter and Chris wouldn't spell out."

He smiled. "Well, if you're trying to decide whether to take the job, you should know the position comes with a lover. Possibly two lovers at Christmas when Rob's back from Cambridge."

"What?"

"I accepted a job doing media there. I told Peter and Chris I'd take it officially after I broke a major story, because they'd need someone to handle fallout. They're going crazy trying to figure out what the major story is. I wanted you to have the honor of telling them about it."

The relief, the happiness, on her face was palpable. "That's wonderful, Mac." Finally, she touched him, throwing her arms around him. "But I don't know about the two lovers at Christmas. As delightful as that would be, I just want the one." She kissed him. "I love you, Mac. I love you for having faith in me, for coming out here to find me. Even after everything."

She felt so good, so right in his arms.

"I've never been out West before," he said. "It's a whole different culture. Fucking in flatbed trucks, for instance."

"Oh, don't beat around the bush, Mac." She raised her eyebrows in the way he loved.

"I love it when you go all sardonic on me. How about it? Beating around your bush?"

"You journalists have such a way with words. Don't blame me if you get sunburn on your butt."

"Ma'am, I'm prepared. I have sunscreen and condoms with me."

They were both a little shy at first, getting to know each

other again. He knew Rob had screwed her ass off while he was here, which for some reason didn't bother him as much as it should have. Rob was a friend. More than a friend—a sort of (almost) platonic lover; he couldn't come up with a good definition for it. But someone he cared about.

"I'm going to cover every inch of you with sunscreen," he said as they lay together on a blanket in the back of the flatbed truck. "You're beautiful in sunlight."

"Put a condom on that before it burns."

God, he loved a practical woman.

Epilogue

Rob, England, one week later

Di was asleep on his shoulder as the airport bus rolled through the village. He saw the roof of Paradise Hall through the trees, and then the imposing iron gates and the gatehouse. He peered down the drive but couldn't see anyone, and the bus moved on.

"Hey, Di." He shook her gently. "We're home."

She opened her eyes and blinked. "I wish we didn't have to come back."

"Is anyone coming to meet you?"

"Yeah, my mum." She yawned. "When are you going back up to the house?"

"In a couple of days. I'd better go and see Graham and my dad first."

The bus pulled up at the pub, and they gathered their bags—Di had tons of stuff, clothes and shoes she'd bought, and presents for people. Rob helped her unload.

A woman and a small girl stepped from a car nearby and Di rushed over to them, babbling about New York and how great it was. Di's sister jumped up and down, demanding to see her present from America.

Rob brought her bags and bits and pieces over. "Hi, Mrs. Brooks. I'm Rob Temple. I work at Paradise."

"Oh, yes, we've heard all about you." She shook his hand.

"Are you Di's boyfriend now?" the little girl piped up.

"Yes," he said, so happy to be able to say as much. "Yes, I am." He put his arm around Di's waist and kissed her.

They invited him back to their house and he said he'd be along later. He needed to see his family and catch up on stuff. And he needed time alone to think about the new, scary, amazing developments with Di.

ROB APPROACHED HIS DAD's cottage, seeing the familiar thread of smoke among the trees. The front gate to the cottage had been repaired—it swung open, freshly oiled—and he noticed someone had started to weed and clear out the flower beds in the garden.

He walked up the flagstone path and pushed open the cottage door, surprised it was open. A tall woman, her blond hair tied back, stood at the stove, pouring water from the kettle into a teapot.

He opened his mouth to say something and a dry croak emerged.

She turned and they stared at each other for one long moment.

"Why are you wearing Dad's pajamas?" Rob asked his mother, surely one of the most stupid questions of his life. And then, footsteps thundered down the stairs, and his dad, wearing only a pair of underpants and a cheerful, stupid grin, joined them in the kitchen.

Rob's face burned. It was too obvious why she was wearing his dad's pajamas and his dad wasn't wearing much of anything at all, and he'd almost walked in on them.

"You're back," his dad said. "Have a good time?"

"Yeah, yeah, great," he mumbled, still staring at his mum. He'd imagined his mother's return so often; how he'd demand apologies and explanations. Now he could only stand there like an idiot.

"Where's Graham?" he asked.

"Off playing with a friend," his mum said. She carried the teapot to the table and reached for mugs from a shelf. Three mugs. "Want a cup of tea, love?" she asked him.

"Uh, no thanks. I've got to go," Rob said, backing away. No way he wanted to intrude on whatever was going on here, not with his dad gazing at his mum like that, and the way she looked at him, like she wanted to… God, it was embarrassing. She put out her hand to Rob. "Come back for dinner? About six?"

"You'll still be here, will you?"

She flinched, just a little, but her voice was steady and calm. "Yes, I'll be here."

"Okay." He almost fell over his feet getting out of the cottage as fast as he could.

He hadn't even asked whether his sister had had the baby, but he supposed he'd find out soon enough. If he'd become an uncle he was fairly sure his parents would have mentioned it, unless they were totally brain-dead from too much sex. Meanwhile, he had an invitation to go to Di's house and that's where he would go.

He left his backpack in the cottage and set off through the woods, back into the village to Di's house, thanking his lucky stars he hadn't arrived five minutes earlier and caught his parents bonking. He wasn't dumb enough to think they never did it, but it was still a surprise to see them together and looking happy about it. Nice, in a rather awkward, cringing sort of way.

And now he'd see Di—he felt rather like one of Lou's dogs, which greeted you with unreserved enthusiasm however long it had been since they'd last seen you. But that was the way he felt about her, full of mindless joy, wanting to talk to her and touch her and find out everything about her. She was at her mum's house, so he doubted they could take a shower together or go to bed for some fucking on English soil, but they'd find a way. So this was being in love—weird, fantastic, finding yourself helpless and powerful at the same time. Better ask Mac for advice, or perhaps not. He was pretty sure he and Di could work things out together.

Lou

THIS TIME SHE MADE HER ENTRY into Paradise Hall wearing blue jeans and tugging wheeled luggage along the gravel drive. She no longer searched for ghosts.

This afternoon a man of flesh and blood lay fast asleep beside her in this low-ceilinged room at the top of the house. Servants' quarters, now that they worked at Paradise, but with a wide bed and soft cotton sheets. Their second room was set up as an impromptu office.

She couldn't sleep, restless and excited, despite her jet lag. This evening they would break the news about the Austen find—and she had to remind herself, nothing was yet proven, but the possibilities were thrilling—to Peter and Chris.

She turned and laid her hand on Mac's chest, her fingers tangled in his chest hair, envying his repose. What a marvel he was, this man of so many contrasts, tenderness and roughness combined. They still had so much to discover about each other, time to deepen and strengthen their bond.

He shifted at her touch and brought his hand up to link their fingers; his dark, strong fingers clasped her smaller, more slender ones. With her free hand, she traced a casual line down his chest and kept going, beneath the sheet. "I'm asleep, Lou."

"Sure you are." She rolled on top of him. "Asleep in Paradise."

★ ★ ★ ★ ★

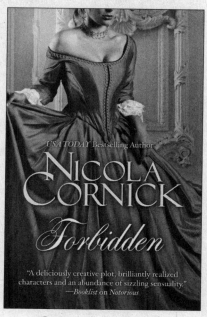

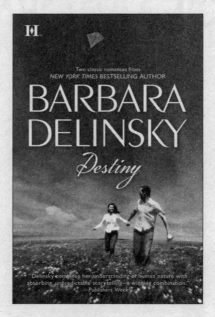

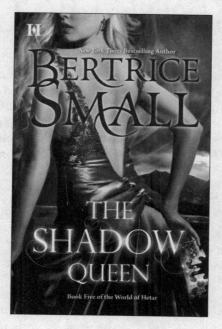

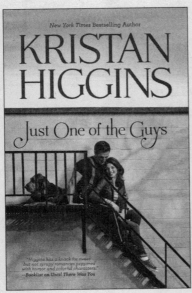

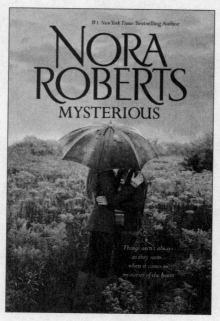